Grand Avenue

AMERICAN INDIAN LITERATURE AND CRITICAL STUDIES SERIES

ALSO BY GREG SARRIS

Keeping Slug Woman Alive: A Holistic Approach to American Indian Texts

The Sound of Rattles and Clappers: A Collection of California Indian Writing (ed.)

Mabel McKay: Weaving the Dream

Watermelon Nights: A Novel

*Approaches to Teaching the Works of Louise Erdrich
(ed. with Connie A. Jacobs and James R. Giles)*

Grand Avenue

A Novel in Stories

by ·

Greg Sarris

With a Preface by the Author
Afterword by Reginald Dyck

UNIVERSITY OF OKLAHOMA PRESS : NORMAN

The following stories originally appeared in the following publications: "The Magic Pony" in *Story*; "The Progress of This Disease" and "Sam Toms's Last Song" in *The Sound of Rattles and Clappers*; "Slaughterhouse" in *Dreamers and Desperadoes* and *Earth Songs, Sky Spirit*; "The Water Place" in *Grand Street*; and "How I Got to Be Queen" in *Talking Leaves* and *The Los Angeles Times Sunday Magazine*.

Portions of the afterword were previously published in Reginald Dyck, "Structures of Urban Poverty in Greg Sarris's *Grand Avenue*," *American Indian Culture and Research Journal* 34, no. 4 (2010): 13–30, and are reproduced here by permission of the American Indian Studies Center, UCLA © 2010 Regents of the University of California.

Library of Congress Cataloging-in-Publication Data

Sarris, Greg.
    Grand Avenue : a novel in stories / Greg Sarris.
        pages cm. — (American Indian literature and critical studies series ; vol. 65)
    A reissue of the 1994 edition with a new preface by the author and a new afterword by Reginal Dyck.
    The 1994 edition lacked subtitle.
        ISBN 978-0-8061-4834-2 (pbk. : alk. paper)   1. Neighborhoods—Fiction. 2. Minorities—Fiction.   3. Ethnic relations—Fiction.   4. Santa Rosa (Calif.)—Fiction.   I. Title.
    PS3569.A732G7 2015
    813'.54—dc23

                                                                2014039222

Grand Avenue: A Novel in Stories is Volume 65 in the American Indian Literature and Critical Studies Series.

The paper in this book meets the guidelines for permanence and durability of the Committee on Production Guidelines for Book Longevity of the Council on Library Resources, Inc. ∞

Contents

Preface   vii

Family Tree   xi

The Magic Pony   3

The Progress of This Disease   25

Slaughterhouse   45

Waiting for the Green Frog   65

Joy Ride   83

How I Got to Be Queen   105

Sam Toms's Last Song   125

The Indian Maid   143

Secret Letters   163

The Water Place   185

Afterword, by Renald Dyck   205

Preface

Twenty years ago, when *Grand Avenue* was first published, critics and other readers took note of the fact that never before had American Indians been portrayed in an urban setting, and they had certainly never been depicted in that setting as individuals from interrelated families all belonging to one tribe. Nor had contemporary American Indian literature had as its subject California Indians, in this case, a tribe of southern Pomo from northern California. While many took delight in the stories, others found themselves perplexed, asking, Who are *these* people? Are there really people like *this*? Why haven't I seen Indians like *these* before? Not surprisingly, a writing professor had asked the same questions ten years earlier when I wrote early drafts of the stories, nearly thirty years ago now.

Thirty years ago, and still twenty years ago, most readers' ideas of American Indians came from representations on film and in books, where the Indians lived, by and large, on reservations in rural settings. The truth is, then and now, a majority of American Indians—more than 60 percent—lives in cities. Los Angeles hosts the largest urban population. Oakland, in the San Francisco Bay Area, comes in second. Many Indian people relocated to these large urban cities during World War II, finding work supporting the war effort, and then stayed. Hence, you find in the big cities Indian people from many tribes throughout the United States—people from large tribes, such as the Navajo from Arizona and New Mexico, as well as people from smaller, lesser-known tribes, such as the Elem Pomo from Clear Lake, California. In the relatively smaller cities and towns, much like Santa Rosa in northern California, where I come from, the Indians living in the town for the most part come from local or nearby tribes.

Grand Avenue is set in Santa Rosa, specifically in South Park, a low-income, or if one wants to be politically correct, blue-collar, neighborhood. I spent a lot of my early years in that neighborhood, which comprised families from diverse—and mixed—backgrounds: local American Indians, African Americans, Mexican Americans, Portuguese, Italians, and many others. In those days, the early and mid-1960s, the streets of South Park were alive with a chorus of different voices and languages. I stayed with a family in which the grandmother and great uncle were Pomo Indian and spoke the language fluently. In the same household, English and Spanish were spoken regularly. The family lived on Pressley Street, which intersects Grand Avenue.

When I began writing in the late seventies, I wanted to reflect in my work as much as possible the experience I had known growing up. And here was the problem: while there was a vibrant outpouring of good and important "ethnic literature," we often saw one group of people, say African Americans, if not in conflict with a racist dominant culture, then at least as a distinct group. Hence, there became an African American literature, just as there was a Mexican American and American Indian literature. This is not to say, of course, that many of our cultural lives are lived in a kind of cultural isolation, an idea that many writers protest in their work. The problem for many writers, then, was that readers who were not from the respective culture seen in the text began to have expectations of what is "black" or what is "American Indian." To them Indians didn't live in cities. Not until *Grand Avenue*.

The Indians in *Grand Avenue*—and the Indians in my family—are mostly urban and mixed racially. While I created a fictionalized tribe called the Waterplace Pomo—so that no reference would be made to persons alive or dead, especially in light of the fact that many of our local tribes have relatively small populations of citizens—the stories I have written are firmly based in history and everyday reality.

Given the horrendous and largely ignored history of California Indians at the hands of the Spanish, Mexican Californios, and early Americans, whose colonizing efforts resulted in the demise of 90 percent of our aboriginal population, it is a miracle that any of us are here today. Many of us, because of this history, are mixed racially, or as I like to say, the history of California is in our blood. This mixing continues—as it does in much of California and the world. One of the persistent themes—and realities—among my Indian people here is that we have become homeless in our homeland. In that regard, then, we are not unlike the immigrants who came to our lands in the past and who continue to come. Certainly, we are working hard, and in interesting ways, to revitalize our indigenous culture.

The Waterplace Pomo is a fictional southern Pomo tribe, a tribe that would be in the geographical area of the Federated Indians of Graton Rancheria (FIGR), which is composed of descendants of coastal Miwok and southern Pomo peoples. The FIGR was formally restored as a federally recognized tribe by an act of Congress in 2000, and since that time has used federal grants, and now revenue from a resort casino, to fund programs to revitalize language and culture, as well as environmental restoration and organic farming projects. Much has changed economically, yet still we live our everyday lives in the aftermath of colonization and the historical trauma associated with colonization. We now have more resources to deal with the various social ills that have plagued us, but by no means are we yet free of those ills. At the same time, we continue to live among many others, and as we work to make and renew a home for ourselves, we are doing it in a world that is always new and changing.

What I wrote about in *Grand Avenue* is a particular tribe, interrelated families negotiating change while attempting to make and keep a home. In that sense, *Grand Avenue* is about a particular group of Indians from a particular, relatively small American Indian tribe, but at the same time, it speaks to the larger American experience.

Shortly after the publication of *Grand Avenue*, the book was optioned by HBO for a three-hour miniseries of the same name. When the show, which I wrote and coexecutive-produced with Robert Redford, aired in 1995, certainly more people were exposed to a cast of urban Indians. The book remains popular today, no doubt because of the ground it broke—and continues to break—in terms of its presentation of American Indians. Just recently in my class on California Indian History and Culture, I asked how many students knew that there were Indians in California. Of 160 students, only about 30 raised their hands. Ironically, I teach at Sonoma State University, five minutes from Santa Rosa and the neighborhood where I grew up.

Today, South Park remains a low-income and culturally diverse neighborhood. Perhaps the greatest change of late is the large number of Mexican immigrants who've moved into the neighborhood. But, really, what is new? Natives dealing with newcomers. Newcomers dealing with natives. All of us, however awkwardly, however successfully, make and remake our home, a home that continues to be transformed and re-formed. One of the main thoroughfares of South Park is Grand Avenue. It is, I think, a good name for a street there and, I still think, a good name for a book.

February 2014

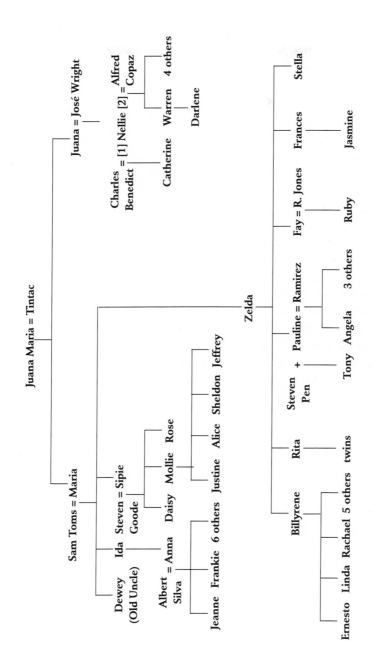

Grand Avenue

The Magic Pony

My name is Jasmine, but I'm no sweet-smelling flower. Names are just parents' dreams, after all. I'm thirty pounds too big and even more dull-faced than my mother, since I make no effort to camouflage it with powder and lipstick. My cousin Ruby is pretty, but it's not the kind of pretty boys see. She's thin and clothes hang on her just so, like her mom, my Auntie Faye.

Us Indians are full of evil, Auntie Faye said. She told lots of stories about curses and poison. We call it poison. Not that we're bad people. Not like regular thieves and murderers. We inherit it. Something our ancestors did, maybe, or something we did to bring it on ourselves. Something we didn't realize—like having talked about somebody in a way they didn't like, so they got mad and poisoned you.

She knew a lot about poison. She said she had an instinct for it. She'd nod with her chin to a grove of trees. "Don't walk there," she'd say. Her eyes looked dark and motionless, like she was seeing something she didn't want to see and couldn't look away from. She traced poison in a family. Take the receptionist at Indian Health, who has a black birthmark the size of a quarter on her cheek. Faye said the woman's mother stole something from someone, so the woman was marked from birth. It happens like that. It can circle around and get someone in your family. It's everywhere, Faye said.

Which is why she painted a forest on the front room wall and painted crosses over it with pink fingernail polish, to keep poison away. She wanted us to touch one of the crosses every day. "You'll be safe," she said.

I knew she was half cracked. I never believed any of her nonsense. I knew what Mom and my other aunts said was true: Faye had lost it. She was plumb nuts. And Ruby, who was fourteen, my age, wasn't far behind her. Ruby talked to extraterrestrials who landed on the street outside. She'd read books in the library and come out acting like some character in the book: Helen Keller or Joan of Arc or some proper English girl. She made no sense. Nothing about Ruby or Faye made sense, but I lived with them anyway.

I wasn't normal either.

I wanted to hear Auntie Faye's weird stories. I wanted to know what the extraterrestrials told Ruby. I wanted to sit at the kitchen table that Faye set each day with place mats and clean silverware and fresh flowers and hear nothing but their voices in the cool, quiet air of the room. I begged my mother. "Auntie Faye said I could live there," I told her. She looked at me as if I told her I had an extra eye on the back of my head. She knew me and Ruby were friendly, but she didn't think I'd go as far as wanting to live there. Seeing how shocked she was, I begged that much harder. I cried, threatened to run away. What could she say? She didn't have a place for us, not really. We lived with Grandma Zelda. Like all of my aunts and their kids when they get bounced out of their apartments for not paying the rent or something. Only Mom seemed permanent at Grandma Zelda's. She could never keep a place of her own for long.

Grandma Zelda's apartment is like the others, a no-color brown refurbished army barracks at the end of Grand Avenue. Grandma Zelda, Faye, my other aunts—all of us lived there. It was like our own reservation in Santa Rosa, just for our clan. Each apartment was full of the same stuff: dirty-diaper-smelling kids, hollering, and fighting. But Grandma's place was the worst. It stunk twenty-four hours a day, and you never knew where you were going to sleep: on the floor, on the couch, in a chair. Babies slept in drawers. And then all the sounds in the dark. The crap with Mom and her men. And my aunts, too. All their moaning and stuff. All the time hoping none of it got close to you.

So you can see how Faye and Ruby's BS sounded to me like water trickling from a cool mountain stream, pleasure to the ears. It wasn't water that could drown you. Sometimes it was even amusing. I'd guess how their stories would turn out because they got predictable. Of course Grandma Zelda and my other aunts were shocked when I carried my things to Faye's. I knew they wouldn't stop me, and they wouldn't come looking for me either. Faye's place was just two down from Grandma's, but it might as well have been in San Francisco, fifty miles away. No one hung around Faye's. If they came over, they'd stay half a second, then leave, like if they didn't get out fast enough they'd catch a disease. I was safe.

Then Auntie Faye found a man, and one day me and Ruby came home from school and found Mom and all our aunts at Faye's like it was a everyday thing.

Billyrene. Pauline. Rita. Stella. Mom. Even Grandma Zelda. All of them were there putting on a show. Big dull-faced Indian women with assorted hair colors. They fooled with their hair and tugged at their blouses, each one hoping Faye's man would take notice. Each one had her own plan to get the man for herself. I know Mom and my aunts. Nothing stops them when they get ideas, and nothing gives them ideas like a man does. First the lollipop-sweet smiles and phony shyness, then the cattiness, the sharp words. By the time Ruby and me got there they had their claws out.

"Did you come from the mission?" Grandma Zelda asked the man, who sat next to Faye on the couch.

He didn't seem to hear her. Maybe he was overwhelmed by the line of beauties that surrounded him. Me and Ruby stood pushed up against the wall. No one saw us, not even Faye, who was looking in our direction. Her eyes weren't strange. They weren't still. She looked back and forth as people talked. I felt funny all of a sudden. I'd seen the man before. There was nothing to him, I saw that right off. He was white, ugly, orange-colored, with thick hairy arms and eyes that were little blue stones, plastic jewelry in a junk shop. It wasn't him that bothered me, really. It was Faye, the way she followed the conversation, and Mom and all them in the room. My stomach slid like a tire on an icy road.

"Did you come from the mission?" Grandma asked again. She was the only one in a dress, an old lady print, with her stained yellow slip hung to her ankles.

"What kind of question is that?" Mom snapped. She smiled at Faye's man, as if telling him not to pay any attention to the idiot old woman.

"Frances," Grandma said, "all I meant was is he Christian?"

Faye laughed, trying to make light of all the talk. She gently elbowed her man to let him know to laugh too.

I turned to Ruby. With all that was going on in front of her, her eyes were a million miles away. It aggravated me that she stood there in never-never land. I grabbed her arm and whispered, "That man's going to be your new father."

She didn't focus, so I said it again, this time loud and clear.

"That man's going to be your new father."

Grandma Zelda looked in our direction. "Hush up," she snapped. She didn't really see me and Ruby. We could've been Rita's three-year-old twins for all she knew. She didn't hear what I said either. No one did.

Then Billyrene piped up, Billyrene in her aqua stretch pants and a white blouse that didn't cover her protruding belly. "Lord knows Faye don't meet men in the mission. Not like some people here." She was looking straight at Mom and Pauline and Rita, giving them an evil gap-toothed smile.

On and on it went. Then out came the beer. They drank awhile, then left. Faye and her man went with them.

I hadn't cooked a meal since I left Grandma Zelda's eight months before. Even with this guy in Faye's life, she hadn't missed cooking for me and Ruby until that night. Tuna casserole, that's what I ended up making, just like I used to for everybody at Grandma's. Ruby set the table. We ate and didn't say anything to each other. Not until we were doing the dishes. I was washing, she was drying. I was thinking about Faye and

Mom and my aunts, all their catty talk. Faye would laugh but she had to know how bad it can get, especially if they're drinking. If they don't beat on one another, they'll go after somebody else. Like the time Pauline and Mom got into it over who used all the gas in Pauline's pickup. They were hollering at each other in Cherri's Chinese Kitchen. Cherri, the owner, tried to settle them down, and Mom hit her over the head with a Coke bottle. The cops came and took Mom, the whole thing. I was picturing all that when I looked at Ruby, who was drying dishes calm as you please. She might as well have been standing next to a sink on the moon. "Your mother's crazy," I blurted out. "She's a freak and so are you."

She finished wiping a plate and placed it in the cupboard. Then she reached for another plate from the dish rack.

"Did you hear me?" I yelled. My aggravation had turned into pure pissed-off. She paid no attention to me. "Damn you, you freak!" I cupped my hand into the sink and splashed her with the hot, dirty dishwater. She was stunned. The dishwater hit her in the face, all over the front of her. But she did just what you'd expect. She got a hold on herself. She dried the plate, even soaking wet as she was, and set it in the cupboard. Then she put down the towel and walked away.

She got out the Monopoly board. I knew what she was up to. She wanted me to sit down and play with her. Whenever I got upset, like with my flunking-out grades at school, she opened the Monopoly board. She cheated so I could win. She wanted me to feel better. I knew what she was up to, but I didn't say anything. I looked at her, sitting on the couch, waiting, soaking wet. I turned, picked up the towel, and finished the dishes she was drying.

The man's name was Jerry. Where Auntie Faye found him I'm not sure. The grocery store, I think. When I first saw him come into the house with her, he was carrying a bag of groceries. He was nothing special, like I said. White, ugly. He'd come each afternoon and visit with Faye. He'd come around three, about the time me and Ruby got home from school, and leave at five, when Faye started cooking supper. He always brought something: flowers, a can of coffee, a pair of candles. It went on like that for a couple weeks, until the day Mom and my aunts came into the house and him and Faye left with them.

I knew Faye was lonely. She had bad luck with men. Ruby's father died in a car crash on his way to the hospital the night Ruby was born. He had been over in Graton drinking. But Faye didn't see it that way. She said she was cursed for loving his brother first. The brother's name was Joaquin. He got killed in the Vietnam war. Six months later Faye married Ruby's father. From the way she talked, I don't think she ever stopped loving Joaquin. She never dated after Ruby's father died. I know because I used to hear Mom and my aunts go on in that dirty woman-talk way about Faye not having a man, and until Jerry came I never saw a guy near the place. It wasn't that Faye couldn't get a man. Just the opposite. She didn't look like Mom and my aunts. She wasn't heavy, plain-looking. She was slender and wore clothes like a lady in a magazine. Everything just so, even the dark pants and white blouse she wore around the house.

But Faye's loneliness was about more than not having a man. It was bigger, more than about Joaquin and what happened to Ruby's father. I saw it in her eyes when me and Ruby left each morning for school. Her eyes got wide, not really focusing on me and Ruby but just staring. She'd be sitting at the table, plates of toast and half-empty bowls of cereal all around, and from the door, where me and Ruby said good-bye, she looked so small, sitting there dressed just so.

When she told stories about poison she looked lonely, scared. She'd sit me and Ruby at the table and tell us what certain pink crosses on her painting meant. She had painted the big green forest first, the dark trunks and thick green leaves, then kept adding crosses here and there with fingernail polish, a pink color she never used on herself. Each cross had a story of its own. When she talked her eyes narrowed. They seemed to squeeze like two hands trying to hold on to something. It was always about what happened to somebody, like the one about our Cousin Jeanne's Old Uncle. It's why Jeanne and them don't live in the barracks with us, why they split off from the family a long time ago, when everybody was still on the reservation. Her Old Uncle—I guess he's our Old Uncle too—liked this woman from Clear Lake, but she was married. He liked her so much he put a spell on her husband. Old Uncle could do things like that, poison people. But the poison turned on him. Something happened. It got his sister. One night she was playing blackjack; the next morning she was as cold and still as a rock in winter. That's how our great-aunt died, Faye said. She held a pointing stick, the kind teachers use with a rubber tip, and aimed near the center of the painting. "And it's why your Cousin Jeanne has cancer," she told us. "She inherited it. His misuse of power, it's living yet."

When she talked about Ruby's father or Joaquin, she pointed to a cross near the bottom of the forest, on the right-hand side. "Man sickness," she said. "Man poison."

Somehow because of that cross and the way she talked about it I figured she'd never have a boyfriend. Maybe she thought she was poisoned when it came to men, so she'd never have one. After Jerry started coming, she stood by the painting with her fingers on that cross and whispered, "Oh, Father, help against this poison. Keep me safe from it. Don't let it turn on me." I couldn't hear her, but I knew what she said. If me and Ruby got the urge to steal something, we had to say these words and touch the cross with the stealing story. If someone wanted to hurt us, beat us up for something, we had a cross for that too.

I never thought much about Faye praying on the man-sickness cross until after Jerry and Faye left with Mom and them that day. Jerry started coming around more, not just in the afternoons but late at night, after supper, and Mom and my aunts visited more and more. I thought about my own words, what I said to Ruby that day about the ugly man becoming her new father. Faye told me more than once I had a mean mouth sometimes and I should watch what I say. Never mind that her daughter made up the tallest tales on earth. She never said nothing about that.

I don't remember if there was a cross for me to touch regarding my mean teasing mouth; what I said turned out true. The man moved in.

Me and Ruby moved out of the bedroom where we used to sleep on the bed with Faye. Now we slept on the couch, with our heads at opposite ends. "You can camp out on the couch," Faye said one night, as if it were something we had asked to do and she was letting us. Our legs met in the middle, and every time one of us moved or turned we got kicked. I thought of Faye in the bed with Jerry. The door was closed. I couldn't hear anything. Still, I couldn't sleep. I tried squeezing my eyes shut, but I kept seeing Faye with Jerry, disgusting things. Either way, with my eyes opened or closed, everything was dark, a perfect empty backdrop for all I was seeing in my mind. I looked to the painting above us, over the couch. The crosses glowed faintly in the light coming through the front window. "Ruby," I whispered, "maybe your dumb mother can find a cross that'll get us a bed."

Of course she didn't answer me. I sat up and looked at her. She was awake, staring, the window light in her eyes. I knew she heard me.

"Damn you," I said and yanked the blankets off her. She didn't move. She was probably in deep communication with a Martian that was signaling her from the back side of the barracks. Hours later I was still awake. Ruby was asleep. I sat up and covered her with the blankets. I woke up that way in the morning, sitting up.

Faye didn't pray at her painting anymore. She dusted it with her feather duster the way she dusted the top of the TV. She'd remind us to think of the crosses when we left for school each morning, but that's about all. No more stories about poison and what can happen to people. No more holding hands after one of the stories, which is what we always did. She'd finish the story, put down her pointing stick, and then we'd hold hands over the table while she said the prayer about Father God helping us against the poison.

Now she talked about ordinary stuff. The ladies she knew at the cannery. Specials at the grocery store. What was in the window at the secondhand shop on Fifth Street. She talked about getting a new place, a house someplace where me and Ruby could have our own bedroom, maybe even out of Santa Rosa. She had it planned. She wasn't going to work at the cannery anymore, where she was laid off half the year. She was going to be a nurse's aide in a convalescent hospital. Jerry knew someone who could get her a job. Once she talked about tenderness, its merits; it makes people smile, she said. It makes them have faith in others. It makes people feel connected. Then she threw her head back and dropped her shoulders, like she'd got goose bumps all of a sudden. "It's like a light's inside you." Jerry was there, and I felt embarrassed, like I was hearing what I didn't want to imagine seeing behind the bedroom door at night.

Jerry was always there, since he was out of work. Temporarily, Faye said. He helped Faye with the shopping and stuff and he still brought her things, flowers and once a coffee mug with red hearts on it. Lots about him bugged me. Like the way he chewed his food. He mashed it, curling his lips out so you could see the food in his mouth. He asked if me and Ruby were cheerleaders. That was funny. I wanted to ask him if he thought we looked like cheerleaders.

But I didn't.

Faye was happy these days. She used to get moody sometimes, just stare into space, and she'd snap at you if you talked to her. Now she was always up, and just by the way she acted you knew she wanted everybody else up too. She'd look at you and there was something in her eyes, something behind the brightness, that was scary. You wouldn't want to cross her. Seemed like Mom and my aunts saw this in Faye's eyes too. They came to the house almost every day now; there was none of their bitchy talk. Everybody was nice, the way Faye wanted. Her and Mom and Grandma went on and on about how they could help Pauline get her two younger kids out of Juvenile Hall. Stuff like that.

It made me nervous. I know my aunts. There was something behind their niceness, something like what I saw in Faye's eyes.

Me and Ruby spent more and more time doing things. It was toward the end of the school year. The days were longer. We took walks. We'd go to the fairgrounds, up to the slaughterhouse on Santa Rosa Avenue, and even to the mall. Anywhere except the library, which I couldn't stand. I'd put up with anything, her stories about extraterrestrials, anything to keep her head out of a book. That's why I got caught up in the horse thing, the magic pony.

It was a regular horse, a small pinto gelding, not much bigger than a pony. She called it a pony. It was at the slaughterhouse with the other horses. One of the things me and Ruby did those days was sit in the rusted-out boxcar by the slaughterhouse and watch the horses. She had them all named: King Tut, Cleopatra, Romeo and Juliet, the Duke of Earl. We didn't talk about what happened to them when the owner took them from the front corral, where we watched them, to the back corral: a loud buzzer, then the gun blast. Sometimes the horses got lucky. If they were gentle and sound, rich people bought them for their kids.

One day this pony darted out from a group of bigger horses by the trough. He was munching a mouthful of hay, and he kept running here and there, snatching hay from the troughs. He moved so fast the others didn't see him. After a while he walked to the cement tub by the fence for a drink. That's when Ruby flew off the boxcar to pet him. True, he lifted his head and whinnied at her. He probably would have done that for me if I had gotten there first. But Ruby didn't see it that way. He communicated with *her*.

That night in bed I heard everything. Far as she was concerned, the pony wasn't black and white but pure silver and gold. A horse who never drank water. He lived off the morning dew and the pollen of spring flowers. A magic pony that carried princesses into fields of poppies and purple lupine. He soared on wind currents over this town with wings stretched wide as an eagle's. He told Ruby he needed a home.

Faye and Jerry were gone, out with Mom and them. I was trying to sleep. I didn't want to be awake when they got home. Ruby wouldn't quit this horse business. "Shut up," I finally said.

Strange thing, though, the horse could do tricks. We went to the slaughterhouse every day. Before long Ruby was in the corral with it, riding it and everything. Smoke, the owner, a tall black man, gave her a bridle. Even he was surprised to see the pony back up and kneel down on command. He let Ruby take the pony into the open field across the street, where the last flowers of spring were blooming, poppies and lupine. He said the pony might've been in the circus. He didn't know much, except the man who dropped the pony off said it had foundered. "Too bad," he said. When he told me this, we were leaning on the fence watching Ruby and the pony in the field. His words fell like dust and piled on my shoulders. I didn't know what foundered was, but I looked back to Ruby just then, and in the early evening light, she seemed to be floating, nothing holding her as she glided above the dried oat grass and flowers.

I told her to forget the pony. I opened her dictionary and pointed to the word "founder." "Nobody's going to want that pony," I said. "You know what's going to happen." I expected her to argue with me, to point out that the stiffness in the pony's front legs was barely noticeable. But she didn't. She took the dictionary from me, set it on the table, and said matter-of-factly, "That's why he told me he needed a home. I have to find him one."

She couldn't think of anything else. Day and night she figured and planned. For two weeks she approached everybody who came to the slaughterhouse, telling them how the pony was magic. She'd jump on its back, without a bridle, and show folks how well trained he was. The pony would back up and kneel with just a little tug on its mane. By this time Ruby could get the pony to do anything. People watched, young pretty-looking girls and white shirt-and-tie fathers. They'd clap, cheer Ruby on, but they always ended up looking at other horses. Finally it occurred to Ruby what I had been telling her all along. Smoke told people about the pony's legs.

Then she went to Jerry, which was the dumbest idea ever. "If he's my father now, he can help me get the pony," she said. Jerry didn't have a pot to piss in, for as things turned out he was living off Auntie Faye's unemployment from the cannery, just like me and Ruby. The flowers he brought Faye he picked out of people's gardens, and the other things, like the coffee mug, he found in trash bins or stole from garage sales. One morning I saw him pocket me and Ruby's lunch money. I didn't tell Faye. I feared that person I had seen behind her happy eyes. But I told Ruby. I reminded her of that and of Jerry's money problems. She didn't listen.

"I want the pony," she told him one night.

He was sitting at the kitchen table, having a beer with Faye and Mom. It was late, after supper. I watched from the couch that I had just covered with a sheet and blankets for bed. Ruby stood only a couple feet from Jerry, determined. Jerry didn't answer her. He seemed surprised, as if he had looked up and just seen Ruby for the first time.

"Ruby," Faye said. "You know we're moving soon. That takes extra money. Jerry and me are saving. Wait until after we move." Her voice was muffled, far away, like a seagull calling over crashing waves. I noticed she sounded like this when she drank.

Ruby looked straight at Jerry. "I want the pony."

Mom took a swallow of beer and set down her bottle. "Ruby," she said, "you should talk it over with Grandma. She could help maybe from her social security check." Mom acted as if she were really interested. She thought she was important these days since she'd found a job at a convalescent hospital.

Jerry, who was still looking at Ruby as if he didn't know her, turned suddenly to Mom. "Your mother's old," he said. "She needs her money." He looked at Ruby. "Go to one of the farmers around here."

Ruby was up against a wall. Finally she quit. She came back and sat on the cot next to the couch. Later, after Mom left and Faye and Jerry went in the bedroom, she said, "See, Jerry did help me. He told me what to do." She was lying on top of the cot, still dressed. She stared at the ceiling, already seeing a thin Indian girl with long straight hair standing before a farmer's open front door.

We walked five miles down Petaluma Hill Road to the dairies. We went to front doors and into noisy milk barns and smelly calf pens, looking for farmers who might want the pony. Ruby never said hello. She didn't introduce herself. "There's this pony," she'd say and go on and on. Most people let her finish before they asked us to leave. One farmer was interested. He was a fat, whiskered man in dirty pants that hung halfway down his white ass. He signaled us to follow him so he could hear us over the loud milking machines in that barn where he and two Mexican men milked enormous black-and-white cows. We went into a dark, windowless room. Metal pipes fed a huge shiny tank, where they kept the milk. The farmer leaned against the wall and folded his hands over his belly. His fingers were thick and hairy.

"You can see him at the slaughterhouse," Ruby said.

"What's wrong with him? Gotta be something wrong with him," the man said. I didn't like the way he took time between his words, and I felt his eyes on Ruby, though I didn't look. I took her hand and gauged my distance from the door.

Ruby took her time answering him. "He needs a home," she finally said. "He gets around good, and he can get up and down with me on him."

The man told us his daughter wanted a horse. Then he said, "I'll go look at him. Meet me back here next week, same time."

I yanked Ruby out the door.

On the way to the main road, we passed a farmhouse where a girl about ten years old stood watering a vegetable garden.

"See, Jerry was right," Ruby said.

"At least he has a daughter," I said. "I still think he's a pervert."

I knew Ruby wouldn't listen to me, but I didn't like the idea of us going back to that dairy. I didn't like that dark room. I felt trapped.

It's not that I hate men. I just know them too well. I've been around Mom and my aunts and seen what they bring home. I've seen it all. The stuff that goes on in the dark, the stuff you're not supposed to see but end up seeing anyway. Like when I saw Auntie Pauline's man pulling off my Cousin Angela's pants in Pauline's pickup, Pauline's daughter who's my age, the one in juvee. Or when that guy Armando hit Auntie Rita in the chest. Or Tito, Mom's last man: the way he tried to get at me at night when Mom was asleep. You develop a sixth sense for it. You see things you don't want to see. You run right into it. It isn't always something heavy like with Pauline's man and Angela. It can be something simple, innocent-looking.

Like the way Mom and Jerry were sitting in Pauline's pickup outside the supermarket. You could say there were a lot of groceries on the seat, or maybe a dog or a child that caused them to have to sit so close together. You knew, though, that they could have put a dog or a child between them. But it's more than their sitting that way; it's something about them that is still, something about the way they quietly turn their faces to each other, Mom looking up so that her eyes meet his, that tells you the whole story, not just in this moment but in all of those in the dark, where Faye hadn't seen them. And you can hear the excuse: "Jerry and me are picking up some things at the store."

I watched them from behind a car in the parking lot. First, I saw Pauline's pickup, the red Toyota, then the back of Mom's head, her teased orange-red hair that was supposed to be blond. I knew the whole story even before I had time to think about it. My stomach turned. I wanted to heave. I started up Milton toward Grand. I yanked my hair just so the pain would take my mind off things. It wasn't that I was shocked by Mom and Jerry or the things people do, sex and all that. I was worried about what was going to happen at home.

Already things were nuts. Faye's place was no different now from Grandma Zelda's or Pauline's. Me and Ruby ate canned soup on the couch for dinner. In the mornings we made our own toast and poured our own cornflakes, since Faye didn't get up with us anymore. The door stayed closed, locked. Ruby did nothing but obsess over the pony. She didn't even do her schoolwork now. I couldn't talk to her. Her eyes were like a pair of headlights on the highway, staring straight ahead, zooming past me. She spent all her time at the slaughterhouse, waiting to see if the farmer or anyone else came to see the pony and making sure Smoke didn't move him to the back, behind the white barn. "The farmer could come while we're in school," I said. But she wouldn't budge. She wouldn't leave the pony's side. The afternoon I saw Mom and Jerry in Pauline's pickup I had left her braiding the pony's scraggly mane.

When I got a hold of my senses, I thought of telling Ruby. I was sitting on Grandma Zelda's porch step. I had come to Faye's first, but when I got to the open screen door and heard all the folks yapping inside, I continued along the row of barracks to Grandma's and plunked myself down. I could hear the loud laughter at Faye's two doors away.

It was a couple of hours before Ruby came up the path at twilight. I jumped up and ran to meet her, feeling desperate to let out everything in my swelled brain. But I ended up saying nothing. I stopped, seeing her face as she turned to go inside, and knew that if I told her what I had seen, her eyes would only look harder and move away from me.

In the days ahead I wanted to talk to Ruby, not just about Mom and Jerry. The weather would have been enough to carry on about, far as I was concerned. But nothing. No way. I'm one to shout, shake her up with what I say, but I could've screamed at the top of my lungs and it would've done as much good as trying to stop a hundred-mile-an-hour train with a whisper. I couldn't stand being in the house. I wanted to kill Mom while she sat nice as could be talking to Auntie Faye. I wanted to pour gasoline on Jerry and watch him burn to black ashes. I stuck by

Ruby. I lived at the slaughterhouse with her. But it seemed to make no difference. I was alone.

We went back to the dairy after a week, just like the farmer said, same time. "We're not going in that back room," I said. But there was no need to worry. The farmer must've seen us coming up the road. He met us in front of the milk barn. He pulled up his sagging pants, then adjusted his stained green cap to cover his eyes.

"That little Indian pony," he said, "I went and seen him. I don't know what you girls was thinking. He's useless."

Of course Faye would find out about Mom and Jerry. For me waiting was like standing on a tightrope, not knowing when I'd fall or where I'd land when I did. I didn't have to wait long. On the last day of school, after me and Ruby got home at noon, Faye explained everything.

Suddenly things were back to the old routine. Faye was sitting at the kitchen table with her pointing stick. She motioned with her chin for me and Ruby to sit down. She was plain-looking again, pale like she was before she'd met Jerry. Her eyes were distant, preoccupied. The table was set, with flowers in a mayonnaise jar. When she lifted her pointing stick to gesture at the painting on the wall, I saw she had drawn circles around many of the crosses and connected them with lines from one to another. She had used what looked like a black crayon.

She pointed to the cross circled near the bottom of the painting. "Man sickness," she reminded us and got up and went to the painting. "Man poison." She looked to Ruby. "Your father and also Joaquin, his brother. I loved Joaquin first."

She followed a line that connected this cross to one that was circled near the center of the painting. She was straightforward, a history teacher giving a lecture for the hundredth time.

"This one here," she said, now looking at both of us, "is Old Uncle's poison. Misuse of power. Do you see how they connect here?"

I sat motionless.

"I'll tell you," she said. She let her pointer hang by her side. "This is what happened. You know I loved Joaquin first. Isn't that right?"

We nodded in agreement.

"You know I loved him. Yes, but I never should have." She paused and swallowed hard, color coming to her pale cheeks. "I stole him from your Cousin Jeanne's mother, Anna. I stole him from Anna. I stole him in the worst way. I plotted with my sisters, your aunts, Billyrene and Pauline. We embarrassed her. We told Joaquin that Anna was poison because she and her mother lived with Old Uncle, who poisoned our aunt. It worked. It split them up. Anna and her mother disappeared. We didn't see them for many years, until we moved here. But that's not the point. What really happened is that Old Uncle's poison found me. Misuse of power. I opened a hole in my heart and it found a place to live."

She took a deep breath and pushed back her hair with her free hand. "I killed two men." She pointed to the two circled crosses and traced the line between them, back and forth. "Each man I love I kill. Each man I touch because the poison in me does that. Now my own sisters are full of the poison. It's growing in them and they're using it against me. They plotted and took Jerry."

Faye walked over and set the pointing stick on the table. "Now drink your orange juice," she said.

I heard her push the toaster down behind us and I smelled the toast. But it wasn't until I saw the buttered toast on the table that I realized how far Faye had gone with her story. Things weren't back to normal. Faye had gone off the edge. "Now hurry or you'll be late for school," she said.

Later that day I followed Ruby to the slaughterhouse to try and talk to her. "Look," I said, "this is serious. Your mother's nuts." Ruby had hardly said a word to me the whole week. "Listen to me," I said. We were standing just outside the corral. "Damn you, you stupid fool, wake up."

She slipped through the board fence to where the pony was waiting for her. Its white ears were perked up and it whinnied, just as it did every time it saw Ruby. She stroked its neck and led it to the front of the corral, by the main road where passersby could see them. The buzzer went off in the white barn; then I heard it, a gunshot. I climbed over the fence and made my way past the bigger horses to Ruby and the pony. She had her arms around its neck, tightly, and its head was over her shoulder facing my direction.

"OK," I said. "I'm sorry. Anyway, it's my stupid mother's fault. I'm sorry." I don't know how many times I said it. But she never turned around. Even the pony ignored me, never perked up its ears. I felt like a fifth wheel. Like I had no business there in the little world that was all their own.

Faye got her time straight, a good sign. When me and Ruby got home, after dark, she scolded us for staying out so late. "Dinner's cold," she said. She was truly angry. She shoved the food she had prepared into the oven and slammed the stove door shut. Ten minutes later me and Ruby were sitting at a table set with flowers, eating pork chops, fresh green beans, and a baked potato with sour cream, my favorite. Ruby talked on and on about the pony, crazy stuff about how it could fly and disappear, and Faye forgot about us being late.

When we finished eating, Faye went to the painting and so did Ruby. Faye wiped her mouth with her folded paper napkin and then got up, and Ruby followed her, as if Faye wiping her mouth was a signal. How else did Ruby know what Faye was doing? Usually Faye went and stood by her painting before dinner or in the morning or early afternoon. Then I saw Ruby's eyes. Walking to the painting, she looked back at me. She looked at me so I knew she was looking, and I felt like I did earlier with her hugging the pony. Only I felt worse now,-1 saw more, even after she looked away and joined Faye, starting in on Father God for help. I saw that Ruby wasn't in never-never land. She was always here. She was always aware of me next to her. Faye was OK too. How could she not know how hard her life had been and that my mother, her sister, had just stolen her man? Ruby knew and Faye knew, just like me. But they believed in something—Faye her crosses, Ruby the pony—and I didn't. I clung to them, and they let me.

We slept together that night. Faye told stories about when she was a girl living on the reservation. She told us the Indian names of flowers. She told us about wild birds. *"Cita,"* she said. "Bird. *Cita, cita."* I fell asleep and must've slept hard because I woke up late, without Faye or Ruby.

I went to the front room, and just as if it had jumped out at me, I saw Faye's painting—or what was left of it—before I even saw Faye. It was black, totally black, the color she had circled the crosses with the day before. Black, except for the edges here and there where you could see a bit of green from the trees underneath. It was as if I were waking up just then, as if in the bedroom I hadn't been awake at all. The fragile peace I had felt shattered like thin glass into a million pieces.

I turned to Faye, who was sitting at the table. Nothing was set, no breakfast dishes, nothing, and the flowers from the mayonnaise jar were laid out around a butcher knife, a halo of green and yellow and purple around the silver blade.

"Faye," I said. "Auntie Faye."

She didn't look at me but kept staring at the painting. It took a minute, and then she started talking. "I must kill Frances—"

"My mother?" I asked.

"I must kill Frances. Otherwise she'll kill Jerry. She's full of poison. She'll kill Jerry. Tonight I will kill her. She is hate. The poison is hate."

"Auntie Faye," I called, but she didn't see me.

I realized talking about it was useless when I saw her eyes. The fearful person I had seen behind her bright eyes the past few weeks had come out now; she was that person. She had told stories to save herself—now she was telling them to excuse herself. Hatred. Jealousy. Anger. Evil. All I had seen in my mother's and my aunt's eyes at different times was here in Faye's. I looked back at the black wall, where Faye was looking, then ran out of the house.

I went to the slaughterhouse. Ruby wasn't there so I ran through the corral and shouted up into the hay barn, where the horses were eating. I hollered and hollered. Nothing. Only the yellow bales of hay stared at me. I went around the back, behind the big white barn across from the front corral, and that's when I spotted the pony. He was there along with a crippled bay mare standing on three legs, a few unshorn sheep, and an emaciated whiteface cow. A large eucalyptus tree shaded the cramped pen. "Ruby!" I hollered. "Ruby!"

Smoke appeared in the door above the chute. "She ain't been around today," he said. "Ain't seen her. Now get, you shouldn't be back here."

First I thought Ruby had run away. But that wasn't like her. I figured she had seen how the pony was in the back. Any day could be its last. Ruby wouldn't give up. She wouldn't run. She'd work harder. She'd go back to the dairies. She'd go farther down Petaluma Hill Road, all the way to Petaluma.

So that's what I did—went back to every dairy we had stopped at, asking everybody along the way if they had seen her. I made up stories, like she needed medicine. I described her, but no one had seen such a girl. I walked clear back to town. One last place, the library—but no luck. The only place left was Faye's.

Faye hadn't moved. All afternoon while I'd been running back and forth to the slaughterhouse looking for Ruby and checking to see if the pony was alive, Faye never looked away from her painting to see me coming and going. I slammed the door. Once I even shook the table. I thought of reaching for the knife, but it was too close to Faye. She might snap, and I'd be within her reach.

I plunked myself down on the couch, and as the afternoon wore on I began hating Ruby. She had abandoned me. Faye was worse than useless. She was worse than gone. I thought of running over to Grandma Zelda's and telling her or Mom. But then what? Have them come down and get stabbed? I thought of calling the police, but why start trouble when it hadn't started? I guess, too, that I didn't want anyone to see Faye like this. They would take her away. I waited and waited. I wanted Ruby to come home, for things to be fine. Maybe Faye would flip back to her old self, I thought, if I just waited.

Faye must have gotten up so quietly I didn't notice. She was standing at the kitchen table looking toward the screen door. Slowly, deliberately, she walked to the door and stopped. "Jasmine," she said, "come here." Her voice was cool, even.

I went to the door.

"A miracle," she said.

And then I saw the sky, where Faye was looking. It was lit by a huge ball of fire, yellow, purple, golden, and red. I was stunned by the sight of it. Then I heard the sirens, and before I could think, I knew. Ruby had set the barn on fire.

I tore past Faye, around the crowds gathered outside the barracks. I ran up Santa Rosa Avenue, past the flashing lights. Horses were everywhere, all over the street, stopping traffic, halting police cars and fire trucks. I was stopped by police and yellow tape, but in the thick of lights and uniforms, through the haze of smoke, I saw a plain-looking girl being escorted to a police van.

There was nothing to do but go back and tell what had happened. There was nothing to hide now. I felt heavy, tired. The first people I saw were Auntie Pauline and my cousins. They were standing on Grand. Then I went in and told Faye. "I know," she said. "I know." She was sitting on the couch.

Funny thing, no one asked me how I knew it was Ruby. Everybody collected in Faye's. They waited for the police car. Something my family always does when there's trouble—wait together. Wait for the details. Auntie Pauline. Auntie Billyrene. Grandma Zelda. Auntie Rita. Mom and Jerry. Auntie Stella.

As it turned out, there wasn't a lot to the story. Ruby had opened the gates and then set the hay barn on fire. She let the horses go. Of course I was the only one who understood the details. I don't mean about how she hid out and poured gasoline on the hay and all that, which we found out later, after she was released from juvee and came back to Faye's. I mean about why she did it. What led up to it. I understood it plain as day even while I was sitting there next to Faye, waiting with everybody else for the police to come with Ruby.

There was nothing I could do. Faye was a crying mess on the couch, and the cops had Ruby. Face it. Face reality, which I always did, which I told myself I should never have stopped doing. I had been hiding at Faye's. With her and Ruby I had been fooling myself. See the road ahead, I kept saying inside my brain. But when I saw Ruby come through the door, a uniformed policeman on each side of her, I stopped. My heart turned and never righted back.

"Jasmine," she blurted out, seeing me. "He's free. He flew away."

I said what made no sense. I said it like a prayer. "Everything's going to be all right, Ruby."

The Progress of This Disease

The doctor takes me alone into her office, as if Jeanne, my JL daughter, doesn't know the truth already, as if leaving her alone in the waiting room won't tell her the kind of news I'm getting about her. I've been through this before. I know all the rooms on this end of the clinic. Both of the beige examination rooms with their striped curtains and oil paintings of plump-faced Indian children. Dr. Kriesel's office is the same. Only behind her on the wall there is a different kind of painting. Against a black background a hand holds a spread of eagle feathers.

"That represents healing," the doctor says, finding me gazing at the picture. "Sit down, Anna."

I sit, glance at her, then back at the picture, then back at her.

"Betty at the front desk said it's a medicine man. Gives me strength as a doctor. You know, in *this* clinic."

I want to tell her I'm no Indian from the bush, that I'm a Christian and don't believe in any of that old stuff. Truth is I don't want to tell her what I'm thinking, because I don't want to think any more than I want to hear what she is going to tell me.

"You do like it, don't you?"

"Oh, yes," I answer. She forgets that we have talked about this before, about what the painting means and whether or not I like it. The conversation always goes the same way. She is confident, knows all about the painting. Then, remembering the kind of news she must tell me, she wilts, slumps in her white coat, listless as a sick gull. Her round blue eyes are like a child's and search the room, maybe for a picture or something that might tell her what to say. I tell her I know Jeanne is sick, and then she straightens and talks about red blood cells and white blood cells. But today she surprises me. Something else happens. She doesn't wilt, says nothing about cells. She hands me an X ray across her mahogany desk, and before I have a chance to study it, before she explains anything, she asks if I understand the progress of this disease.

"Yes," I answer.

It is still early when Jeanne and I walk back to the parking lot outside the clinic. The sun hovers above the hills, hitting the clinic roof and the tops of trees in the lot. Jeanne skips a few steps just before the car, then turns and announces, "We're going to the ocean today. Right now, Mom." Her resolute voice is at odds with the lighthearted skipping from a moment ago. You'd think it's just another sign that at fourteen she is still flip-flopping her way into adulthood. Like the way she experiments with makeup and then spends hours arranging and rearranging her dolls. But she is sick and she knows it. The pain in her back last week, the three doctor visits, the now-and-then loss of feeling in her legs. I must be careful with her today, I keep telling myself. Follow routine. This is about all I can do, given what just happened in the doctor's office, what I saw. For her sake, stick to routine.

"We're Indians of the road," she says as I pull the one-eyed Ford out of the lot.

"Onto the road," I say. She stares ahead with eyes like oversized marbles in her thin face. Her skin looks yellowish, her lips too dark, the color of blackberry stains on a person's fingers. I say nothing. She is determined, almost fierce. Like me, she's stubborn, insistent. We know our limits; we have our ways of doing things, like the trips we take after the clinic.

I pinch from what little I have for these trips. Jeanne and I eat at restaurants I can't afford. I leave my seven other children all day. We go east to Sonoma, where Jeanne likes to have lunch in the park and watch the ducks and geese. Lots of times we go to the coast and sit on the beach. When she was stronger, we used to pick seaweed for Grandma and Uncle, my mother and her brother. I always tell stories, fill the road with talk, mostly about things I remember from my youth, when Mama and I moved from place to place after we left the reservation. So much has changed. In some places endless rows of new houses cover the land. But I see the signs—an old gatepost that a contractor missed, an apple tree left from an orchard—and I am amazed at how quickly I remember things. Today I take 116 west, and where the two-lane highway opens onto the scrub-oak-dotted hills, I tell about the dairyman's wife. She was so fat she couldn't get out of bed. Mama worked all morning just to get her to sit up so she could push her into the special chair the dairyman had built. Still, the lady often missed the chair, so she dripped in fleshy gobs to the floor. Then Mama's work was really cut out. She had to get the woman up.

"She ate too much butter," Jeanne says. "Now tell about the sheep farmer."

I nod, and as I start about the farmer and his errant sheep, I see the late spring sweet peas, pink and white along the road, and the clumps of bright yellow Scotch broom on the hills like billowy clouds, soft as feather pillows.

I talk until we reach the ocean and then go north to Bodega Bay. Jeanne wants to eat at the Tides, where we can watch the fishing boats. I tell her it's too early, the place isn't open yet. She says we can wait. The ocean is flat, clear as glass. We're quiet until we get to the pier, where I park in the empty lot and Jeanne and I find a bench by the water.

We watch a large fishing boat berth at the dock below us. Curly-haired men in overalls come onto the deck from nowhere and jump to the dock, working with ropes quickly, frantically, to secure the vessel. The men disappear for a time; the boat looks empty. Then slowly two or three come back and jump onto the boat, then two or three more. A short heavy man in a blood-smeared apron pushes over a wooden cart nearly as high as he is. And then we see the fish, piles of silver salmon in a cage being lifted by an automatic crane from somewhere in the boat's insides. The huge cage drips water and the fish jump and writhe, their metallic silver bodies catching the sun. I tell Jeanne how we used to come here and get big salmon for five cents a pound, and how Grandma remembered when us Indians had them for free.

"White people," Jeanne snarls, imitating Mama in a bad mood.

"Remember your Bible," I say. "All people are equal. Some of us just behave better."

She is suddenly sleepy, I can see it in her face, and she does not respond to me. Usually I get a *humph* or *tsst* when I mention the Bible. Like any kid, I suppose. The morning sun is warm now, bright in her face. It will be a scorcher in Santa Rosa today. I hope Mama will take the kids to the Swim Center. She got her social security this week.

"Gee," I say. "Mama and me used to come here all the time. Hitch a ride with the dairyman, when we didn't have a car."

"Mom," Jeanne says, as if far away, already half asleep, "you and Grandma were real Indians of the road. You went everywhere. We've never moved, just stayed in the same house in Santa Rosa. We never go anywhere."

"We do now," I say, but I'm talking to myself. Her eyes are closed, her head tilted against the back of the bench. I put my arm around her, under her head, and wait, watching the men below me tossing the fish, one at a time, into the wooden cart on shore.

I'm not surprised, given the doctor's office and all, that I should find myself on this pier. Funny how things turn out. I can picture Mama standing not far from where that wooden cart sits, her hair and tattered calico dress flapping in the cold wind.

"I'll clean fish," Mama hollered. "Clean fish," I remember her repeating, as if Old Man Jones couldn't hear.

Jones's boat rocked up and down in the rough water, strained at the ties, and he stood on the deck before a stack of empty crab nets and looked at Mama as if he couldn't see any better than he could hear. He was half white. He had fine features, but the sun and his shabby white beard made him look even darker than Mama.

"Clean fish," she yelled at the top of her lungs. "Any amount." He squinted. Mama called again, even louder. She waited. At last he seemed to recognize her, but he said nothing. He planted his feet, and his eyes shot back, crazy, pointed like a mad bull's. He took a deep breath. "Cursed!" he roared. "Cursed!"

Mama's calico blew in the wind. She stood, unflinching. He told her to leave. "Bad luck," he shouted.

"You're no Christian," Mama burst out. "You're no highbrow like they say. You're a goddamned low stinking Indian worse than your white-man's-whore mother!" Mama hollered on, her face colored with rage. But it was no use. The wind pushed her hateful words back into her throat. Jones, with his arms crossed over his chest, wasn't touched. Mama wouldn't get the job.

I didn't realize how sore and tired I was until I picked up my cardboard suitcase again. We'd already come ten miles, not on any road but mostly through the bush, picking our way along fences and black woods. Mama hoisted the gunny sack holding everything we owned over her shoulder and started off the pier, stopping once to look back at Jones. She spit and laughed. We followed the coast highway south. Luckily, we didn't walk far. We came to a bridge, and like a wounded animal Mama dropped under it.

A shallow creek ran below the bridge. Mama knelt as if she was going to wash her face,- then she slumped back against the gunnysack and fell asleep. I put my head on the suitcase and tried to do the same, but the cars and lumber trucks over the bridge kept me awake. Mama slept like a log.

It was all I could do the night before to keep up with Mama and lug my suitcase, and now I couldn't sleep. The world sat still, but my mind raced on. I looked to Mama and saw clumps of watercress with tiny white flowers by her feet. I couldn't ask her what happened, given her mood, even if she was awake. She was temperamental, and you knew to stay out of harm's way when she was irritable. I knew Auntie Sipie had died, but I couldn't figure what else had happened. I was nine or ten and my mind couldn't take in an adult's amount of knowing. I needed Uncle, Mama's brother who lived with us and took care of me. He cooked, even washed my clothes, when Mama worked or took off with a man friend. When she came back grumpy and empty-handed, I kept under him like I would an umbrella in a storm. He'd answer my questions. Once, after some kids teased me, I asked him who my father was. "Your mother doesn't know," he said, plain as day. Then he took the gold watch that always dangled from his coat pocket, rubbed it between his thumb and forefinger, and whispered, "So you're magic, daughter of every flower that grows." He said this was my secret, that it was like the doctoring songs he sang when I had a cold or stomachache.

Somehow in the events of the last day Uncle got lost. He wasn't home when Auntie Sipie's man came with the news. When Mama went down to Sipie's house, which was just a few doors away on that tiny ten-house reservation, he didn't come in. And still later, when Mama came back acting crazy, like a chicken with a coyote in the yard, he still didn't come. Mama bolted the door and pulled the shades. Later, someone came back and asked for Uncle, and Mama went outside. The next thing I knew we were packing, and when Mama finally grabbed my arm and yanked me out the front door, away from the sleeping reservation, we were alone.

It must've been almost noon by the time Mama woke. She lifted herself up and stretched. She looked around, and when she spotted me, she seemed surprised. She leaned over the creek, cupped her hands in the water, and patted her face.

"We're moving," she said resolutely. "I know what we're going to do." She seemed lighter, refreshed. She straightened her hair and brushed the sand off her dress.

"Now, come on, get up," she said and turned, starting up the bank to the highway. She swung the gunnysack over her shoulder.

"What about Uncle?" I said.

She stopped. I'd come up behind her on the slope. She turned, and the only thing I could think of was a giant, a bear. Her face got darker and darker and I couldn't move. "Don't you ever mention him again," she snarled. "Don't you let me or any Indian ever hear that name. It's all his fault. His foolery. He caused your Auntie Sipie to die." She leaned her fierce face into mine. "I'll leave you in the woods, you hear? I'll leave you with the white people."

I didn't look away. I needed her to forgive me.

Mama's a big woman, wide but also tall, which is unusual for a Pomo. It's what the dairyman must've noticed when he found us trudging south on the highway. We'd hardly been up from the bridge ten minutes when he pulled his truck off the road. He was a burly man with a head of black curls and a face the red color of a cooked crab. He asked Mama to lift one of the heavy metal milk cans off the back of his truck. He said he'd pay her. She set her sack on the road and, without saying a word, lifted a shiny can and set it on the ground. She lifted another, then another, until she had half a dozen cans down. The man watched and then told her to put them back.

"You want a job, don't you?" he asked Mama when she finished. He was looking at me and Mama's gunnysack.

She never said yes or no, but the next thing I knew we were riding in the back of the truck, bouncing around against the milk cans. Mama couldn't have known where we were going, she couldn't have known about her job, about the dairyman's wife she would care for and lift in and out of bed. But bracing herself against the cans, she looked peaceful, her head lifted triumphantly as she watched the road disappear after each turn.

The dairyman put us in a one-room shack next to the milk barn. It had a wood-burning stove that heated the place good, and that's about all it had. Turned out the dairyman and his wife were Portuguese, like half the other dairy farmers in the county, and from that first afternoon until the day we left we ate Portuguese food: stew, soups, and sweet bread. We ate in the front room, where the lady—Marie was her name—slept and took her meals. The kitchen table was there, and the radio. Mama and Marie became more than friends,- they became inseparable, which was odd, given Mama's dislike for white people. Marie smelled sour, just the way Mama described white people, and she felt sorry for herself, which was something else Mama didn't like. She'd cry about how she was fat and sick, rubbing her tiny round hands into her massive face. Still, Mama would sit with her all afternoon talking and looking out the window to the fields of black-and-white cows on either side of the rutted road that led up to the house. At night the two of them played cards until the wee hours of the morning. The dairyman became a stranger in the house, if he hadn't always been. He came into the front room as if asking permission to do so. It was no surprise when he moved our pallet beds into the house.

Mama changed. There were no men in her life and no drinking, none of her moody hangovers. She didn't talk about people the way she used to. When we'd see Indians in town, she'd look the other way. She pulled her once loose hair back in a tight bun, and even though she got her dresses from Saint Vincent de Paul she wore them like new, clean and pressed stiff. But there was more. She doted on me. She watched to make sure I ate all my meals. Each morning before school I stood at attention as she straightened my dress, evened my shoelaces, and added a ribbon to my hair. She walked me to the bus stop, and she'd be there waiting every afternoon. She went over my lessons with me. If she didn't understand something, she'd ask Marie, my other mother. At night, she stayed with me until I fell asleep. She sat straight and hard, her body shaped into a perfect rectangle by the corset she cinched herself in each day.

Mama and Marie argued sometimes, about things like what time to eat or how much salt to put in a stew. Mama had an obsession about beating Marie at cards, and once after Marie won five nights straight, Mama asked me to stay up and watch to see if Marie cheated. I watched the longest time, then I fell asleep.

When I awoke, sometime in the early morning, there they were with the light still on over Marie's bed: two big women, the light one sprawled back in the bed, the dark one slumped in a chair, and a pack of cards scattered between them on the crumpled white sheets.

For all Mama's hard work, Marie got sicker and sicker. Marie wasn't well to begin with, after all. But Mama wouldn't see it. She fought Marie's failing health with the same mad determination she had for everything else she did in those days. When Marie couldn't sit up by herself, Mama pulled her forward in the bed and then let go of her, leaving her to sit by herself for as long as she could. Mama counted the seconds on her wrist-watch until Marie collapsed on her pillows. Toward the end Mama got so crazy with this it seemed she was torturing Marie, whose lifeless arms and head flopped this way and that each time Mama pulled her up. And when the moment came Mama couldn't coax another breath out of Marie, Mama sighed and looked as if she'd just lost a hand of cards, her eyes searching the bed, the still body, for a sign she'd been cheated. She pulled the shades over the window, looked back once at Marie, propped up in her bed and staring blankly, then left the house forever.

We didn't have to move. The dairyman never told us to go. He knew after Mama asked him to move our pallet beds back to the one-room shack that we wouldn't stay. Turned out he helped us move. He got us a job with the sheep farmer five miles down the road. After the dairy ranch we just went from place to place: the sheep farm, another dairy, the orchards. Mama's size and determination made her the best at whatever she did, whether it was digging postholes for the sheep farmer or milking cows. And she always kept herself clean, in a dress, with her hair pulled back in a shiny bun. Somewhere along the way she picked up the Bible and spent all her evenings and spare hours reading furiously. She would be the one who decided when we needed to move on. Certain things set her off: twin calves drowned in a well, the sheepherder's cousin who carried a talking parrot on his shoulder. "I can't tell them that bird's scaring the sheep off," she said.

'They won't listen. They can't see the truth." She quoted the Bible. She had answers for everything.

I came to detest her doting care. She was plain overbearing. Of course now I was sixteen, the age to revolt, and a boy named Joaquin Jones gave me good reason. It was on an apple ranch, where we lived in a nice cottage next to the rancher and where Mama was the field foreman. Which are the two reasons the Indian workers didn't give Mama mind to leave right away—she didn't have to live in the tent camp with them, and she didn't have to talk with them about anything beyond business. Some were our own relatives from the reservation: Mama's sister Zelda and her daughters Pauline, Rita, and Billyrene, girls my age. I was happy to see them, make friends, never mind Mama's proclamations that they were heathens and dirty. It had been six years or more since I had talked to other Indians.

Joaquin was the kind of boy a girl notices. A boy whose mouth moves just so when he talks, whose black eyes settle in yours like nothing before, who makes you senseless. I was a late bloomer, sixteen, like I said. I knew he liked me. He'd hide behind the apple trees along the road waiting for me to get off the school bus, and later, down by the creek, where I'd hide from Mama and visit my cousins, he'd sit with the other boys and watch me. What I didn't know was that half the other girls liked him too.

After school I changed out of my new skirts and blouses into dungarees and sleeveless work shirts. I wanted to look like the other Indians, who didn't go to school. I knew Mama was suspicious, given my absence from the house after school, and I should have figured she'd follow me one day. When she did, she found me with the others, and for the first time I was sitting in the grass next to Joaquin. She stood above the creek, a dark, imposing figure casting judgment on all of us. I was the only one who had to answer to her.

That night it was warfare, the quiet, smoldering kind, Mama's specialty; it was what happened before her spewing proclamations, so you never quite knew when she would erupt. I'd seen it when she was mad at a boss. I watched her explode alone in the house. Now it was me, her and me. Finally, at the dinner table, it started but was over as quickly as it began.

"That boy's your third cousin," she said, matter-of-fact.

I was surprised by her tone, expecting something worse. "We're tangled up with everybody," I retorted.

She looked at me for the longest time. "That's right," she said. Then her voice cracked and she whispered, "So don't get any ideas."

She excused herself and left the table. I didn't know it then, but she was a hundred feet under water in her own loneliness.

I cared only what the others thought, my friends and Joaquin. None of the Indians liked Mama. They said she was stuck-up, white-acting. Rumor had it she had married the dairyman, since people saw her in town with him and had no idea about his sick wife at home. So I used Mama's finding me with Joaquin to tell the others all the things that I found wrong with her: the rock-hard corset, her Bible preaching, her friendliness with the white bosses, which wasn't quite true but which would certainly stir up my friends. But something was wrong. At first I thought maybe they pulled back from me because I was disrespectful of my mother. Then I worried they thought I was too much like her, white-acting with my going to school and all. They wouldn't talk to me, just listen, their shared silence signaling their collusion.

Joaquin brought me flowers every day. We held hands, and once, above the creek bank away from the girls, he kissed me. I was embarrassed when a couple of his friends jumped out from behind the brush hooting and hollering. So was he, since he was the rare kind of Indian boy who didn't make hate and insecurity his best friends. He didn't need to show off. He was a gem. Believe me, if things had been different, Mama would've blessed us both, had us married in a heartbeat. But that would never happen, Mama or no Mama. Billyrene, my older cousin with the mouth, fixed things just the way the girls wanted.

It was at our hangout place by the creek.

"Your mother's no Bible lady," Billyrene cracked, breaking the silence.

I didn't really understand her, what she meant.

"She's cursed, a witch, just like her brother who killed our aunt."

Joaquin sat up straight, resting a bouquet of snapdragons on his knee.

"Oh, don't try to defend her, Joaquin," Billyrene said. "I can't believe you don't know. You're probably already cursed just by kissing her Tell him, Anna, tell him what *your* uncle did."

I watched the other girls shift in the grass. They looked with confident amusement back and forth at Joaquin and me.

"Go on, tell him how *your* uncle cursed some lady so she died and then it backfired on Sipie. . . . Tell him how the lady died all covered with gray snot and afterbirth. Yes, and how we found Auntie the same way. Tell him how you're cursed. The only reason you and your mother live is because you're evil too. Tell him."

Billyrene's voice echoed. I saw the snapdragons strewn on the ground next to me. I didn't look back at Joaquin, but before I left I saw all I needed to—the girls' jealous faces emboldened and relieved by Billyrene's spiteful victory.

Of course I knew we'd move after I told Mama. But I wasn't thinking that far ahead when I finally burst out with everything at the dinner table that night. I just talked on, let go with everything, but my voice was small and broken with all I knew for the first time.

When Jeanne first got sick, we used the word "ache." It started that way, just below the abdomen. That and tiredness. Then chemotherapy and no more ache. But eight months later ribs and hipbones showed under skin that was not the right color, and the ache was back and everywhere.

"Cancer" was the word Billyrene told Jeanne. Billyrene with the mouth. Billyrene who moved up the street to haunt me with her forked-tongue kindness. "Oh, Anna, is there anything I can do for you? Watch the kids while you're at the doctor's? It must not be easy with Albert in the bars again. So glad you and me are neighbors now, Anna." Go ahead, I think, rub it in, Billyrene. No one invited you with your how many kids from how many men to this place. The United Nations flag should fly over your front porch. You turned out just like your mother, who'd pass out drunk so the men could carry her on a stretcher from room to room. But I don't speak. At least I can stop my tongue, and I'm ashamed that what I shouldn't be thinking comes up so fast.

When Jeanne came through the front door with the word "cancer" I surprised myself. I sat down with her calm as day. "Yes," I said. I was relieved, and as I talked, in a way Jeanne could understand, the word actually felt good. The only time Jeanne asked if she would get better was right then. "Yes," I said.

I took myself to the library, read books, learned so much about the disease I came to speak its language, which is a hollow tongue of numbers and strange words. That's why Dr. Kriesel goes on with me about counts and cells. But I moved beyond her. I read about Laetrile, coffee enemas, diets of brown rice and sprouts, support groups—none of which I had time or money for. Visualization seemed the ticket. It's free for the effort. Picture the body healthy. See flowers and things. Green is a good color.

At first Jeanne and I took rides to find open pastures where we parked the car and sat, letting the color green fill our eyes and enter our bodies. Jeanne saw cows and got bored. Then, to keep her happy and fill the road as I drove frantically look-ing for an empty spread of green, I started telling stories. I told about me and Mama and all the different people we knew, and Jeanne seemed to like the stories. Now all I do is call up the same stories again and again while we drive here and there for lunch or whatever. Truthfully, Jeanne's not crazy about the stories. I know. It's the ride that pleases her. It's the break from home, where monotony leaves the door wide open to pain and fear. "Grand Avenue," she complains as we turn onto our street.

When we first moved to our place I marveled at all the room. Three bedrooms, such a big house. And the name of the street had a ring: Grand Avenue. Even if it was at the south end of Santa Rosa where the poor and what-have-you's lived. I'd walk out in the evenings with my two kids in my hands and look at that street sign like it was magic. Here I was a free woman living in the city. A woman like any other, with two kids and a husband. No more running from pillar to post so Mama could help half the countryside live and die. I put the rent down, first and last months, and Mama came to live with me. Stores. A shopping center. Parks with goldfish ponds. No one we knew.

Reality is like the sun on a summer morning. It burns right through the fog. As I always think in looking back, Vietnam got Joaquin Jones and Albert Silva got me. Two kids become eight, and a husband's earnings become a welfare check. I peel apples at the cannery when there's work, and Mama's burdened caring for my kids. Half the Indians in town live up the street or around the corner, and of those too many are on the front porch asking for Uncle.

We found Uncle preaching on a street corner uptown. He wasn't poor, even though he lived in a room above the Sixth Street mission. And he wasn't crazy. He'd organized a Bible study group for Indians at the YMCA and took orders directly from the local minister. Mama and I were stopped at a light when we spotted him. "Pull over," she said, and before I stopped the car she was out and making her way across the street. When I caught up, he was reading from his Bible. He was so much smaller than I remembered, shorter than Mama. He wore the same Stetson hat and dark suit, but his clothes fit him loosely, and there was no gold watch chain dangling from his coat pocket. Mama answered him, naming the chapter and verse he read. This went on for half an hour, him reading and stopping long enough only for her to identify the passage. What I didn't see, as I stood there waiting, was all that was understood between them.

They never inquired about each other's lives. They never said good-bye. Uncle closed his Bible and Mama and I went back to the car.

We were on our way to the unemployment office. I'd managed to hold enough time at the cannery to stand in line there. We drove in silence. Mama didn't say anything about what just happened with Uncle until I was parked; she waited until I stopped the motor.

"What happened was in the past," she proclaimed. "The rest is the devil's black heart feeding itself on those uncertain souls who know no better." Her voice was so plain and even you'd have thought she was reading. She skipped a beat, then added, "Uncle's always lived with us. His social security will help us out now."

She made herself clear: Whatever Uncle did or didn't do didn't matter. He was coming to live with us. That much the two of them understood.

It happened like clockwork, the next day. Uncle showed up in his dark suit and Stetson hat with a shopping bag full of his belongings in each arm at eight o'clock in the morning. By noon he was washing the kids' clothes with Mama. He was a regular fixture in our house. Even the kids didn't notice him anymore.

Mama and Uncle turned out to be two peas in a pod. They found in each other what they had missed for years: company. They did everything together—shop, cook, clean house, disappear each night for their Bible meeting at the YMCA. For the first time I saw how they were brother and sister. Their broad dark features, that slant in their eyes, the fat hands and short fingers. But more than that, more than anything else, it was something about their posture that drew my attention to them as two people. Something I'd seen in Mama the last few years but never really thought of, and something I would see in Zelda, Billyrene's mother, and the rest who'd come to the front porch for Uncle. They were slightly stooped, bent in a way each and every one of them understood. It was what Mama and Uncle showed each other straightaway on the street corner that day.

It bothered me.

There was something secret between them. When they peered up at you from their lowered faces, they seem to be telling you that they knew something you didn't know. At first I thought a lot about the unspeakable: Uncle and what happened to Auntie Sipie. Mama only alluded to the matter, saying it was in the past, which was the first and last time she talked about it since that day many years ago when we were under the bridge. I'd heard about it, though, and not just in front of Joaquin. At the dance hall when I was around the other Indian girls, I'd catch the words "her uncle" and see the furtive glances full of suspicion and curiosity. I ignored them. But there was nothing furtive or suspicious about the eyes of Mama or Uncle or any of those folks who came for Uncle, nothing that spelled out whatever happened in the past. It was something bigger, bolder, something you see in the eyes of religious zealots bent on converting you. A secret you could know for the asking that would change your miserable life.

But there was nothing for me to ask. I read the Bible and I struggled the best I could.

More and more people came for Uncle, which brought me added aggravations. Billyrene, for instance. Zelda's on friendly terms with the family, and Billyrene learns all about us from her. Perfect setup for Billyrene to come in each night after her mother leaves with Uncle and revel in my hard luck. This wasn't the first I'd seen of Billyrene since she snuffed my romance with Joaquin. She'd be at the dance hall, around the time I was dating Albert. She was somewhat pitiful, so overweight and plain. She was the last girl the boys asked to dance, the first to have their babies. She asked me once what Albert was. "Portuguese," I answered proudly.

She's never mentioned the Joaquin incident, and she'd be embarrassed if I did. True, she's nosey and jealous. But I suppose she's not unusual; I've found lots of women like her. It just seemed like she was always sitting in my house, all two hundred and fifty pounds of her, absorbing every detail of my life and reminding me of it. After Jeanne carried the word "cancer" from her to me, I had an excuse to strike back. "Billyrene, you've got diarrhea of the mouth and nothing in your brain to stop it. You've always been like that," I told her. And I could've said a lot more, but there was no satisfaction in it. She hung her head, the way she used to when she was standing against the wall at the dance hall, and like the sorrowful and spiteful fool she was then, coming back each Saturday night, she'd keep coming back to me.

I try to be charitable. I make a point of it. I take what's good in the Bible and use it in my life. Like I said, I can stop my tongue from spilling what's in my head. But things got to me when Jeanne got sick and then sicker. My snapping at Billyrene was just the first sign. I got so bad Billyrene left one day without me having to ask her. Albert had an excuse to stay out and drink all night. I got to be like a porcupine using its stiff quills to keep the world at a safe distance. I couldn't stand it; everybody knew my business. A hundred pairs of eyes were on me, offering prayers, condolences, and secrets I didn't want to know existed.

Uncle wasn't the jolly man I remembered. He was quiet, solemn. Neither he nor Mama push their ideas at you with their tongues. Neither one asked if they could pray over Jeanne. I asked.

One night while I was punching down fry dough as if I were killing a wild dog, Mama took my arm. She surprised me, since she is not the kind of person to touch you out of the blue. It was early, before dinner, and she took me out the back door. We sat on the porch step overlooking a backyard of junked car parts and untamable weeds and blackberry vines.

"It's a mess," she said.

I didn't know if she was referring to the yard, Jeanne's situation, or both.

She turned and took my arm again. "Honey," she said, as if I were ten, "you can't let this bother you so. You got to relax, let go." I still wasn't sure what she meant by "this." But it didn't matter. Her voice was like cool water on a burn. I'd pushed and pulled the world too long. Made lunches. Made doctor appointments.

I looked at her soft brown hand on my parched, dough-dusted skin and fell into her uncontrollably. "Pray for me," I cried. "Pray for Jeanne."

It was a weak moment, as I would find out. That same night Uncle and the congregation didn't go to the YMCA. They settled in the front room, about a dozen of them. Jeanne lay on the sofa, her tired face propped up by a pillow. The lights went off and the crowd of hunched men and women gathered over her. I didn't like the darkness and the flickering candles that Zelda and Mama held. Hocus-pocus. Staging, and a lot of trickery, so that the secret in the eyes and bent backs might reveal itself.

"Our Holy Father, forgive us our sins," Uncle started as he stood between Zelda and Mama with his open Bible. "Forgive us," he continued with rise. "Forgive us who knew no better. Forgive us the pain in our lives." He kept on about forgiveness, which angered me. Then in my anger I saw their secret. They accepted their sins, admitted guilt: Zelda her numerous affairs, Mama her lonesome pride, Uncle the deaths of two women. I picked up the secret in Uncle's first words. They were praying for themselves.

Eventually, Uncle turned to Jeanne and invoked the Holy Ghost. He was earnest, faithful. He put everything in God's hands. It was God's will whether Jeanne got better or worse. The way he prayed, he couldn't lose.

Now, after sitting on the bench for over an hour, Jeanne and I go into the restaurant. We are its first customers. We sit at a table with a view of the fishing boat, now emptied of fish. She has taken two bites of her tuna sandwich, maybe a couple of spoonfuls of her chowder. She looks out the window and she is very pale. Already one trip to the bathroom. She can't hold anything down.

"How long did it take them to empty the boat?" she asks, turning her head on her stick shoulders. She is trying to make conversation with me, follow routine. But her voice is thin, strained, like fine lace stretched to its limit.

I help her. "About half an hour," I say, and look at the vessel secured tightly to the dock.

She looks at her food, then out the window, then at me.

"Mom," she says, "Rachel has been nice to me."

Rachel is Billyrene's daughter, a year or two older than Jeanne. She's like her mother, petty and jealous. *Why shouldn't she be nice to you?* I want to say and follow routine. But that's not what Jeanne wants now. Her voice is broken, torn. She has given up on our routine. This is it. I must talk.

"Mom," she says. "Mom, everyone's nice to me now." She keeps her eyes on me.

"Yes," I say.

"Mom, they know I'm gonna die, huh?"

"Well. . . ." I pause. "People should be nice no matter what."

She looks back at her food, then out to the blue, blue water beyond the fishing boats. She *knows*. She knows *I* know. There, as much as I can say. It's out. Acceptance. What I should've seen two weeks ago when Uncle and his congregation prayed. My sin: my blinding drive against hard luck, against the curse. It was like a train coming all along. You watch it, hear the whistle blow, the rumbling of the tracks as it draws nearer and nearer. But then it's something else, something that hits you in the back while you're watching the train. Jeanne knew I'd been hit. Our routine, our drive today, wasn't working. I tried, we both tried. But I'd been hit. She just couldn't see how. Couldn't see Dr. Kriesel hand me that X ray. Couldn't see my face, feel my insides burst, as I glanced at the picture and saw not the dark masses in a sea of lighter gray, not the tumors, but the pieces of snot and afterbirth that covered Auntie Sipie, the story that wouldn't die.

"Yes," I repeated to Dr. Kriesel, letting out all I held within me. "Yes, I understand."

I wrapped Jeanne's sandwich. The soup I couldn't take. I hate waste. As we drive silently into Santa Rosa, I wonder what will change, if anything. I'm thinking about little things that have been a part of our lives. Jeanne's skipping after the doctor visits. My endless stories. I think to tell her that our ancestors are from this place, from a village along Santa Rosa Creek. That was so long ago, before the tribe got split up and the handful of survivors went west to the coast or north to the reservations. But what's the point? Because it's something I haven't told her, I tell myself. Something she should know. . . . Then, in my mind, I hear what she would say: So we all came back.

She's slumped in her seat, drowsing, her head showing just above the window. The prescription Kriesel ordered last week is stronger. Jeanne sleeps longer. She's more dopey. I look at my watch. Forty minutes, I think, which was how long ago she took her pill, just before we left the restaurant. She should be feeling better.

"Are you OK?" I ask.

She nods and then says yes so I can hear.

I drive through the hot, crowded town. Women in shorts walk the streets with their blond-haired boys and girls. Businessmen in nice suits hurry in and out of buildings, across crosswalks. Old people shield themselves with purses or newspapers from the sun. At a stoplight, I catch our reflection in a storefront window. An old Ford. A mother and daughter. Even a daughter slumped down, sick, maybe, or just sleeping. The light changes, and I continue home.

Slaughterhouse

I was fourteen. Thirteen, maybe. I was worried I couldn't shoot: I mean, take care of business once I got there. That's all us guys talked about. And I had a girl who would've let me. Her name was Ruby. An Indian who lived in the Hole. Eyes pretty as nighttime sky in the country. Believe me, fine. And she's looking at me like I'm something, even I'm an Indian, but a half-breed. I'm scared, but luck gives out on me and I win a trip inside that slaughterhouse barn and I know I'm a man no matter what.

The barn was down Santa Rosa Avenue, where folks had animals and stuff. There was chickens in the yard, cows. But the houses didn't look like anything, no better than ours, small and needing paint. Stuff like refrigerators and washing machines here and there where you could see them if you looked, hanging around the sides of houses, on back porches and in garages, like folks thought stuff that didn't work wouldn't stand out. Either that or they wanted you to see the stuff, like it was something, which everyone knowed was nothing. Falling ragged barbed-wire fences surrounded the places, except for the slaughterhouse, where there was thick plank boards. Along the street plyboard was nailed to the planks so you couldn't see the horses. On the plyboard you seen advertisements for things in town: Coca-Cola. Cherri's Chinese Kitchen. Hamburger Dee-Lux.

It was two barns at the slaughterhouse. One was in the middle of the corral. Its roofline sagged like the swayed back of one of them horses. It's where the hay was, where the horses fed. From there we watched the goings-on in the other barn across the way, three stories high and painted. I say watched the goings-on, but we couldn't see much, just trucks carrying in horses and carrying out pet food. But it was no secret what happened in that place at night. Smoke and Indian Princess Sally Did sold girls.

Smoke had eyes the yellow color of his straw hat. The eyes looked out from his black face like they was set in a dark wall. Folks said they was goat eyes, square in the iris. I wondered if the white people who came about the horses seen his eyes that way. Smoke looked like the devil. Indian Princess Sally Did was worse. She had balled-up black hair with a white stripe down the middle. She never took off her sunglasses and she dressed in a purple getup and high heels. Thing is, she thought she looked like she was society. I remember seeing her in the market on Grand Avenue. I thought she couldn't see I was looking because she didn't pay attention to anything that was no use to her. She was reaching for a can of coffee when I seen it on her leg, just above her knee—a tattoo that said *1946*. Whatever that year was to her. "What you looking at, smelly Indian scoundrel?" she snapped, scaring me half to death. Made you feel she had something personal against you.

Anyway, it was out of Sally's Cadillac we stole the girlie magazine, one showing everything on a body. Me; Buster Jones, the oldest and the leader of our gang; Micky Toms, another Indian, like me and Buster; Victor Patrick, who was black; and the angel-face Navarro twins, Jesus and Ignacio, who we called Nate. I seen the car parked in our neighborhood, and it was Buster who spotted the magazine and told Micky to reach in the open window and take it. There was paper and stuff like phone numbers, which flew out the magazine as we tore down the street and made our way to the barn. "Good thing," Buster said, "because if we get caught with this there's no proving our connection to it. Like it could be anybody's." It was summer and we was too young for the cannery and too old for our mothers.

Up in the hay Buster started looking at the pictures. From where I was I seen the curves of naked women, the pale color of a half-cooked hotcake. Micky, who don't have much of a neck to stretch, sat next to Buster. The rest of us looked from where we sat, even if what we seen was upside down.

"Turn it so we can see," Victor said to Buster, who hogged the pictures on his lap. But I knowed what was next.

"Just picture it like it's real," Buster said.

See, Buster couldn't control himself. He made it like if we didn't follow we wasn't cool. We had ourselves a hideaway in the barn, a fort made by moving hay bales around so we couldn't get seen. Just then it looked like Buster was going to share the pictures because he put the magazine in the middle of our circle. But it was only so he could get his drawers down and have us look at the pictures and do the same. He wouldn't be alone not controlling himself.

"Close your eyes," Buster said.

By this time we was exposed too. Or partway. The closing eyes part I went along with. You know how guys check each other out, and no one compared to Buster then, least of all me and the Navarro twins. Which caused the shooting worries. But I seen Buster's eyes closed but not closed, all glassy, like hard murky marbles over them pictures. He was gone already. Then I closed my eyes completely. I tried to keep seeing the picture showing a woman in black stockings. Never mind the hay poking my ass and the back of my legs, I was starting to feel pretty good, like things was working, when what I seen was Ruby. It was her come to my mind, and I kept on.

I thought first it was them stray cats, which had a way of coming out of nowhere in that barn and scaring the hell out of us. I heard Buster jump, then the others. I opened my eyes. Buster and them wasn't there. They'd moved, over the side of the hay looking down on the mangers. I blinked a few times; then I pulled up my pants and joined the others. Buster turned and put his finger to his lips. I moved between Micky and Victor and seen what Buster was looking at. It was Smoke and some black girl talking.

"You just shut up and never mind," Smoke was saying. He chewed her out like nobody's business.

"Well, I—" she started to say with her hand on her hip.

"Well, you nothing," he said. "You jealous 'cause you an old whore. Let me and Sally run things. And tonight we doing a run and it ain't just you."

It was like he said something that all of a sudden took the air out of her. Her hand fell from her hip and she stood there looking foolish, standing in that short black skirt two shades darker than her skin. Standing in high heels sunk flat in the dusty horse shit. I could see the black where her orange hair growed out.

"Now you just get," Smoke said. "You go through the fence there. Go up the railroad tracks and don't be coming ground here in broad daylight. You look worse than you is."

The black girl disappeared. Smoke lifted his straw hat like to cool his head. He was dressed in overalls, like someone who just works with horses. After a minute he left too, through the gate to the other barn.

"We're going in there tonight," Buster said, like he'd been thinking it over the past two days. We sat back in our spots, and Buster closed the magazine and stuffed it between two bales of hay.

"We can't all go in," Victor said, "because there's a big pit in there full of dead horses, and we could fall in."

Nobody really knowed what was in that other building. Sure, they killed horses in there, and folks talked about a hole where they ground up the meat. But Victor was just talking to cover over what we was feeling. It was dark, scary. The only way to get in that place besides the front was to sneak up the chute in back where they took the horses to kill them. No one wanted to go through that to see what tonight was all about. No one had the guts.

Buster acted a smart-ass. "We all die," he said. But he had things figured out. He played on what Victor was saying. "If we're dead, then there's no way anybody knows what's going on in there. So one of us is going to stand near that chute and the rest is going to watch outside the fence"—he stopped for a second, breaking up his line of words like he was in a movie—"oh, and in case you all forgot, *one* of us is going inside."

He grabbed six pieces of straw and started arranging them in his hand, like he couldn't see what he was doing. "There's one short one," he said.

Victor's eyes popped out of his head. He must've been picturing himself drowning in a hundred feet of molding horse intestines. He had a sister who rode off with Smoke one night, somebody said, and when one of us, I forgot who, asked him about it, his eyes got big, and he looked over his shoulder like his mother or somebody was listening.

"Think of the girls," Buster said.

I must've looked as scared as Victor. Thinking of girls in that barn didn't help none. I picked the short straw.

"Micky, you stand by the chute. Me and everybody else stand guard." Now Buster was all business, a commander of the troops making his strategy. He looked at each of us, then stopped on me. "Frankie, if you don't show up . . ." He stopped and spit and looked at me again. "Get some points, Frankie."

The plan was to meet at nine o'clock, when it was dark. I was standing outside the market on Grand, just about home, and I seen on the store clock it was only three. Six hours, I thought, and I'm superstitious. Six ain't a good number. Buster and them split, went home. I couldn't just sit. I went back to the slaughterhouse, probably just to see where I was going.

Nothing seemed the same in that hay barn. I thumbed through the magazine, but without the guys there I felt like a pervert or something. I seen the cobwebs on the old roof boards and the way the main beam swayed under the weight of the roof. Like them endless spiders had eyes and was seeing me with my secrets. The beam would snap, coming down, and the whole world would see me with them pictures in my hand. I thought of

Mom or Sis finding me like that, and Uncle Angelo, who always visits Dad: "Can't you get the real thing, boy? That's OK to study, but don't be no fool. Remember what I tell you." That drunk talk of his with me and my friends, about what you're supposed to do with a woman to make her happy.

I put the pictures back between the hay bales and crawled to where I could see the other barn. Sally's gold Cadillac looked small, miniature-sized against the large white barn growing up all around it. In the corral just below me, horses stood swatting flies like they had a million tomorrows. I couldn't sit still.

I went out behind the barn and made my way along the railroad tracks. Lots of times us guys followed the tracks, which cut right through town, from the slaughterhouse north to the station on lower Fourth, where there's bars and pool halls. The tracks pass back of the white place where you can see the chute they take the horses up to meet the gun, the place where I was supposed to go in a matter of hours. I came to the fence and saw the burlap hanging from the top of the shoot, covering half the gaping black hole that led inside. All at once an old white cat appeared. It stopped and looked at me, then came down the ramp like I was nothing. In the sunlight it was old and matted, white hair gray and dusty-looking. It moved slow, stiff-legged.

It was then I decided I needed luck.

Do a good thing, Grandma says. I thought of her cousin, Old Nellie. They didn't talk much, even though Nellie lived just up the street. It was about something Nellie did a long time ago, which had Indians mad at her. Something about who she married, a white man. Folks don't talk. Point is, she was alone most of the time. When I got to Old Nellie's, I seen her front door was open, and I walked up and tried looking through the screen.

"Auntie Nellie," I called.

She came through the kitchen into the front room, and her face was all pushed up, set hard. It was like she might not talk at all, refuse to answer up to all the things folks accused her of. Then she let up, and her eyes came out big and watery. "Frankie," she said, pushing open the screen.

"Auntie," I said, "them weeds out back of your house, they going to catch fire and burn you down."

She giggled and covered her mouth with her hand, like a young girl. "Oh, gee," she said, and you'd think I told her her slip was showing. I seen lots of old Indian ladies do this. Grandma does it, and it's her way of covering what she's thinking about a situation. Old Nellie, I should've figured the range of her thinking after I'd just found her face hard as the porch I was standing on.

"Now come in," she said, shaking the screen door she held open.

Inside Old Nellie's place you'd think time stopped. The world hadn't touched her. Not a speck of dust. Not a scratch. Not a dent or sign anyone sat on the puffy couch or rested their elbows on the pressed white doilies over the armrests. The purple and pinkish blooms of her African violets in the windows seemed fake, clothlike. It looked like she'd just put the pictures of her kids and grandkids in new frames and placed them perfect on the walls that morning.

In the bright yellow kitchen her redbud and sedge roots for basketmaking sat on the table in neat coils wrapped and tied with strips of yellow cloth. Like my grandma, Old Nellie was what they call a Pomo basketmaker, but there were no signs of her weaving except her roots, no peelings on the floor or wet hairy sedges drying on newspapers. She poured me a glass of milk, placed it in front of me on a napkin, then stood by the counter, like she was waiting for what I wanted next. I sat down. I felt like she'd been waiting and hoping all day for me to come, like she had that milk just for me and the house perfect.

"I don't have much to do today, Auntie, so I thought I'd take care of your weeds out back and side of the house." I sipped my milk.

She shifted on one foot. "Oh, dig them out? That's too much work." Her voice was steady.

"Someone could throw a match, Auntie, and that's it."

"True," she said, shifting again. She looked old. She wore a red scarf, and wisps of white hair stuck out bright against her sagging brown face. Her slip showed below her faded print housedress. "That would be nice," she said finally.

She offered me a plate of cookies, but I wanted to start on the weeds. I went out the front door and started pulling the tall oat grass that lined the sides of her house and filled her garden. I seen a couple of her window screens was rusted out. Really, her place was like anybody else's, only she had no junk, refrigerators and stuff, sitting around. In-town-reservation living, we called it. I was working at the oat grass half a minute when I realized I couldn't pull it out. It was too far in summer, and the tops of them dried oat stalks just busted in my hands. I should dig them, I thought, turn over the soil. But that would take too long. The earth was dry clay, packed tight as stone. A small plot was all I could do.

Then I seen the scythe. It was leaning upright against the fence. Its wooden handle growed out of the grass like something looking at me. I walked over and seen the blade was rusty, but it cut. Not good, but it cut. I'd do the whole place, surprise Old Nellie. I swung that scythe like crazy, and in a hour or so I'd hit everywhere, alongside the house, in front by the rose hedge, the whole back.

I was standing catching my breath and admiring the territory I covered when Old Nellie stepped out on the back porch. I started to gesture with my free hand, as if to say, Look, when I seen she was chuckling to herself.

"Oh, gee," she said. She was looking down where I butchered her small roses by the porch, not just those but the ones beneath the back window.

There was nothing sorry about Old Nellie now,- her whole body started shaking, the slip and housedress jumping up and down, and she done nothing now to cover that laugh, like a crow calling, and shrinking me to the size of a pea. I wanted to apologize about the roses, but she was laughing so loud and hard I couldn't get her attention. She stopped a split second and her face changed hard. She looked at the chopped oat grass, then at me, and before she busted up worse than ever, I seen what her squinting bird's eyes said: Throw a match and that's it.

I went home and sat in the shed back of our house, just plopped myself on a prune crate in the dark. I seen my luck: the short straw. Old Nellie's cursing laugh. She'd seen what would happen the minute she found me on her porch, and she let me fall in. She tricked me into entering that strange clean house where nobody lived, because Old Nellie wasn't a person. Tricked me with them watery eyes like she done that first time at the grocery store so I would carry her groceries. The old folks knowed. Old Nellie was a witch, a poisoner. Why else would Grandma and them keep away from her? Not because of a white man. Indians around here got secrets. Don't want people knowing certain things. But they wasn't hiding nothing from me. Old Nellie seen where that straw torn me wide open. She seen the hole and hooked herself there, and then like she had that straw in her hand, she tickled me with it for no reason except to laugh at me and feed her evilness.

I had to turn things around.

I went to Ruby.

That movie we'd seen in the barn was still going in my mind. I wanted a different picture, and it was Ruby I thought of, because no matter how low I was I felt high as the tallest tree around her. And none of the guys was around to make fun of me and her. I'm not lying, she was fine. But she was different.

"She's weird," Buster said. "Stinky virgin."

That was on the first day I really noticed her. Buster and me and Micky was sitting on the bike racks in front of the market and she come walking up the street. Looked like a schoolgirl, white bobby socks and tennis shoes, pants rolled up at the cuff, plain white blouse. She tossed her black hair around to keep it out of her face, and the way she walked she could've been anywhere, going down the hall at school, at the fair. Maybe that's what caught my eye, because to me just then there was something womanly about her. She wasn't no schoolgirl.

"Hah! She's your cousin," Micky said, laying one into Buster.

"Shit, I don't know them drunks. Stinky Indians," Buster said.

I knowed she was Buster's cousin first day in history when the teacher called her name: Ruby Jones. That, and her mother was one of them Toms ladies who's related to Mama. So I guess me and Ruby was related somehow too. Hell, all of us is related. Me, Buster, Micky. But it wasn't till just then on the street I seen Ruby's potential.

That same afternoon I went to the Hole, where she lived, and played like I was visiting old Grandpa Toms, the grandpa of half the neighborhood. The Hole is in our corner of town called South Park. Only it's in the worst part, on the south end of Grand Avenue. It's two lines of brown army barracks separated by a dirt road. All kinds of Indians end up there. Blacks, too. Grandpa Toms lived in a place toward the end, just across from Ruby. I found him sitting on his ripped-apart piss-stained couch halfway in the middle of the road. He sat all day like that, watching folks and sucking his empty pipe. I greeted him and sat on the wobbly armrest. He asked how Grandma and Old Uncle was and then laughed, showing a long yellow tooth, his big belly with his pants pulled up quaking up and down, causing his half-undone zipper to come open more and more.

"*Mata,*" he said, which means woman, and I seen Ruby come out her door.

The old man's Stetson hat was on the couch and I picked it up and made like I just took it off my head for Ruby. Like a dude of high class. "Good day, lady," I said.

It stopped her short. She studied me. Her eyes focused and then I seen her face changed like she knowed me half her life and just then remembered. "Good day, sir," she said, in the same kind of voice I'd used.

That's how I got to know Ruby, and how I knowed she was different.

I struck a lucky note. Ruby loved games. We played we was different people. Used accents and that stuff. Sometimes we'd be married and discuss our children. Oh, Peter has such a problem with his homework. And what is it, my dear husband, that keeps our Allison brooding? Mostly Ruby. She'd start up out of nowhere. We're just walking along or sitting back of the fairgrounds, and she'd start into something. I couldn't keep up with her. She lost me.

"You read too many books," I told her.

It was me started the Romeo thing one day. Except she thought it was a damsel in distress story. Point is Juliet wanted same as Romeo, which Ruby hadn't figured. We was in our spot under the cypress trees back of the fairgrounds. I helped her down where she could sit.

"Thank you, kind sir," she said. "I narrowly escaped."

I kissed her, started pressing on her. I moved up her skin, under her blouse. She pushed up and hunched over. She was that girl again, the one I didn't look at in history class. Only I seen her now, and when she turned to look at me I was something cool, the toughest guy on earth.

She looked away and let out a sigh like she was tired. But she was already somewheres else. "Peter got another note," she said, disgusted-like.

It was almost six when I knocked on her door. It was bright outside still. Grandpa Toms was watching from under the Stetson hat that shaded his face, and his big belly started heaving again. I turned away. I was about to leave when the door pulled open, then closed just as fast, like a window shade popping up and down. Now you see, now you don't. The door opened a couple inches, then slowly a couple inches more, until Ruby's mother appeared. Her face was just there, come into the light, and wasn't attached to nothing. It was a mask, painted orange lips the same color as the nails on the door, pencil brows, and false eyelashes, one of the lashes drooping over her eye like on a busted doll. She moved so slow and strange and stared with that drooping eye, like she was looking at something beyond me.

"Ruby, your boy's here," she said without expression.

I waited; then Ruby came out and the door closed behind her.

She was bright-looking, clean with her white blouse and tennis shoes and socks, her pants rolled up just so. Only thing, she didn't give me them eyes. No princess look. Not the wife, either. Nothing. She didn't even look at me. She brushed past me. "Come on," she said. Grandpa Toms was laughing so loud I wanted to kick him one in that fat gut.

I figured Ruby was mad on account I hadn't come by for a while. She was stepping fast and big, like she knowed where she was going. I trailed behind her and kept asking over her shoulder what was the matter. I thought it might be her mom being so weird and all. Living with that puppet head couldn't be no pleasure. But it wasn't her mom. It was me, what I first suspected.

She led me to the cypress trees and then sat down. I caught her eyes once, but she looked away.

"You're just a dumb boy," she said.

Her voice was different. Nothing I recognized, none of the voices I knowed from her. She had her face in her hands, the long fingers up her cheeks, and she was looking back down the street, toward Grand. The sun showed her eyes, but I couldn't see her straight on.

"I been looking for a job," I said.

"You lie, Frankie. You can't get no job." She wasn't moving.

"I want to do something. Not just sit around here all day like a nobody bum."

"You're a nobody."

Her voice was ten miles away same time it was right there. I wasn't stupid. She was mad on account I kept reaching for more than she wanted to give and then stopped showing up to see her. Which was the truth. She pushed me to it.

Then I put my arm around her. I felt good. But she was hard as a rock, unmoving.

"I never went to the park with Buster to see them other girls."

The soft sell. I figured I'd play it from her point of view. I was telling the truth, even if the truth was them girls around the park moved too fast. But nothing seemed to matter to Ruby. I had to approach it different.

"Me and Buster's going to do something tonight. I'm—"

"Probably you are," she said, "because you're a nobody."

It was like she cut me off without thinking about it, like her voice come out of the sky and then was gone so you didn't know whether you'd heard it or not. It sounded something like a disgusted mother, but it went too fast for me to say for sure. It wasn't what I wanted. I heard my own words about tonight, me and Buster, and I remembered why I was sitting there just then. I'd started to feel good with Ruby, but now I was sinking. The stakes were high. I had to win. I held on to her like she was a card I could will into an ace. Time was all I had. I knowed if I just held—and I would've held till dark—she'd give in. And I was right.

The sun dropped two fingers' worth in the sky. That's how I was measuring time, with my free fingers against the sun. I first seen her kicking at the dirt, just a little with one foot; then she adjusted her shoulders. I started moving too, but not where she could see. I leaned over and kissed her. Her eyes was open and holding the sun in little dots of light, and if I hadn't closed my eyes just then and kept looking I would've seen the mountain range, everything in her eyes clear to the ocean and back. She put her arms around me like never before. I felt her hands back of my shoulders holding on. I leaned her against the tree. Then, all at once, she twisted and bolted upright, and when she pulled away my hand was caught in her blouse, which pulled her toward me and made her pull back again. We was caught together, and when she jerked free she flew against the tree and hit with a thud.

I jumped up to her, then coiled back. Her eyes shot through that tangled mess of hair like I was the devil himself. She pushed herself upright with her elbows, still glaring at me, then faced the sun and started clearing the hair out of her face.

"It's no use," she said, "You're like all the rest. It's all the same. Mama's right."

I didn't follow her. Everything changed so fast. She arched her back, stiff. The wife, I thought. I worked my throat so my voice would be the husband. Ruby's lips moved, but nothing came out. Then she wilted and folded up into her lap.

"It's no use," she said into her hands.

She crossed the line. She was gone, and I felt we wouldn't be friends after that. I cramped up, felt sorry, because just then I also knowed I liked her special. I found out too late. I felt sorry and mad at the same time.

She braced herself, hands on knees, then she was on her feet. I seen the sun glistening down one side of her face. Then she was running. She'd gone halfway down the block before I could move. I chased her far as Grand, then quit.

I was just plain mad. Mad at her, Buster, everybody. Mad at myself. Damn this sex business, anyway. Damned if I did, damned if I didn't.

I went home.

The house was noisy and stuffy-smelling. Kids everywhere. The TV, Mom cooking, Dad and his brother, Uncle Angelo, their six-packs of beer at the kitchen table. Mom over the stove with the pink plastic curlers in her hair from morning. Grandma and Old Uncle in their spots next to the stove, two old Indians, sitting like they was in the park or on the front porch, watching.

"Frankie, you want some beans here?" Mom asked without turning to look at me behind her.

She's like that. Got a sixth sense where she knows each of her eight kids without looking.

She dished a bowl of chili from the big pot she was stirring. "Get yourself a spoon," she said and then dropped a spoon in the bowl she handed me. I looked for a place to sit. The chairs and couch was filled in the front room so I sat at the table across from Dad and Uncle Angelo. I didn't want to do it on account of their getting drunk and loud. Mom handed me a warm tortilla in a paper towel. "Where you been?" she asked, turning back to the stove.

Just then Uncle Angelo's fists hit the table, causing my plate of beans to jump half an inch. "Son of a bitch, the bastard was in his car already," Uncle Angelo said.

It was something about somebody Uncle Angelo wanted to beat up at work. Him and Dad always talked like that when they was drinking. Fighting and women. They was more drunk than I first figured. Both of them cussed up a storm. They looked the same, curly black hair, lightish skin, tight faces that opened and cracked in lines when they laughed. And when they was drinking, their eyes got small, black beads like rats' eyes, so you couldn't tell what they was thinking and what was coming next. I looked to Grandma in the room with all that talk. She seen me and giggled, putting her hand to her mouth. Mom lifted the pot of beans to the sink. At least I got interrupted and didn't have to think of an answer for her about where I'd been. I could thank Uncle Angelo's fists for that.

Most of the time I wanted Dad and Uncle Angelo to leave, get on with their routine, which was drinking out on the town in the bars and pool halls on lower Fourth. Uncle Angelo picked on everybody: Old Uncle about never being married, me if I got a piece of ass yet. I started thinking about the scene, about Sally Did and Smoke. I thought of asking Uncle Angelo about Sally on account his wife was related to Sally, sister or something, which is how we knowed Sally was just another Indian from around here and not a princess from some faraway tribe like she was claiming. See, I was thinking if I could find out something about Sally and the goings-on in that slaughterhouse, I wouldn't have to go all the way inside. Just fake it, go in a little, then tell the guys a story.

But I wouldn't get a chance to ask Uncle Angelo nothing.

Everything got quiet. Just the TV and Mom taking plates from the cupboard. I kept my eyes on my food. I kept eating. I felt Dad and Uncle Angelo move past me, behind me. Uncle Angelo was going to tweak my ear, pinch my chest. I could even hear what he was going to say. "You get your whistle wet, boy?" All that stuff. I just kept my head down, chewing my beans, and because the longest time went by, I figured the worst possible thing would happen. Like he'd hit me a good one upside the head and then I'd have to sit there watching him and Dad laugh at me. Like I was supposed to be quicker and outsmart them. What could I do? Then from the corner of my eye I seen Mom picking up the empty beer cans. Dad and Uncle Angelo was gone. I turned clear around until I seen the open front door.

Mom put plates of beans on the table for Grandma and Old Uncle. The two of them sat down with me. But I didn't look at them. I seen only the open front door and the streetlight shining beyond it. It was my time to go too.

I had nothing to take out that door with me. No luck, only a empty barrel. I looked at my sisters and brothers in the front room and then at Grandma and Old Uncle. I was alone all of a sudden. I started to shake. I thought of Buster and them out back of that slaughterhouse. They'd be waiting for me. Points. Points. I had no points. I was washed up, broke. Then something come to me, something just gave up in me and let me go. What was I holding on to? What did I have to lose? What I had was one more chance to turn the whole picture around. The short straw, Old Nellie, Ruby. It was my only chance. So I got up and left.

It was cool, clear. The night opened itself up for me. I slipped down Grand and up Santa Rosa Avenue like a eel in water. Nothing stopped me until the slaughterhouse fence. Turns out I was the only one there. Seemed like forever, but Victor and Micky finally showed. Buster didn't turn up for another half hour. The Navarro twins didn't show at all.

"OK," Buster said, "it's just us." He looked at me and then started explaining how I just walk up the chute. He talked like it was some technical maneuver, as if I couldn't figure out how to walk up a ramp and hadn't thought way beyond that the whole time I was waiting for him. But he was going through the motions, saying stuff so he could still play Buster. He didn't know what to do after going up that chute. He couldn't say if he had to and he knowed it. Nobody could. It was a big deal. "All clear," Buster said, but I was already through the fence.

The chute had cross boards like steps so the horses wouldn't slip back or fall. That struck me funny. Like to make sure the horses would go in and not hurt themselves and miss out on dying. But soon as I was under that burlap and in the dark I had to pay attention. I couldn't see worth a damn. But funny thing, it never crossed my mind to lie just then, like I planned at home. I never thought of stopping and hiding in the dark. I already done more than Buster or any of them.

I followed a fence railing. I walked sideways, like a crab, never letting go of that railing. I was thinking. The pit of horse guts was on my mind, and I took little steps, holding onto the railing and testing with each step to make sure I had solid ground. I looked back to the light from the chute hole every once in a while. Then something happened. I couldn't see anything, frontward or backward. My way out was gone. I couldn't see the chute hole. I must've rounded a corner. Things shifted. The railing stopped and I was clinging to a flat wall. I froze up, spread-eagled on the wall. I was completely lost.

I thought of tearing out of there, making a mad dash for the chute hole. The place had no windows. There was no way out but the chute and the front door, and I was a far ways from there. I was on the second floor somewheres, and the front door was on the first. I almost panicked. But I had enough reason left to tell me that tearing off in that darkness was likely to land me in the horse pit or something worse. I stood there awhile, my palms flat against the wall. I was facing the wall like I was caught and waiting for cops to frisk me. Then I started moving real slow, going sideways, with the toes of my tennis shoes and my palms holding to the wall. I'd gone about five feet when I heard it. Actually, I felt it, a vibrating sound in the wall, like base pounding through the wood. I stopped, then moved a little backward, then forward. Forward it was stronger. I followed and it got louder. It was music I was hearing. A clear beat, a drum-beat for some rock-and-roll song or something. Still I took small steps, testing that I had solid ground beneath me. I kept moving sideways. I started smelling something like meat, a thick copper-like smell that was warm and damp. It choked me. I felt like I was moving between flesh. Like it was hanging on either side of me, all around. But I kept going, following the music. Then just as fast as that meat smell come, it disappeared, and I was standing on a landing looking down a flight of stairs to light below.

It was the Supremes singing "Back in My Arms Again." The way was clear, just down the steps. But I was more scared than ever. Down those steps I would see the goings-on firsthand. I could hear people moving and talking. What if it was nothing, just some folks partying? What if it was something and I got caught? Like I seen something illegal and they killed me so I wouldn't tell. It was this last thing pushed me on. Fear, what I knowed best. Not Buster and them. They was far behind me now. I was alone and scared to death and if I stopped I might've lost my fear. I went down one step at a time. The boards creaked, but by now the music was so loud nobody below could hear. Two steps from the bottom I stopped, and when I peeked around the corner, bracing myself against the wall, it all come into plain view: the room with Smoke, Sally, and the girls.

I moved down one step and situated myself so I could watch. It wasn't really a room but a clearing of cardboard boxes stacked nearly high as the ceiling. That was three walls, and Sally's gold Cadillac made the fourth. A big transistor radio sat on the hood of the car and a black girl in a short dress that looked like a pink flowered towel around her body played with the dials, trying to find another song. The rest of them was in the middle of the room. But they hadn't stopped. They was still moving like the music was still playing. They wasn't dancing, really, but walking in a pack slowly around the room, going in a circle. Like in some ceremony. Smoke was out in front a little with a wine jug in a brown paper sack, in his straw hat and overalls. Sally was in the middle, her skunk-striped hair standing out in the small crowd. They turned so they had their backs to me, and when they turned again, coming in my direction, I seen a smaller girl in the middle, between Sally and the orange-haired black girl. Sally and the orange hair was holding on to her arm-in-arm, walking her along. Sally yelled for the pink dress by her car to hurry and find some music. The girl Sally was holding wore a dark shawl, and when a song came booming into the room, I seen the fringes of the shawl start shaking, dangling. I must've had my eyes fixed on that shawl because I didn't see if any of them started moving faster or not. I didn't see that the girl had stepped out of the crowd. Not until the shawl dropped on the floor did I look up and seen the girl was Ruby. She was still moving, taking little steps, one at a time by herself, wobbling some, like she was just learning how to walk or had had too much of Smoke's wine. Ruby with lipstick and done-up hair, and even in that tight red dress that would never let me see the color red again in peace, she looked to me like a butterfly just out of its cocoon. Nothing I had known before. And she was looking right at me, her eyes in mine and mine in hers, and not knowing it. Then she looked up, like she was looking to heaven. "Over here," Smoke said. He was next to the Cadillac, holding the door wide open.

I pushed myself back up the stairs to the landing. Somehow I had sense enough to know if I stood there any longer I'd likely fall forward out of the stairwell in front of all those people. Somehow, even when you're dead inside, you think how to live. I should've just collapsed there, letting Ruby and everyone else see how small and dumb I was. But something takes over. A million things raced through my mind. I thought of rescuing Ruby. I pictured myself charging down the stairs and whisking her out the front door and us running along Santa Rosa Avenue to safety. I must've been standing there awhile like that because I heard Sally's car start. I thought of Ruby. But it was no use. Things was bigger than me.

I groped in the dark and found the railing. Going out was easier. I came up under the burlap and stood on top of the chute. You'd think I was a king or something by the looks on the guys' faces. I had a long view of the empty railroad tracks leading into town. I didn't want to move, but I was already going down the chute.

"What'd you see in there?" Micky asked.

"Nothing," I said, crawling through the fence.

Victor stood with his eyes popped out of his head. I looked to Buster, who was quiet. He knowed like the rest I'd seen something. Must've been on my face.

"Just some people dancing around. That black whore with orange hair. There's no horse-gut hole or nothing," I said and spit. My voice scared me. Like telling what I just won was nothing to wear a crown about.

"Man, you *did it,*" Micky said.

"Shit," Buster said. "It ain't no big deal." He spit to outdo me. But he didn't believe himself, and nobody else did either.

I looked back at the burlap hanging over the top of the black hole.

"Shit, let's go to the park and get us some chicks." Buster was still at it. He turned up his T-shirt sleeves to show his muscles.

We started making our way back to Santa Rosa Avenue.

"Frankie, you smell like meat or something," Victor said, first time opening his mouth. "You better go change your clothes."

"Yeah," I said, and looked up, and there was nothing in the sky.

Waiting for the Green Frog

I am an old woman now, like any other, except for what I am going to tell you. You want to know about me, don't you? OK, then.

It's no secret what I am.

When my son was a young man, when he thought of nothing but what he could do with that thing he thinks makes him a man, I pulled a tiny rabbit with the tail of a crow from the center of his chest. I used my flint piece. I cut him open, the same way the white doctors use a knife. Call it surgery. I caught that rabbit by the ears, between my thumbs, and pulled up. The entire room of people heard it squealing for its life, which I would end. And Alfred, my husband, when he was giving his hop-picking money to the Catholics in Santa Rosa and everything else to Old Lady Hatcher, I danced sixteen nights and sang every song I knew and some I didn't so he would live. A part of me wanted him to die, given what he put me through in those days. I admit it. But that's the part I put aside for this business. My medicine is good. I danced and sang until that jealous spook Sam Toms quit, until his curse, which came each night in the form of a great blue light, faded into nothing outside our back door.

I won those fights. I won all my fights, which is why I am still sitting here today.

I say fight, but it might make more sense if I say game. It is like gambling, a crapshoot. Every time I stand to sing doctoring songs, when these hands locate the pain in a person's body, the game is on. I gamble with my life.

It's not like in the white-man books you read about us Indians. It's not me. I do not have the power. These hands and the songs are power. They are what I use in the game, my weapons against the odds. I must outwit my opponent. If something goes wrong, if the disease gets the upper hand, it would finish me, leave me a mumbling old hag with death my only prospect. So I use the songs. The words charm. They put the disease in the patient's body to sleep, make the disease forgetful. Then the hands move like pieces of metal to a magnet.

OK, so how do the hands get this way?

With my basket, that old basket shaped like a canoe with the butterfly design. I make baskets, but I didn't make that one. It was given to me by the old man, my father's uncle, when I was sick. I didn't want to do this work. I wanted to chase the boys and drink wine at the train station in Santa Rosa. I wanted to do just as the others did. So I went down. Call it a coma. Darkness. Felt like I was in a tunnel. I heard this voice: *You don't see what I am telling you. You are going to spend your time on earth like this, throwing your life away.* That was the spirit talking. Then I realized I wasn't in a tunnel at all. I had been under water. When I came to, I was holding on to the side of a canoe, my head just above water, and then I saw the old man. He was singing and leading me around the front room with my hands fastened to the basket.

"This is what you are going to use," he said. "Your hands will have this basket power to pull up sickness from people."

Later, my aunt, the one who raised me, told me the basket had been his. He died not long after that. He told me he wanted me to have it. At the time, when he was doctoring me, I didn't know much. I just knew he was singing and talking and tugging on the basket, pulling me around the room.

It turned out true, everything he said.

And that gets me back to the other part of this, which is the songs. "You have to sing those songs," my father's uncle said. "Sick people will come."

One day a song hit me, just as if someone hit me with a stick, on the side of my neck. And the pain spread until it was singing in my throat. That was my first song. Then another and another; on it went like that for many years. I never knew when I would get hit. My aunt said I was becoming with power. Several people prayed for me: that coast woman, then Lily Rosario, and that north man. All of them danced and sang. Each one gave advice. But like I said, I didn't want this life.

It was sometime after my father's uncle gave me the basket that I heard singing by the shed out back. That was on the old land by Sebastopol, near the lagoon. The others had gone to town, over to Santa Rosa, because in those days we couldn't get supplies in Sebastopol. Maybe everyone was working in Santa Rosa, I don't know. I was alone doing the laundry, which is how I took time off from work in the fields and orchards. I was folding shirts and things in the kitchen. We had a big table there.

I heard this singing. I thought I had been hit with song again. But I felt no pain, no whack on the neck. The singing wasn't in me. It was a man's voice, outside, just as if someone was under the window. I looked out. I could see the shed and as far as the tules that lined the lagoon. Nothing. No one. A couple of chickens the raccoons hadn't caught and my aunt's pig. Then I thought of someone trying to spook me. I figured a person was behind the shed, where I couldn't see.

I was foolish in those days. I grabbed a butcher knife, thinking that could stop a spook. The shed sat hardly a hundred feet from the house, and I went out without stopping, butcher knife in my hand, clear around the back. Then I went inside. I checked behind the broken carriage, looked in the dark corners where we kept the tools and feed. I cussed. But the singing didn't stop. Show yourself, I kept calling.

One thing, I didn't go down to the tules, where someone could have been hiding, watching me. The voice was right there in the yard. It was everywhere around me, pounding the way songs did in my throat, only now the songs pounded against my body, like a pulse, squeezing me from head to toe. The only thing that was free was my throat, and I hollered things that must have shook St. Rose church ten miles away.

By this time I was sitting on the bench under the kitchen window where my aunt's husband hitched the horses. I knew something out of the ordinary was happening. I didn't know I was struggling for the last time with that which would change me forever. By nightfall I would have a new life. In four days I would have my first patient.

With the knife across my lap, I sat facing the shed. Something told me the voice was coming from there. I don't know. Maybe I was telling myself that. I set my eyes on anything that moved. It was three or four o'clock in the afternoon, a late autumn day, and the sun caught on shiny things: stones, the door latch, a chicken's eyes. I guess that's how I first noticed the frogs, shiny-backed little things hopping in front of the shed, coming from around the corner, circling the building counter clockwise. Frogs up from the lagoon, I thought. We had frogs in the yard all the time. Sometimes the pig ate them. Just then I looked for the pig. The place was empty: the stones were dull gray, the door latch the color of lead. Only the frogs sounded alive, more of them coming and going the same way, and they stopped in a certain place each time, right in front of me, before they moved on.

At first I thought the little green things with black glinting eyes were cute. They were something to think about while the songs that pounded the buildings and everything in sight squeezed me tighter and tighter. Then the yard emptied: no yard, no shed. There was only the pounding, like a hammer, knocking away whatever I knew, all I could see, except for those frogs. Then I realized something. It was only one frog, the same frog going around and around the shed, and each time it came from the corner it was bigger. I had no sense of time. How long had it been since I had first seen the little green thing?

I wasn't myself. Do something, I said to this frog. Stop this or I am going to die.

It winked at me.

I wanted to keep talking, but I couldn't, because my voice was singing and I was on my feet, dancing in place with my whole life in front of me. I had no breath. I was beating, as if I was only my heart, with the songs and me inseparable. Of course those songs I'd heard and was now singing were the power songs, the ones that had been making a home in my throat all along.

And there was a chorus, all those women and men who would stand behind me singing these songs as I wrestled with disease. I saw all of them, from the beginning to the end. My cousin's aunt, Filomena Jones. Even Sam Toms's sister. They were singing, keeping time with the red clappers. And the frog was talking to me and showing me the instruments I would use for curing the sick: the old canoe basket, the flint piece, a tobacco pipe from a mail order catalog, and a cocoon rattle. Only the frog wasn't there anymore. Just the voice, and it said in four days my cousin from Tomales would come. She was full of little black minnow fish. I was given a song to net them.

Then I heard my aunt and her husband fighting.

"You have overworked my niece, and now she has taken her life," my aunt said. My aunt was the excitable type. Her husband was not.

"Lucy, go jump in the water."

"Look, the knife. The end of her."

"There's no blood. Turn her over, check her back."

I opened my eyes just as my aunt started to turn me. I was sprawled in the yard, in front of the shed. My aunt was crying, her face full of water, and her husband was behind her holding the lantern. Beyond was a sky bright with stars.

The next day, the next afternoon, I wove a net of fine willow branches, just as I had been instructed. I can only collect willow at certain times. I fast. Whatever I am told. My aunt's husband didn't believe at first, but after my cousin appeared just as I said she would, after I calmed and healed her writhing body, he .never doubted again. Who would doubt a catch of black fish?

So wherever I go I have a shed. I call it the frog's house, where that frog can hop round and round, like the first time. When we moved to the Indian land in Mark West Spring, my aunt's husband built a place a hundred feet behind the new house. I worried that because we weren't near the lagoon I might have left the frog behind. Two weeks went by. Then, sure enough, it came around the corner sounding the whole place with songs. That time I had a patient coming from Lake County, a young man poisoned by his in-laws. And when I married Alfred he knew my conditions. Use the shed for your tools, I said. But I know now I needn't have said anything. Even with his riding to take communion at St. Rose's every Sunday, he never questioned me. That's how I know in looking back that, in spite of that church and Hatcher and everything else, he loved me to the day he died. He never doubted me.

Only now folks say this is hooey. Like my granddaughter Darlene, for instance. She says she wants to make baskets. Teach me, Grandma, she says. I say, There are rules about weaving, collecting the sedge and bulrush. I go even though I know she hasn't listened to a word I said. One part of me says I need help digging the sedge roots. That's the part of me that's old.

And look what happens.

She picks me up. It's twelve noon and she's got both kids with her.

"C'mon, Grandma. Sorry I'm late. Jenny's sick, had to pick her up at the child care. Then I had to fill out papers for the damn social service woman."

I am eating a piece of bread and the leftover soup her mother dropped off. Because of my sugar I can't go that long without eating. Little Jenny peeks at me over the top of the table. She's sniffling, snot coming out her nose. The other one, the little boy, hides behind Darlene, trying to make sense of the four-legged aluminum contraption next to me that is my constant companion these days. Darlene drops her keys on the table, as if evidence that she is here. I see on the key ring a metal plate with the words LOVE ME OR LEAVE ME.

"Are you on your period?" I ask.

"No, Grandma. You told me the rules. I said I'm sorry I'm late."

When my nose was good, when I still possessed the fine-tuned senses of a wild animal, I could tell if a woman was menstruating. What difference does it make? I think. I told her eight o'clock the latest, and no kids. I told her about fasting and about the time it takes me to pray over the place I am going to dig sedge, not to mention the time it takes us to drive there and me to shuffle from the road to the creek bed. Already enough rules are broken. But, like I said, I need help.

We stop for gas and the man shortchanges Darlene. It was a mistake. Before she is half finished telling him what happened, he hands her the money.

When she gets back in the car she slams the door and mumbles something mean about the man so he can hear her. I see the shadow on this side of the station garage. It's past one o'clock.

"Is something wrong, Grandma?" she asks, handing me the change from the gas. I tell her to keep it, buy something for the kids. By now I know we won't dig a single root. I just wonder what will happen.

Along the highway I see the buildup, the housing tracts and apartments. Only one dairy is left; here and there, along the streets and in the front yards of houses that look the same, a pear or apple tree from the old orchards. When I was little I helped my mother and aunts pick acorns under huge oak trees.

"Used to be dirt road here." I jump, hearing myself thinking out loud, then say something to sound deliberate. "This road was just a dirt road."

"See, Grandma. I got to get that all down. Your life. That teacher at the junior college was going to help me. Then I had to quit school. I got mouths to feed."

Little Jenny leans on me, sleeping. The boy, between Jenny and Darlene, is quiet too. I have a hard time pronouncing his name, that Mexican name Darlene says too fast. Out of Santa Rosa we go north.

"But Grandma, it doesn't matter. I can still write the book."

"What?" I ask. It's been some time since anybody said anything. I can't think what it is or what book she is talking about. My mind wanders. Then I figure about the book, since the last couple months Darlene has been talking about recording me.

"I don't need that teacher to help me," Darlene says. "Anyway, he's white. Those guys just want to get their names on a book. They don't really know about us."

I tell her where to turn off the highway. We follow the road along the creek. I see the earth is damp, good for digging. I forget myself. I don't want to listen or pay attention to Darlene. I don't even hear little Jenny struggling to breathe through the snot in her nose.

"Anyway, I got someone else to help me. And this is what this whole conversation is leading to. I got something to tell you."

She pauses to make sure I am listening and know the importance of what comes next. She's like my mother that way, her great-grandmother. If Darlene didn't have her hands on the wheel she would be wringing them in her lap.

"I have someone special in my life, Grandma. I didn't want to say until I was sure. You know I haven't had the best of luck in the men department. This guy is different. You'll be happy. Guess what? He's Indian. Sioux Indian all the way from South Dakota. I met him at Indian Health."

"He's interested in Indian things, isn't he?" I say.

"Yeah. See, I told him how you are, how you know things. I told him how we're Pomo Indians right from this area. And you know what he said? 'There's no such thing as Pomo or Sioux. That's just a name the white man gave us.' See, the same thing you always say. 'OK,' I said. And that's why he said us Indians have to write our own books. White man doesn't know anything and thinks we're dumb. You see it all the time, like that man back there at the gas station. . . ."

Darlene is still on the white-man kick when we cross the cattle guard onto McGill's property. I don't know. She's talking a mile a minute. I tell her to stop at McGill's house to let someone know we are here. Half a dozen times I try to interrupt her. She stops only where the road ends, which, as it turns out, is where we get out and start the walk to the creek. Like I said, it's no easy chore for me, that walk.

So I let Darlene fuss with the kids and pack the trowels and small pickax while I start off, my four aluminum legs in front of me, my dress dragging behind. Must be a sight. But I'm not thinking of myself. I'm smelling the damp warm air and seeing how the sun hits things this time of day. The oaks. The willows near the water. That's when I stop to rest and look up from the cow stuff I must dodge in my path.

I get to the sedge beds below the willows. I forget what I know and start praying anyway. The creek reflects quivering sunlight on the willows, and I see what I am being told. I see in the flickering light the motion of the diamondback's rattle. I look quickly for Darlene and the kids. "Don't go near the water," I holler. "Come back!" But I don't plead anymore. I am singing the power songs for safety with all I have.

I am lost in song and that's why what happens next isn't all clear. I hear a loud whir, like thunder behind me, and dogs barking. Darlene is running up from the creek, the boy in her arms, little Jenny just behind. Then the world turns clear around and the next thing I know I'm looking straight up at McGill. Behind him is the sun, and it's calm on the sides of his black Western hat.

"Mrs. Copaz, are you OK? I'm sorry. Nellie, it's me, Charles McGill."

Darlene is screaming for him not to touch me.

"Nellie, it's me," he says. "Are you hurt?"

He looks old as me, the poor thing, pockmarked beak nose and white whiskers. I wonder how he is going to get himself up off his knees. With my aluminum walker, which I am under, I suppose. When I can think where I am and what's happened, I'm embarrassed.

Darlene gets me to my feet. I hold the walker for McGill to pull himself up with even though he shows me he doesn't need it. Darlene has called him every name she can think of. I think, Lucky she lost the pickax, or she'd have threatened him with it. He displays the kindness to ignore her and offers me a ride back to the car. Of course Darlene objects. No way to treat the man who has kept this tract of land over fifty years for me, I am thinking, as he makes his way to the jeep and the barking dogs. "Hush up, bastards," he says.

I start back to the car.

"He ruined our whole day," Darlene says, with the kids yapping on both sides of her.

He saved your life, I think to myself. Something terrible would have happened. What, I don't know, but I saw it coming.

In Santa Rosa we stop at Indian Health to pick up my medicine, which was part of the plan. I let Darlene go in and I sit with the kids. I think back on what happened. Someone once showed me pictures of cave drawings Indians did of people with lines around their bodies. I don't know those Indians, where those drawings are from, but it's like that. I have four lines around me. Spirit lines, protection, so nothing will get into me. Hah! Out there in McGill's pasture those lines held me up like a dummy. They are stretched, worn like old tendons.

I turn to wipe little Jenny's nose, and when I look up, who do you think is coming out of the building? This tops off the day. It's Old Lady Hatcher, fat and on her cane. Breasts that half the county enjoyed now hanging like the udder of a ten-year-old cow. Hands that cast half the spells I fought now crooked with arthritis.

I straighten in my seat, throw my shoulders back, hold my head as if I were twenty again. This after I have just fallen in a cow field, like a wild mallard shot out of the sky. Just in case Hatcher should see me. I'm still here, Hatcher. Remember our meeting just two weeks ago?

And that's what I'm getting back to, what just happened.

You see, we go way back, me and Mary Hatcher. Like two different flowers in the same field, we come out each spring, show our colors in the summer, cast seeds in autumn, then sprout with the first good rain and find where the other has taken hold for another round. Love and jealousy tangle with business. Throw hate in there too. Our battles over the years cover the length and width of all that is human. She is a poisoner, and she stole my husband.

I hate her when I think of it. I am jealous, I admit. After all, I am human. For nearly ten years my husband was charmed by that woman, taken in by her love songs and made crazy by everything she had under those fancy city clothes she wore. She was highfalutin-looking, nothing like what you see today, just another old Indian. With that light skin and long wavy hair parted on the side just so, she looked as if she were Spanish or a pretty Mexican. Of course, the stories told about her today are true. She operated a house, hired the girls, and took money from the men. I believe she sat in her parlor in that place on West Seventh and drummed up business with song. I see her sitting among her fine things, lamps and cherrywood furniture, in her store-bought dresses, with crystal charm stones in her cupped hands. Or maybe on the second-story balcony, casting powder from the dried remains of an orange-bellied salamander into the moonlit air. I can't prove any of it. She did coerce nearly every man within her reach, white and Indian, one way or another.

My husband was special to her, and it pains me to say this. He cared enough to give her two children and never to forget them. Yes, Alfred Copaz, my husband, is the father of Mary Hatcher's two children, her only two children, and the whole county knows it. Each Sunday Alfred drove into Santa Rosa, and after he had communion and swept the walkways for the priest, he took the two kids out for the day. Dinner, clothes, what-have-you. This went on long after him and Hatcher called it quits, until those kids were grown. What was I to tell six needy faces each Sunday, Your father is working? Hatcher sacrificed the boy some years back when her attempt to poison someone backfired. The girl is alive and well, with children of her own. Who do you think was helping Hatcher out of Indian Health the other day?

It's rubbed in my face all the time. So I should hate morning, noon, and night and then some. But I cannot carry on my life that way. That's the difference between me and Hatcher. With her it doesn't matter. Poison is the handmaid of hate. It works where we are weak. It plays on the sourness in our hearts. If Hatcher hates me, if she is jealous and greedy, all the better for her. Her life depends on it.

Indian people know about poison. It has been with us from the beginning. Poisoners know how to use disease and pain. And they know where. In the old days a poison man or woman lived separate from the camp, where the camp and everything else could be seen. Poisoners watched enemies. Nowadays you can't tell so easy. The way we live, a poison person could be next door, in your own house. And what a field day for that person. We are so full of hate and ignorance these days we can't see two feet in front of us.

Hatcher was a perfect candidate. She comes from two different tribes somewhere up north. I forget now. But the story goes that her mother died and she was raised by her father's people, who hated and distrusted her mother's people. She was passed back and forth. You know how old Indians are. They suspect what's in the blood. So by the time this girl was five years old her heart was weak enough that anyone listening could hear it crying, and no one listens better than a poisoner. And that's what must have happened, because old Salvador King took her as a child. She would be his last pupil, his fourth leg. Salvador King was so full of poison he needed four people to carry it for him, four legs: his daughter; Sam Toms, who lived by the fairgrounds in Santa Rosa,- the half-breed or whatever he was, with blue eyes, who sat in the park; and Mary Hatcher. Toms and Hatcher are the only ones still living. They say she sleeps with King's pipe.

Sam Toms was the one who introduced me to Hatcher. Oh, I had met her before, her and Sam Toms and the rest of them, in the songs, charm stones, insects, animals, and whatever else I found in my patients' bodies. Poison was nothing new to me by that point in my life. I can tell my patients what's happened to them. The voice tells me where that frog comes from. But I never set eyes on Mary Hatcher until just before Sam Toms tried to kill my husband, until just before I sang and danced that blue light into nothing. In fact, I would have figured someone, Sam Toms or whoever, was after me because of my medicine and got my husband instead.

I would have been wrong.

I can see what's happened to my patients, but I can't always say why. Hardly a week before that incident with my husband, I found out the truth simple as seeing a stop sign on the road. Far as I'm concerned, it's the only honest thing Sam Toms ever did.

I thought he poisoned me. I was shopping at the market in Santa Rosa. We had a car by this time and I was one of the first people to drive in these parts, so I was alone, only a couple kids with me, the smaller ones. Not like in the old days when everyone jumped on the wagon every time it was hitched up because it was their only chance to go someplace. I was bent over pulling a sack of flour from the pallet on the floor when I felt a tug on my coat. It was the rainy season and I wore a heavy overcoat. I thought it was one of the kids. But just as I looked up and found both of them in front of me I caught from the corner of my eye a dark hand. Sam Toms, the same as always, winter or summer, in that buttoned-up suit and Stetson hat, with only his black face showing.

"Excuse me," he said.

Excuse me nothing. I got my groceries and the kids and drove straight home. I could hardly grip the wheel. I went to my shed, sat there in front of it, and prayed. But nothing came, no protection songs. When it became dark I gave up. Maybe I should call someone good to pray for me, I thought. Then, when I was inside sorting the groceries, which had been sitting for hours, up from my coat pocket floats the note. At first I thought it was my grocery receipt. But I saw the scrawl. He spelled it out direct and simple, the affair and the time and place.

I looked at the clock. My mind was upside down, my life inside out. I warmed leftover beans and put the oldest child in charge. The rest you can guess. I drove back to Santa Rosa and found the place on West Seventh. But, oh, it was pitiful, my husband's horses and old outdated wagon parked among the shiny new cars. What testimony. Pitiful and so beautiful and true I felt as if my heart dropped on the car seat and was beating for anyone to see under the pale streetlight. There was nothing I could do to retrieve it.

Later, notions about other women in that place dissolved into thin air. No matter what excuse I made, no matter what other story I put together to cover up my eyes, Hatcher and Alfred broke through and stood together for me to see bright as day. It was just as Sam Toms said. Jealous Sam Toms, who told the truth only because he was a fool for Hatcher too.

That night I drove home not knowing my own name. What I was thinking I don't know. I don't remember. I got home, I know that much, because I can say I didn't go into the house. I didn't see my children. I was seated in front of that shed caught up in the songs, hearing that voice. Something about a girl from the coast who would come the next day with her grandmother. I had to go through with it. I had to go on with my own life, leave behind my hurt, my hate. Like I said, I saved my husband from Sam Toms after this. But when I think about it, I'm happy that my life has destroyed so much of her work.

In those days I was busy. It wasn't just Sam Toms and Hatcher and King's daughter and that man in the park. Old Man Miguel was living in these parts and going strong. And there were others. People came to me from all over, seven days a week. Sometimes half the tribe. I doctored back to back, twenty people at a time. My yard overflowed with the sick. For certain kinds of poison I must build a fire to burn the poison as it sits in my hands. Once I held my hands in the flames for one whole night. My son kept asking, "Mother, when are you going to get up?" I suppose he was tired of bringing wood. But he knew, just as my other children knew, this work was our bread and butter.

I was paid well, though I never asked for a thing. My patients offered whatever they could. That's the rule. Some people gave beautiful blankets, expensive clothes, fifty-dollar bills. Others gave a bag of acorns. One woman brought a dozen white hens and four spotted pigs. I remember because she had them tied up or strapped down, whatever, in the backseat of her Model A Ford. And for good reason. We couldn't keep those things locked up anywhere. The chickens flew into trees and the pigs rooted under fences. But we had eggs and meat. We never went without.

A lot has changed.

For me things happened gradually, passed unnoticed, until one day I was sitting and realized I had been sitting for some time. Where once there was this or that, now there was nothing: no clothes to fold, no lunches to get ready. Time opened up a space, and I found myself sitting in the middle of it. I saw the distance between me and those clothes and lunches. I counted the days, then the weeks and months, between patients. Of course once the space was opened and I saw how I was sitting, I knew by the aches and pains in my body that things could not be otherwise. Time's trick, I suppose.

The old poisoners are gone, except for Hatcher and maybe a couple of others I haven't heard from lately. Sam Toms is alive and they say living with an eighteen-year-old white woman. I guess he's putting what's left of him in that. I don't know. The thing is, poison hasn't gone anywhere. It's everywhere so people can't see, and what they can't see they don't believe. Maybe in time it will take new songs, new words to stop the poison. I don't know. Sometimes I think I'm done for.

Funny thing: I took up cards. It gives me something to do, since I can only weave baskets so long before my eyes give out. I play solitaire and it's fun. I mention this because it leads to what just happened.

I was holding a card in my right hand, just the card I needed to finish the game, the queen of hearts, when I got stuck. My arm wouldn't move. I thought of my arthritis or a stroke. The card dropped. Then I turned and took hold of my walker. I knew what was happening. I could feel it. It's just that it had been so long, at least a year, since the last time.

And then I can't recall the details, except to say the next thing I knew I was standing in front of the shed and the little green thing with black glinting eyes came around the corner and I was full of songs. The songs pounded the buildings and everything in sight, and I listened to the voice and found out about the work I was to do the next day. I was listening where I couldn't see the frog anymore, just like in the beginning of things.

And it turned out true.

The next day that boy came with his mother and father, the football player from Santa Rosa. I'm proud to say he's Indian and just as handsome as the papers make him out to be. And strong, a large boy, who looked as frightened and small as a trapped finch when I opened the door and first set eyes on him.

"Do you still doctor the sick?" his mother asked in Indian. She didn't speak my language but a language close enough so I could understand. Besides, I knew what she wanted.

I backed up, pulled my walker out of the way. "Come in," I said back in her language.

The boy had been sick for some time. The medical doctors figured a blow to the head from his football game, but they could find nothing from their tests. For six months he'd been forgetful. He wandered here and there away from home. I sang and danced. I used my cocoon rattle, smoked angelica root in my pipe, and held the canoe basket until my hands were ready, until they moved to that young man's forehead and seized upon something that twisted and squirmed with all its might against me in the center of the boy's mind, something that when lifted out could not be seen with the naked eye but was heard by everyone as a woman singing.

I held the voice cupped in my hands for just a moment. I knew it was Hatcher. I didn't know why, whether someone had hired her to harm the young man, whether someone was jealous or wanted him, or what. I knew the song and I knew the voice even as it was that of a young woman, sweet and high. But something happened. I got a funny feeling. The song was touching me. It was a nice feeling, gentle, hitting my heart the way leaves touch down on a dry autumn earth. I wanted to embrace the voice. I was full of gratitude. So much came into my eyes.

Then I became frightened. I wanted to hold the voice forever. Of course I couldn't. So I turned ever so slowly and held it over the burning candle next to me and waited until it was silent.

Afterward, after everyone had left and the house was quiet again, I sat at my kitchen table for the longest time. The window was open and I could see the sky. I took a deep breath, then another and another, marveling at the endless stars.

Joy Ride

The sixteen-year-old girl sitting next to me uncrosses her legs. "C'mon, Unky," she says, "let's go somewhere."

Streetlight hits her legs, travels up and down her shiny skin. My heart pounds. I know where there's a motel, a room I can get for twenty-five bucks. To the left at the end of Grand. Or maybe we could take a ride to Montecito Heights, park, and look at the view. Just up Pressley here and out of South Park, five minutes across town. But I can't turn. I can't stop circling the block, passing my house with its yellow porch light.

This girl is a ghost. This sixteen-year-old snapping bubble gum and tossing silky black hair climbed into my pickup to haunt me. She tricked me by the side of the road, turned her face from the headlights so I couldn't see who she was until it was too late. I want to drop her off, get rid of her now and forever. I want to go in and come clean with my wife. But she keeps talking, this girl, reaching with her painted fingernails across the seat. Her words form the stories that are my life. Her breath is the same as it's always been, as long as I can remember, sweet bait hiding the sharp metal hook. She's an Indian, after all, and nobody fishes like an Indian.

I've known them all my life.

Worse than niggers, my father used to say.

We'd see them on the streets, lots of times down by the train station on lower Fourth. The men glassy-eyed, holding wine in paper bags. They'd sit in the shade under the trees, or against the gray stone building if it was raining, and pass one another the bottles. Women were with them, heavyset dark women with scarves on their heads. Sometimes even the kids sat there.

"Lazy drunks." My father scowled.

For the longest time I didn't know what a nigger or a drunk was. I knew we were Portuguese, and that's about all. Niggers and drunks were something bad, like when he called me and my brothers no-good sons of bitches. Which we heard a lot. He was easily pissed off. He didn't mince words when he told us his life would be easier if he didn't have kids to look after. "Saddled" was the word he used. "Your mother up and died and saddled me with you," he'd say. He'd blow up if we questioned him about anything he said or did.

Like the time my older brother Frankie asked why he always drove into town on the west side. No matter where we lived, and we lived lots of different places, the old man would take pains to drive into Santa Rosa from West Seventh, past the old bottling plant and warehouses. The day Frankie asked my father about this we had circled the entire town, a good while out of our way. It was hot, a fall day after the prunes, and we were parked outside Ben's Used Clothing, each of us sitting in the back of Father's forty-nine Ford pickup with our summer earnings clenched in our hands for school clothes. The old man's grizzled face reddened as he stood alongside the truck. He looked up and down the street, and instead of shouting like he would at home, he whispered. "Frankie," he said, "do you know what shame is?"

Frankie didn't answer.

"Give me your money," he demanded, and Frankie opened his hand, letting the crinkled bills drop into my father's fingers, which curled up like prongs on a garden trowel. "There, there," Father said, grasping the money. "You'll know what shame is when you go back to school in old clothes."

He bought my sister a dress that day with Frankie's money. It was a hideous thing, orange with frayed bows up and down the front and on the shoulders, an old lady's castoff. He didn't want Frankie to forget. He made my sister wear the dress day in and day out until Christmas. My sister never protested. She never said anything to him. She never said anything to anyone, not to me or Frankie or my other older brother, Angelo. Never. She didn't talk, Marie. My father would drop sacks of potatoes or flour by the back door, sometimes meat wrapped in bloodied butcher paper, and she'd fetch in the things and quietly get to work, peeling or whatever. She was dark, what we'd later call Mediterranean-looking, and she kept her thick hair pulled back with a plain barrette on each side of her head so you saw nothing but her downcast eyes. She was a mother and didn't want to be.

Me and my brothers took off every chance we could, cut away from the house. When we lived on the Nunes dairy we'd skinny-dip under the willows in the irrigation ditch. Swimming in the cool green water, hidden from where anyone could see us, we had a world of our own that summer. No cares. No grouchy sister, no father complaining about every little thing we did or didn't do. The naked wienies, we called ourselves.

We lived on lots of dairies. Our father milked cows. Portuguese people owned many of the dairies, and he could get work, I guess, because we were Portuguese too. For a while, though, we lived on the Benedict place, harvesting and then pruning their grapes. It was when the old man was between dairy jobs, which happened all the time. Portuguese or not, he'd fight with a boss or co-worker and we'd be up packing in the middle of the night. There was always something wrong with someone. The Benedict job was rough. Long hours, sunup until sundown cutting and hauling grapes. A rush job because the sugar was just right for making wine. Only my sister didn't have to work with us, just like she never had to go to school. The boss, Old Man Benedict's nephew or something, said the best workers could stay on rent free after the harvest. Already our father was complaining about people. It was about the Indians who worked alongside us in the vineyard. "Watch them," he'd say. "They'll steal your full boxes of grapes faster than you can blink." He told us not to walk alone through the tent camp. "They'll catch you and tie you up."

Old Man Benedict, the owner of the place, was crazy, senile. He sat in a tall hay barn at the edge of the vineyard and mumbled to himself. Me and my brothers found him one day. We had a couple of hours of free time, while we were waiting one afternoon for the boss to deliver empty boxes. After hearing so much from our father about this loony in the barn, we wanted to check him out. Our father talked about him after supper one night. It was like a ghost story. We ducked along the grapes until we came to the barn. Then, taking dares, we went in. Angelo went first. He signaled us to follow, and coming through the ajar door, I saw the old man right away. He was tall, standing in overalls against the stacked bales of hay, his featureless face and bald head like a dull lightbulb burning in the dark barn.

He was facing us but I'm not sure he saw us. He put his hands in his overall pockets and spun himself around so fast I never had a chance to really see his face. Then he started moaning, half sobbing, like, and screeching in a high-pitched cracked voice. We tore out of there like bandits.

Father must've known we went there. He must've seen us across the field. He never said anything that afternoon when we started working again, but after dinner he called us to where he was sitting on the ground under a walnut tree. He didn't yell. He just looked at us, letting us know he knew where we had been, and talked like he was picking up the story where he had left off before.

"You see," he said, "a Indian lady hanged herself in that barn." He told us in detail how she wrapped the rope around the roof beam and then placed the noose over her head and jumped from the hay. Like it was happening just in front of us. Then he said the Indian lady was mad. Betrayed, he said. Old Man Benedict had betrayed her. The Indians got mad. "He thinks they're still out to get him," Father said. "And they might; they'll get you when you're not looking. Cut you in two with a butcher knife. Worse than niggers."

Me and my brothers went back to the barn after that. We made a game of it. We'd chuck rocks at the side of the barn and holler, "The Indians are coming, the Indians are coming!" and then tear back across the vineyard.

"There's nothing but a bunch of Indians in there," the girl said to me when we first passed my house.

She must've seen me looking. Maybe I slowed down a bit. I don't know. At that point, before she started talking, before she mentioned the Indians, she was just a dark-skinned girl who waved me down as I turned onto Grand from town. A couple beers with my brother Angelo and then home. That was the plan, and I was almost home.

I stopped when I saw her waving, and she ran around the back of the truck, came up and opened the door, and climbed in. "You're cute," she said. She wasn't even looking at me. She was still pulling the door closed. First I thought maybe she was a hooker, lost her way in these parts from over on Santa Rosa Avenue. She was dressed like one, short dress and makeup and all. But then there was something about the way her Levi's jacket hung on her that made me think she was just a kid. That and the way she chewed her bubble gum. She was fresh, excited, not cool and collected like the streetwalkers. She didn't ask me what I was up to. She didn't talk money. She got in the truck grinning, smelling bubble-gum sweet, like any girl wanting a good time.

I know lots of women check out my decked-out Ford Ranchero. Clean, with mag wheels, the whole thing. Maryann liked my truck, the girl me and Angelo met in the Fiesta Club. And I don't look my age, thirty-eight. So why not, why wouldn't this girl take a look and want to go for a ride? Of course, until she started talking, I had no idea she was sixteen. She looked older.

She faced straight ahead for the longest time, so I couldn't see what she really looked like, the details of her face. We were halfway up the block when she finally turned and I could see her. She was dark, like I said, and beneath the silky hair cut in bangs over her forehead, her dark eyes slanted up, Asian-like. She looked different, like maybe part Chinese or Filipino. Her eyes caught the streetlight, and then that same light was in her smile and then down her legs. "You're cute," she said again.

First things first, I thought without thinking. Which is what a man like me does in these predicaments. He goes on a kind of automatic pilot to save both his home and his desire so that one doesn't cancel the other out. Get across town, at least out of the neighborhood, where you can sort these things out while both are still in your hands. Get out of South Park, I thought. But already I had turned again, onto Grand, where I live, and when I saw the house with its yellow porch light and heard her mention Indians, things changed. Tricky, the way she turned her face away in the headlights and then showed herself only when the light on her face and body blinded me. Never mind the slanty eyes, the part Chinese or Filipino. She knew who was inside my house. She's one of them. Indians in there, she said.

That's what my brother Frankie said years ago, outside that sagging tent by the water. I was fourteen. The three of us—me, Angelo, and Frankie—standing there in the dark. "She's in there," he said. "The Indian." My teeth started clattering, and I looked away from the faint light showing through the tent flap. I saw the moon spread in a wide light over the river. It was late summer and the river was low, motionless, but looking at it just then I thought of the water below the moonlight as wild and bottomless.

"Remember what I told you," Frankie said. "Remember the plan." He was talking to both me and Angelo, but without looking at him, just hearing how he was talking, I felt he was addressing me in particular. My clattering teeth must've shown my fear. That plus the fact I was the youngest and hadn't done anything like this before. "You each know what to do?" he asked.

I looked away from the water. "Yes," I answered.

How could I have forgotten, even scared as I was? He had drilled us all day with his plan. How he was to go in first and then signal us if things were all right. How Angelo was to watch the path from the road for anybody coming. How I was to keep an eye along the river and on the tents a few hundred yards beyond this one. We practiced a bird call, a short, then long whistle we had to use if someone was coming or if something went wrong.

All during lunch break we went over the plan and practiced our whistle. We walked down to the water, scouted the area around the tents. "That one there," Frankie nodded. Even while we were working, picking prunes off the hot dusty ground, Frankie kept talking, motioning for us to work close to him, away from the others. Which was unusual, I mean for Frankie to be talking while we were working. He wanted us to work as hard as he did, focus on what we were doing. He was our boss, since Father seldom worked with us in the crops these days.

Father had settled permanent on the Gonzalves dairy, just south of Santa Rosa. He mellowed. He didn't pick on us the way he used to. I figured it had something to do with my sister leaving. He had a fit, ranted and raved around the house for days, calling her every name in the book. He smashed the pies she left sitting on the sink, threw pots and pans. Then he got quiet, calm, and stayed that way. What could he do? She was over eighteen—nineteen, actually. She met this guy, Manuel, another Portuguese. Actually, she saw him, this guy walking up the road by the mailbox with peaches-and-cream skin and golden hair that was curly tight as a black person's. She walked out, apron on and everything, introduced herself, and never came back, not for her clothes, nothing.

Me and Angelo took over the cooking, since we were the youngest and had been around our sister the most. We couldn't bake pies or make anything fancy, but we got by with the basics: spaghetti, fried chicken, eggs. No one complained. Frankie took jobs after school, first in a grocery store, then in the shoe factory, where he made good money. We were poor, nothing like the rich kids who played sports on the school teams and got elected to class offices, but you'd never know it by looking at Frankie. Pegged Levi's, black wing tips, pressed new shirts,- everything those kids had, Frankie had too. And he was a star athlete, with letters in baseball, basketball, and football. I guess you could say Father's lesson years before struck a chord. Frankie wasn't going to be shamed ever again.

All kinds of girls liked him: blondes, brunettes; rich, poor. But he was strange in this department. Not the blonde whose father owned Satter's, the tony clothing store uptown. Not Christi, the redhead who drove out to the dairy in a Mustang convertible for six weeks trying to find him. He liked Angie, this plain-looking Mexican who didn't go to school. And the Toms sisters, big Indian girls who lived out by the coast. Girls tucked away in places a regular guy couldn't find. Work camps. Indian reservations. That's what Frankie liked. He sniffed them out. Like Rosie, the whore. He went nuts over her. Where did he find her, unless he went in that place on West Seventh? Who would go there but an old man or Frankie? He'd dress up every night after dinner, late when he got home from work. I watched him comb his hair with Vitalis and slap cologne on his neck. "Albert," he said to me once, "you know what Rosie says to me? She says, 'Frankie, I can't take it anymore. Stop.'" He grinned at me, his teeth white, a dimple in his cheek, and I pictured him showing this Rosie the same grin.

He had to work hard for the clothes and things he wanted. And he bought me and Angelo stuff too, clothes, baseball mitts. But there was more to his working hard. He had this thing about outdoing everybody, and he wanted me and Angelo to be like him. So it was unusual, like I said, for him to be going on about his plan while we were working that day in the prunes. Even if it was about women.

He had talked all week about this girl in the tent, ever since we started work. "She's just right for you two," he said to me and Angelo after work the first day. "She's working here with us, but I'm not going to tell you who she is. It's a surprise." He went to see her that night and for three or four nights afterward. I think just talking, because there was no way for him to get alone with her without someone looking out for him. Then one morning he told us it was OK, he had the whole thing planned out with her. He was serious when he talked, as if it were about work or sports, and I felt like I had nothing to do but keep up with him and go along with the plan.

All week I tried to figure who the girl was. Since it was a surprise, I imagined someone special. I knew she was Indian, because the tent was in the Indian camp by the river. And Frankie told us that much right off, that she was an Indian. So I narrowed it down to two girls: a light-skinned girl who was older, Frankie's age, or the girl with long black hair who wore low-cut blouses in the orchard. She was older too. I picked the light-skinned girl. Angelo picked the one with long hair. With my knees shaking and my teeth clattering, I started picturing the light-skinned girl inside the tent, lying on a blanket just beyond the flap. Then Frankie turned and said, "Her parents are upriver drinking, but they could come back any time. Watch close, you hear."

Standing in the willows close to the water, I kept thinking of that one girl. I kept my eyes open, where I was supposed to, along the river and on the other tents, but I kept seeing that girl. Even after Frankie came back and traded posts with Angelo. And after Angelo came back and traded posts with me. Going into that tent, crawling through the flap, I expected to see her, her light skin, maybe just a sheet or blanket over her.

So I was surprised.

Not because it wasn't her, but because it wasn't any girl at all. It was a child, a kid who by the look of her couldn't have been more than twelve years old. She was stretched out, resting back on her elbows, an army blanket covering her to the neck. I was so shocked I forgot what I was thinking. I froze there on my knees, face to face with her.

"Well, what are you waiting for?" she asked. "Take down your pants." She slid the blanket off her body so I could see all of her. Below her kid's face, with its pudgy brown cheeks and chipped-tooth mouth, she was a woman. Curves. Breasts. I felt my insides turn. Waves of warmth rolled and broke in me.

"C'mon," she said, stretching her foot with its chipped pink toenails to touch me. "C'mon." Her voice was deep, husky, not like something you'd expect from a kid with that face. It came from her body, which knew much more than mine at that point.

Then I did a crazy thing, something totally unnecessary. I took off all my clothes. I mean my shoes and socks, shirt, everything. I guess I saw her naked and figured I had to be the same way. I wasn't thinking, like I said. When I stood up to slip off my Levi's, my head hit the top of the tent, nearly bringing the whole thing down, kerosene lantern and all. She laughed. I looked at her face, and that's what I kept seeing, focusing on, when I moved to her. It made sense to me, even when I touched her, excited as I was. And all along, until after, when I felt from her body something older and more powerful that her face had hidden.

I jumped up and felt the cool air where I had been with her. I gave out our bird whistle, loud and clear, perfect pitch. I thought of water. I crawled out of the tent, naked as a jaybird, and dove into the river.

I swam madly. I made it to the other side without coming up for air. I ran up the sandy bank and stretched my wet body in the cool night air. I touched my toes, reached over my head, but when I looked, when I focused across the water to where Frankie and Angelo should have been waiting, I saw people, Indians, coming down the path from the other tents. A couple men and a woman, I think. One of them was carrying a flashlight. I ducked into the willows and started downriver, toward the place Frankie had parked the car. Then I saw him and Angelo waving from across the water. I dove in, swam across.

"Stupid fool," Frankie said as I got out of the water. "What in the hell's wrong with you?"

Him and Angelo turned and started finding their way to the road through the brush. I followed and didn't realize how badly I had cut myself on the twigs and stuff until I saw the bloody gashes on my legs and arms as I rode home naked in the backseat of the car.

My first thought was my clothes. My shoes and pants. Not that I didn't have others, but I wanted my clothes back. That's what I kept saying to myself. Me and my brothers worked only two more days at that place. I never saw the girl. And with both my brothers pissed at me, I did nothing to ask about her. "It's just a damn good thing we didn't get caught," Frankie reminded me.

We moved on to another place, north of Healdsburg. More prunes. Lots of Indians and Mexicans. Frankie found a Mexican girl, and me and Angelo found ourselves waiting hours in the dark for him to give us a ride home. One day after work, Angelo said he wasn't going to wait. He decided to hitchhike back to Santa Rosa. I went with him. We got a ride into Healdsburg, but then no luck. We walked across the Healdsburg bridge, tired from work and fifteen miles from Santa Rosa. "Let's go sit on the beach for a while," Angelo said. So we did, for about an hour, until it started getting dark. Then, on our way through the parking lot back up to the road, I saw the girl. She was looking straight at me from the passenger side of an old Rambler. "Hey," she said.

Angelo was up ahead. He didn't see her. I only half stopped, but it was long enough to hear her say, "Meet me here Sunday morning." Then she rolled up the window.

I felt there was something urgent in her voice, something she couldn't tell me just then. Like maybe her parents caught her that night, found my clothes, and gave her some kind of cruel and unusual punishment. Or maybe she was pregnant. I thought all kinds of things in the days ahead. But like I said, I wanted my clothes back, and I kept thinking maybe that's what she wanted—to give them back to me.

I never told Angelo I had seen her, that she was sitting alone in the Rambler he had walked past. I didn't tell Frankie either. Sunday morning I was there at eight sharp. I don't know why I picked eight. It was like a church date or something. I had to get there. And it was church folks who picked me up on the highway and took me clear to the Healdsburg bridge.

She was sitting on top of a picnic table next to a barbecue grill, a kid in Levi's and a faded sweatshirt. She blew a bubble with her purple gum, popped it loud in her mouth, and half smiled. I felt funny again, the waves rolling inside my body.

"My clothes . . ." I said.

She laughed, throwing her head back, showing her soft little neck. "Man," she said, "you're nuts."

I felt embarrassed, remembering how foolish I had acted that night. But when I looked at her, I saw her mind wasn't on that night at all. She wasn't thinking of what I just said, she was looking right at me. I looked across the beach to where the river was dammed, the water wide and smooth. There wasn't a soul in sight. An occasional car clunked above on the bridge.

"C'mon," she said, climbing off the table.

We went below the dam, away from the main beach, where the river continued on its course. I followed her inside a grove of willows. We sat in the sand, facing the water. She didn't say anything. I smelled her grape gum. She tapped her fingers on the top of her knee. I looked at the river rippling in the morning sun through the leaves. I thought of my clothes again. Then she said, "This time keep your pants on."

I saw her after that, lots. Same place, same time: Sunday mornings, Memorial Beach, in the willows below the dam. Her name was Mollie. She lived with an aunt in Healdsburg, close to the river. I never learned much more. She wasn't talkative.

Each time I wanted to ask her about my clothes, what happened to them, since I figured by this time I'd never get them back. I'd go over the whole thing in my mind when I left the house each Sunday. Standing on the highway with my thumb out, I pictured myself asking her. Then I'd get there and couldn't say a thing. She was just a kid, but she had the power to embarrass me. All she had to do was make me think of that first night.

I'd get nervous sitting there with her. Once, when I felt jumpy, I snapped off three willow branches and braided her a necklace. She liked that. It broke the ice, made things easier. After that I started giving her presents, packs of grape bubble gum, once a cheap silver bracelet. Now, when I left the house on Sundays, I wondered what to get her.

Then one day she disappeared. She didn't show up. It was well into fall, colored leaves fell all around, and the dam was down. I waited until noon, when a couple Mexican families fixed their towels and things on the beach and sat looking at the scummy river bottom where the water had been all summer. I thought something had happened to her, trouble. But then something else told me she just got tired of the affair, called it quits, went on to somebody new. I thought of that first night, not of my foolishness but of Frankie and Angelo in the tent with her. How many other guys did she have in her life? She was no kid. She was a conniver who tricked me. I was dumb. I clutched the dollar-ninety-eight red carnations in my hand and headed back to the highway, relieved, thankful I hadn't told my brothers about her and that she was behind me now.

But I kept thinking about her. I wanted to find her just to sit there, so she wouldn't have anything on me. I went back twice but no luck. Then the rains came. I got busy with school and things and hoped I'd never see her again.

Other girls came into my life. A few more summers passed. I blinked and found myself graduated from high school. The Vietnam war was on. Me and Angelo got high numbers in the lottery. Not so for Frankie. He went and got killed inside his first month of action.

If my sister's leaving the house cooled off Father, Frankie's coming back in a flag-draped box froze him. The old man didn't talk for a month. He'd milk the cows, then sit in front of the TV without the sound on. Then one day he started talking, all this stuff about how the world was upside down. "Hate everywhere," he complained. "All people do is hate." He started doing nice things around the house, making homemade ice cream, washing and ironing the curtains. Since I was the only one left at home, no one else ever had the benefit of knowing his kindness. I figured since we had seen Marie and her two kids at Frankie's funeral, he would pay her a visit and make up with her. But this never happened. About two weeks into his change, he took a gun to his head and left his brains on the metal stanchions inside the milking barn.

I went to live with Angelo and his wife, Toni. Since they had only a one-bedroom apartment, I slept in the front room on a sofa, which wasn't that comfortable, not to mention their kid, who cried every other hour of the night. Angelo got me a job with him at the cannery, driving a forklift. Full time, permanent. "It's just you and me now," he'd say, which made me happy to be with him, lousy old sofa or not.

We got to drinking, me and Angelo, after work. At a place in Sebastopol, near the cannery. First just on Fridays, then, before long, every day. I was just eighteen, but somehow I never got questioned. Angelo said I wouldn't. He knew the bartender. He knew practically everybody there, a lot of the guys we worked with. I had a hard time at first. I was what you'd call a cheap date, since I hadn't been a drinker and got buzzed so fast. Shots of tequila, beer chasers. It's a lot if you're not used to drinking. After a while I got so I could keep up.

One night after we left the bar, Angelo didn't drive back to town. He drove west into the hills above Sebastopol. "What are you doing?" I asked. He didn't answer me. He spun his truck onto a dirt road and parked where we had a view of the lights in the valley below. "What's going on?" I asked again.

He looked at the lights a long while, then reached under the seat and pulled up two beers. "Here," he said, handing me a can. He raised his can toward the lights. "For Frankie," he said.

I looked at my can, pulled the lift top, and toasted.

"You know, Albert, I used to bring chicks up here," he said, turning to me. "Yeah, I did." He looked back toward the city. "Wasn't it great when we were kids, running with Frankie, nothing to do but pop the babes? Shit, it seems so long ago." He kept rambling on, but I knew then what Angelo was up to. He didn't want to go home.

True, him and Toni weren't happy. They fought all the time, mostly about his not coming home. I saw her point. There was a baby, after all, and Angelo should've been responsible. But you had the feeling that if she hadn't gotten pregnant, they would have split up. They had given up liking each other long ago.

Things got worse. Angelo started gambling: five-card stud, blackjack. Not at the bar in Sebastopol, but in that dive in Graton where you were likely to get a knife in your back. Especially over matters like cards. And women,- yes, women. The women were nothing beautiful in there. Indians and Mexicans who looked as if they'd been drinking too much, too long. At least that's what I saw when I glanced around the dark bar. But I didn't look too long, lest one of those guys in there thought I was checking out his woman. Like I said, they'd dust you over cards or women. They were mostly Mexican guys, a few Filipinos. The Filipinos were temperamental, hot to start arguing, worse, I think, than the Mexicans. They gambled hard, serious. I watched Angelo's back. I watched him lose his shirt night after night, leave the bar with his empty pockets inside out of his pants.

Then he started with the women there. First some Mexican he gave twenty-five bucks. He drove off, left me in the bar for an hour. Second time around I wasn't going to stand for it. But it was more than my impatience with him. Actually, my anger when he slipped out of the bar with a broad-built Indian prevented me from putting together certain facts. Like the woman's features and the silver bracelet on her wrist. Then I flipped.

Even though I drank, I watched my money. I never played cards. I saved for a truck. That night I paid some guy to give me a ride. "Thirty bucks," I said. I didn't want him to say no. And sure enough, there was Angelo parked on the dirt road above Sebastopol, all the lights below him.

I flew to his truck, pulled open the door. "You son of a bitch," I said, "get out."

He got out, standing unsteadily. "What . . . ?"

"I'm tired of you!" I screamed. "Go home and tell your wife what you're doing, man. Or just end it. Get it over, Angelo. Just leave."

"Where?" he asked. He sounded as if I was asking him to leave that spot on the road, as if he didn't get the bigger picture about his marriage. He shrugged his shoulders.

"Leave," I said, and this time I meant for him to leave that minute.

I gave the driver another ten bucks.

"You want this bitch?" Angelo asked. "Is that it?" He was gesturing over his shoulder to his truck with his thumb. The driver, a good-sized Mexican, stepped toward Angelo. Angelo looked at him, then glanced back to me. He started laughing. "Go ahead. Take her. She's seven months pregnant," he said and walked off with the big Mexican.

I waited until they were gone, until the taillights vanished beyond the apple trees. Then I climbed in. I don't remember what we said, me and her: a few words, maybe. My mind was white light, blank. We were in a truck, no backseat, so she turned on her side.

Afterward, things started to fill the vacuum that was my head. Features, the bracelet on her wrist, why she didn't show up at the beach ever again. Then from out of left field, I asked her who the father of her baby was.

"Guess," she said.

She had the same girlish smugness I knew from her before, even though now she was grown. She must've been about sixteen, but she was large, older-looking, like twenty-five or so. She was the kind of heavy you see on some women where you can't tell if they're pregnant just by looking. Her clothes were dark, baggy.

"I don't know," I answered her. "Probably some Mexican."

"Nope," she said, shaking her head, as if I was guessing which hand had the M&M.

"Some Indian?"

"Nope."

"A black guy."

She started laughing. "Nope," she said. "How could that be? You're the only nigger I know, and I ain't been with you for some time. How long? You and your brothers, you're the only niggers I know."

Nigger. First I thought she was just slamming me. But then something changed when she brought up my brothers. Something about the way she said it. "What do you mean?" I asked.

"Nigger Marie," she said.

I thought she was referring to my sister, her dark skin and wavy hair. But just then I thought of something, even before she said it. My mother, who I never knew, was named Marie too.

"Yeah, my aunt, all of them, called her Nigger Marie. Then she died and everyone felt bad."

"We're Portuguese," I said.

"Part," she said, "like I got Irish in me. But your father too! You're all part nigger."

I thought of mentioning our name, Silva. I thought of other things, like the way lots of Portuguese, even Italians, are dark. But I said nothing.

Later, when my mind settled on this moment in my brother's truck, on those days in the weeks and years ahead of me, I would think of a lot of things. Like how a Portuguese could be a black person: you know, mixing with the Moors and all. Or how a black person could be a Portuguese, mixing with a Portuguese. It could happen either way or both. I'd never know in our case, since there was no one to ask. Maybe my father didn't know. But I'd think of him, and all of us, during these spells of mine, about his meanness when we were kids, and his driving all around town so we'd always come in on the west side. And my sister, how she stayed locked up, hidden, until she saw someone like her and took the chance of her life by asking him to let her go with him. And me and my brothers, even if we didn't know this part of the story: Frankie with his out-of-the-way women, who could never put him beneath them. The whole picture of our past looked different to me. It was the picture our father couldn't escape, even with his short-lived kindness, until he blew his brains out.

But that night, sitting in my brother's truck with Mollie, I flip-flopped to make sense of things. Nothing came up but anger,

anger and something else. Anger because this girl, this woman, got me again, took me senseless. I was mad at myself now, but it was something more, something that made me mad. I couldn't stop feeling Mollie's tight, swollen stomach in my hands or seeing her dark pleated dress thrown up, covering her face. It was my story, my particular version of what plagued everyone in my family, my shame.

My wife, Anna, is a good woman. Honest, devoted, hardworking. She loves our kids. She loves my family: Marie and her kids and husband, Angelo and his kids. She's strong, keeps the peace. She's held us up and half the neighborhood too. She loves me. She's everything I thought she was the moment I met her, though she'd be hard pressed to say the same about me.

About two weeks after my skirmish with Angelo, I moved out. It wasn't over Mollie, the Indian girl. Me and Angelo never said a word about that. And I never saw her again. In fact, I made a point of avoiding Indians. I'd look the other way if I saw an Indian woman coming. I moved out because the fighting between Angelo and Toni reached the pot-and-pan-throwing stage, and I didn't like being in the middle of it.

I got my own place. It wasn't much, a studio in a converted motel way down Santa Rosa Avenue. But I fixed it up good: new curtains, art posters, and a couple of plants in macramé holders. With the money I saved while living at Angelo's, I bought a car, a sixty-eight Mustang I cleaned up and polished to a bright blue, like the sky. I felt good, kind of like I did when I was in high school. I quit getting drunk. I led a clean life. I met nice girls at local dances, like at the union hall and the vets' building. They were girls like the girls I dated in school, clean, the kind that reminded you of everything you were doing every step of the way.

Seemed like there were lots of girls, dates at the movies, concerts. I wanted someone permanent. I wanted to settle down with someone, not get married, not for that. Then I met Anna. Like I said, the moment I saw her I knew she was special. A girl in clean white tennis shoes, wholesome, with long dark hair that wasn't curled up or teased like the other girls around her. She wasn't rich. You could tell she was from the country. But she did her best. She made me think of myself, or the way I wanted to be.

It was at a dance, one of those at the union hall. Even though she looked as if it was her first night out, she seemed to know people. She talked to the regulars, women you saw there week after week. Like the Toms sisters, the big Indian girls Frankie used to fool around with. Those girls smiled at me all the time. I figured they knew who I was, that I was Frankie's younger brother. But I was wrong. When I went up to them to get them to introduce me to Anna, they asked what my name was. They didn't know me from Adam. I had figured they told Anna all about me. But again I was wrong. Anna knew nothing.

I told her both my parents had died, not much else. She told me she never knew her father, and her mother took care of somebody's kids on a dairy. She was boarding with an old maid in town while she was doing housework and taking classes at the junior college. She wanted to have a preschool. We talked outside the union hall until dawn, until the gray morning light showed the empty gravel parking lot all around us. We couldn't get enough of each other after that. We fell fast and heavy, so fast that when she told me she was pregnant I didn't know what to say or do. I should have told her right then and there I'd marry her. I just didn't think of it.

Once, after the news, she took me to meet her mother, at a dairy in Sebastopol. A tall blond woman in her midfifties answered the door. But that wasn't her mother. I blinked and an Indian woman was standing where the blonde had been. That was her mother. A clean tidy-looking woman, but no doubt Indian. The dark woman had us in and served us tea in fancy cups. I couldn't believe it, that this fair-skinned girl I loved came from this woman. But why not? I had been so careful not to bring up the details of my family that I never asked about hers. I watched as she hugged this woman good-bye and kissed her hard on both sides of her face. I heard the way she said "Mama," loving, for all the world to hear. I had always thought we were alike, me and Anna, more or less like orphans with no ties. But just then I saw we were different; she wasn't like me at all. On the way home that day I asked her to marry me. I told her we'd have a big wedding for all our families to see.

You dream and plan, plan and dream—and then there's life, the everyday way of the world. It's like ivy. It looks pretty at first, the way it climbs a tree. Then it takes the life right out of the tree, strangles it. You have your firstborn and it's the most beautiful thing you know, so beautiful you decide to have the second one, which you didn't plan for, even though you can hardly afford the first. Then the third and fourth appear, but it's all right because your mother-in-law moves in and helps with her social security check. You open your eyes and realize you're too far under water and haven't taken a breath of air for some time. You learn to live without breathing.

Angelo never quit his wild ways, not with his second wife and not with his third, who was Indian. Once in a while I'd have a beer with him after work. But I'd leave when he got too out of sorts with the drinking. I never understood why he even bothered to get married. He angered me. One night, after a couple beers with Angelo, I was coming home and came upon a car parked off the road, half in the ditch. Clearly there was no danger, but what caught my attention was a head on the passenger's side, someone slumped down. It was dark, quite late, maybe nine o'clock. I was going too fast to stop. I pulled around the corner, then came back up the street behind the car, slowly, with my headlights out. Why I turned off my lights I don't know. Maybe I sensed what was going on. But when I walked up on them, the two kids, I was stunned. Not that they were butt-assed naked but at their wild abandon, the madness that left them oblivious to the dark figure standing over them outside the car.

My heart thudded. My knees shook. Somehow I made it back to my truck. But I had a hard time making it back to my life. It was like a first kiss that tells you there's more you could do, even if you weren't thinking about it before. It was like seeing a naked girl for the first time. I started staying out for that one extra beer. I flirted. I fell more than once. I hated facing my wife. Worse, I hated seeing Angelo, whose life I detested.

"Nothing but a bunch of Indians in there," this girl said to me as I drove past my house. "Don't stop," she said. "Don't stop."

A bunch of Indians in there. In my house, yes. Not just my wife and children and my wife's mother. It doesn't stop there. It goes on. Now my mother-in-law's brother, the Indian preacher man, and half his congregation pack in our house every night with their Bibles and prayers for our sins. And when Jeanne, our oldest, got cancer, it wasn't just the old preacher and his troupe of hand tremblers but all the Indians in the neighborhood. They came out of the woodwork. Long-lost relatives like the Toms sisters. Yes, turned out Frankie's big girls are Anna's cousins. Everybody's connected to everybody. Seemed I'd leave the house to take a breath of air and then come back, only to find the space I left filled by another Indian.

So after this girl mentioned "Indians," after I collected my thoughts and made it around the block once, I figured she was a relative of some kind, that her family was visiting my wife. Then she started on this Unky business. I wasn't the only one who had done some figuring. So had she. She knew who I was.

I've heard Indian girls call their uncles and other older men relatives "Unky." It's sweet, respectful. Not this girl. And she talks openly with me about her life, about stealing and getting in trouble, as if I'm a kid, just another guy. She doesn't care who I am.

She doesn't care about anybody. She goes on and on about people and things. But I've stopped listening. I stopped after she talked about her mother, after she called her mother a lowdown whore, after she said her mother had screwed every man in the county, that she'd been doing it since she was a young girl living with an aunt near the river in Healdsburg. "People say she took ten Mexicans at a time into the willows there," she said. "I've heard them say that, that she was just a kid and doing that."

Something turned in my brain, rolled, and came up right. No white light, nothing emptying my better senses. No rage, like when I went back to Healdsburg time after time, or when I got into it on that dirt road with Angelo that night.

I wanted to drop this girl off.

But where? If I drop her off in front of the house or a hundred miles away, it's all the same. She'll be back. And what's to keep her from blabbing about riding around with me? No matter how you look at it, it's not right. I didn't go straight home. Already she's got me on that score. I bit the bait: her short dress, the naked legs on the street. Now I can say I don't want her, and I don't, but what do I do? She's a mean girl, vindictive, no doubt. She could talk. Each time I pass the house, I make things worse. I can't stop circling.

"C'mon, Unky," she keeps saying. "Let's go someplace."

Not a motel. Not up to Montecito Heights. Maybe for an ice cream. But even that isn't innocent. I'd like to throw her like a stone out of my sight. I picture her as a small hard rock in my hand, and Fm tossing her with all my might, like when I was chucking rocks with my brothers at an old barn, when I didn't know any better.

How I Got to Be Queen

I watched Justine across the street. I seen her from the window. Even with Sheldon and Jeffrey asking for lunch, I seen clear enough to know she was up to her old tricks. I said to myself, That queen, she's up to it again. This time it was a boy, a black boy whose name I'd learn in a matter of hours. Justine wastes no time. But I pulled away from the window, in case the two little guys might see what I did. Kids have a way of telling things, after all.

Nothing was unpacked, not even the kitchen this time. I pulled a towel from boxes on the floor and dusted the paper plates left from breakfast. What food we had was on the table: half a loaf of Wonder bread, two large jars of peanut butter, two cans of pie filling. Justine went for another loaf of bread, jam, and a packet of lemonade mix. She got as far as the store, which is kitty-corner, just down the street, in plain view from the window.

She stood on one side of the bicycle rack, by the newspaper stand. She stood with a hand on her hip, her head lifted and tilted to the side. Like she was taking a dare, or fixing on some scheme. It makes people notice her. She draws them in that way. She looked black as the boy straddling a bike on the other side of the rack.

I wondered what Mom would do if she seen her there. That's if Mom wasn't at the cannery with Auntie Anna. I think it's bad the way Justine and Mom talk to each other when there's trouble. "Damned black-neck squaw," Mom says. "Dirty fat Indian, you don't even know which Filipino in that apple orchard is my father," Justine says. On and on it goes. Of course, Mom doesn't say much any other time. And if Justine goes on long enough, Mom goes out or watches TV. Like nothing was ever started. Like she does with just about anything else.

I took the longest time setting two pieces of bread on each plate. I found things to look for: the aluminum pie tins, the plastic cups left over from Cousin Jeanne's party, the rolling pin. "I'm going to make a pie," I said to the boys standing at the table. "We'll have a party with pie and lemonade." They shifted on their feet with no patience. "All right," I said. "You act like starved rats and you look worse than pigs. Now wash up." I spread peanut butter on the bread, then sprinkled on some sugar. "I don't want no complaining," I told them when they came back.

Justine came in about four, an hour before Mom.

"Now what good's that?" I asked. She put the bag of groceries on the table. "You might as well go back and get the burger and tortillas for dinner. And get flour. I got canned pumpkin for pies."

"Don't give me no shit, Alice," she said. Times like this she plays older sister. She wasn't listening to me. She just shook that silky hair and said, "I'm in love. And he is *fine*. Oo-wee, Sis, the boy is fine!"

She was talking like a black person. It's one of her things. I don't mean talking like a black person. Justine does things so you notice. She goes for a response. Like what she started with Jack, the boys' father. Which is behind us coming to Santa Rosa. Mom said it's Justine's fault. I said Jack was old and his family would come for him sooner or later anyway. Giving Justine credit just fed the fire.

It started with a social security check that wandered to the bottom of Mom's purse and stuck itself into something or other. Since a week went by and it didn't come up for air, Jack started to get edgy. "My money, where is it?" he kept asking. He was at the point if his dinner wasn't on time you was trying to starve him. If a door or window was left open you wanted him to die of pneumonia. It didn't surprise me he called Clifford, his son.

"What do you mean, you lost it?" Clifford said to Mom.

I heard Jack make the call, so I figured trouble. Clifford and Mom have a history, and Clifford was all along dead against Mom being conservator and signing for Jack. True, Jack wasn't in his right mind half the time, and his insides was shot. "Like a sponge that doesn't suck water" is what the clinic doctor said. But Mom wasn't no crook. I opened my huckleberry jam. I made toast and set the table. But Clifford, who's more stubborn than a ass and looks worse, seen none of it.

"What's the matter, Mollie, you start on the bottle again?"

Mom was sitting next to Jack. I looked at the place mats and the food. Anyone could see the old man was cared for and fed.

"Cliff," I said. "Why not put a stop on the check? Go to the social security." I felt funny saying "Cliff." For a while it was "Dad."

"Yeah, and what's my father supposed to eat in the meantime? You kids is using up his money." He looked at Mom. "I'm telling you, Mollie, I'm sick of what's going on here."

He brushed past Justine, who stood in the doorway. I said the check would turn up. Justine said, "Who cares?"

But Justine seen how to use the situation to her end. She never liked Jack. "He nags Mom," she said. I said, "How can he give anybody else attention when he's half dead?" Justine didn't see my point. And it was Easter vacation, no school and no work in the orchards, which means you had nothing to do, no one to see. Or, in Justine's case, nowhere else to pull her stunts. So there was time for thinking.

All of a sudden Justine was dressed up. I mean dressed up every day. She found clothes I never knowed existed in that house. She mixed skirts and blouses in different ways. She wore down her eyeliner pencil in a week. Each morning she worked her hair into a hive the size of Sheldon's basketball. And when that was done, she sat at the kitchen table painting her nails the color of a red jellybean. Then, when Mom went to register at the cannery, she started on how she was going to buy a stereo. "I put down fifty dollars at the Golden Ear," she said.

That got Justine a response.

Clifford made it from the reservation in one hour. And he wasn't alone. His sister and his white woman was with him. The white woman opens her mouth only when her nose is plugged and she can't breathe. Her I wasn't afraid of. It was Evangeline, the sister, who'd just as soon spit as say hello. She hated Mom. She looked at me like I was Mom's bare foot and she wanted to smash it under her work boots.

I knowed the old man went into the bedroom and called someone. I figured one of his kids. I just never put two and two together. And neither did Justine. She never got the pleasure of being falsely accused of stealing.

Clifford left his woman and his sister guard. Like we would lift the last penny from Jack's pockets. Then he came back with suitcases and boxes. "Come on, Dad," he said. "Evangeline is going to take care of you. She won't spend the money on *her* kids. Not like this lot of swine."

Mom wasn't legal with Jack. There was nothing she could do. It was agreed about the checks only because he lived with us. Since the car was Jack's, it was gone now too. Even so, she walked to town, then took the bus to Santa Rosa and canceled the check at the social security. Of course three days later it floats up from the mess in her purse.

Auntie Anna drove her to the reservation, but it was no use. Evangeline wouldn't let her see Jack. She didn't care about the check. I know what Evangeline said. I heard it before. "You screwed my brother, then went for my father. Dirty whore. I don't believe those two kids are my father's. Now get." I reminded Mom that we are from Healdsburg. "We're not from that res," I said.

Justine unloaded what I first sent her for, then tore off for the dinner stuff. This time she was back right away. She kept the boys out of my hair. I got busy. My nerves pushed me. Rolling dough for pies, I thought of things. This is a way I calm my nerves when working won't do it alone. I didn't like what I seen at the store, and my imagination started to get the best of me. I thought of Jack, I guess because I hadn't made a pie since we left Healdsburg and came here. I thought how he'd settle down his griping when I cooked. Mom called me whenever he started screeching. He acted drunk, though the hardest thing he took those days was ginger ale. I rolled pie dough and didn't notice when he picked berries or apples or whatever it was out of the bowl. He was quiet. I thought that's what a grandfather would be like.

I set the pies in the oven. Then I got to work on dinner. I turned meat in one skillet and warmed tortillas in the other. I sent Justine to the store again, this time for cheese and chili sauce. The skillet of meat and a plate of warmed torts, sliced cheese, and toast was on the table when Mom got home. Her place was at the head. It's where I put things, like the cheese and chili sauce she likes on her meat.

She didn't say anything. She was tired, I know. She finished eating, then cleaned up and went to play cards with Auntie Anna like she did every night. "Tomorrow, we'll start on the boxes," she told me before she left. She was standing in the kitchen then, combing back her washed hair with Sheldon's pink comb. I kept on with the dishes. It's been two weeks, I thought to myself. Then, with my hands in the greasy water, I resolved to start unpacking myself, no matter what she said. We couldn't wait to see if we was going to stay here or not. Tomorrow, I told myself, first thing. I heard the front door slam.

I was still scrubbing, finishing the damned skillets, when I turned to tell the boys to take a bath before I gave them pie, which I had cooling on the sink. I thought Justine was behind me, seated at the table. But she wasn't. She was standing there with her friend.

"This is Ducker," she said.

First thing I noticed, the boys wasn't there.

"They're taking baths," Justine said, seeing how I was looking at the empty seats.

She was referring to them not seeing Ducker. I never heard the door open since it slammed behind Mom. My ears pick up on those things, so I was caught off guard.

Justine didn't have to embarrass me. "Close your mouth," she said. "You look like Clifford's wife."

I thought of the boys again. The bathroom door was shut. Then I thought this Ducker might think I'm stupid or prejudice on account of him being black. My mind was going in several directions at once. I said what made no sense, given the circumstances.

"Here, Mr. Ducker, sit down and have some pie." I put a pie on the table.

Justine started laughing. I knew she thought I was in shock seeing this black person in our house.

"It ain't *Mister* Ducker," she said. "It's Ducker. Ducker Peoples."

"Well . . ."

"We don't want pie," she said. She looked toward the bathroom, then to Ducker. "We're going for a walk."

"Nice to meet you—" he said, stopping when he got to my name.

"Alice," Justine said.

"Alice," he said.

I was still standing in the same place after they went out the front door. I tore to the window. Then I seen what he looked like. When they was across the street, almost to the store, I remembered who it was in front of me two minutes before. Funny thing about Ducker, he wasn't a man. Well, I mean grown. He was a kid, looked like. Bony arms hanging from flapping short sleeves. His face shiny smooth, no hair. Like he should be chewing bubble gum and keeping baseball cards. Not holding on to Justine, who was sixteen and looked it.

"Who was here?"

I jumped around, half scared to death. It was Sheldon and Jeffrey out of the bathtub, drying their naked bodies.

"Go dry off in the bathroom," I said.

"Sound like a nigger."

"Hush up, Sheldon."

"Who was here?"

"Nobody."

Next day something concerned me. Mom was in the kitchen, putting things in cupboards. I heard her even before I got up. Even then I didn't think she'd make a day of it.

"It's Tuesday," she said. "Day off."

She finished with the kitchen before I started breakfast. I had to open cupboards to find things. She was in the bedroom by the time I could help her. Her things she put in the closet first. I seen her red dress from where I was standing, opening the boys' boxes. It's crinoline with ruffles. She wears it with her black patent leather shoes with the sides busted out. Like at Great-Auntie Effie Goode's funeral. Or when she came home with Clifford. Same thing with Jack.

"I guess this means we're staying here," I said.

This move was a trial. Ever since we came to Santa Rosa seemed nothing worked for very long. First that house on West Seventh we couldn't afford. Then the one by the freeway which no one told us they was going to tear down for development. Got two months' rent from us, anyway. And now this, which Auntie Anna, whose idea it was for us to come here, got from the landlord she knows.

"What choice do we have?" she asked.

The way she said that matched her business putting things away. Seemed to me just then, anyway. Like I said, it concerned me. I was the one who put things away, after all. No matter what she said before or after. It was just this time she made such a big deal about the neighborhood. Then I guess we moved so much. Just three months in Santa Rosa, and three times already.

"Well," I said. "I like it here. It's a change."

"A lot of blacks," Mom said. "Auntie didn't say so much about that."

"Not everyone can be a Pomo Indian," I said. Since Mom had her stuff on the bed, I spread the boys' things on their sleeping bags, which I hadn't rolled up yet. I sorted underwear on my knees. I thought of reminding her that Justine is part Filipino and I'm part Mexican. But that is what Justine would do.

"It's nice having Auntie up the street," I said. I liked the way Mom called her cousin Auntie, which she did for us kids. "I like hearing Auntie tell stories."

"Ah, don't listen to that old Indian stuff."

Auntie Anna cooks good. She's got recipes. And she's classy. Slender-bodied, not like me and Mom. She knows how to talk to social workers, those kind of people.

I got up and put the folded things in the boys' drawers. Mom was hanging up me and Justine's clothes. "Is this OK?" I asked, seeing how she was putting things where she wanted.

"Your sister, I don't know what she'll do here. Run with them kids out there. Niggers, anything/'

That made it click. My worries took form in a picture. Justine and Ducker. Still, I wasn't certain about Mom just then. Did Sheldon or Jeffrey see last night and tell? Mom says things by not saying them, which puts you in a place where you don't know if she's saying something or not. That's far as she'll go. Unless it's with Justine in a fight.

I was caught, trapped, and bothered just the same. Mom kept working, her back to me.

"Don't worry about Justine," I said.

We had a normal family dinner that night. I fixed chops and fried potatoes. I cut celery sticks and carrots. People need greens but this family don't eat them, which is one reason there's so much crabbing. They're stopped up. Mom stayed and helped with the dishes before she went to Auntie's. Of course while things looked peaceful I imagined a disaster. Like Ducker knocking on the door. I wondered if Mom was hanging around in case that happened. I saw loudmouth Sheldon saying, "It's him, it's him!" But nothing happened, even after Mom left.

The boys opened drawers, looking to find where I put their clothes. They kept bugging me about getting the TV fixed and hooked up. Justine moved stuff in the closet to her liking. Me, I only wanted a long enough couch in the living room. I was sleeping on the floor with the boys. I can't sleep in the bed with Mom and Justine. No rest, even with them out like a light.

Next day Mom went fishing to the coast with Auntie Anna. Auntie's mom and Old Uncle, they sat in the car when Auntie came in for Mom. The old lady stuck her white head out and said for me to come along. I stood on the front porch to say hello. "I can't," I said. Then she said to me in Indian what men used to say in the old days when they set out fishing. "Get the grill ready, then."

"Damn cannery's so cheap. Got illegals instead of working us extra days," Mom said when she came out.

"Don't think of work, Mollie," Auntie said.

Justine padded up and stood with me to wave good-bye. She was still waving after the car left. I thought she was nuts until I seen it was Ducker she was waving forward. Bold daylight. He walked right up the front porch.

"Morning, Alice," he said.

I thought of my mouth this time. I kept it closed, not shocked. And I thought what to do. Already the boys seen everything. I got some bread in a plastic bag and headed for the park. I carried Jeffrey part of the way. Sheldon I just about dragged by the hair.

"What's so big about seeing goldfish?" he said, whining like he does. A sure trait of his father. Proof I would have for Evangeline.

"Shut up," I said. "You damn-ass brat."

"You just don't want us there with that—"

I slapped his face. Then he started crying like I tied him to a stake and burned him, which I wanted to do. We was at the park by then. I put bread in the water for the fish. But nothing worked. Sheldon screamed so the whole park could hear.

"I'm telling Mom!" he said. Then I thought of the opposite of fire: water. And I had it right there.

"Shut up," I said, "before I rub your face in dog shit. Now shut up, damn you." Then Jeffrey started crying. "Now see," I said. "Stop it, Sheldon. Please."

I threatened the police. Sheldon quit some, but I knowed what weapon he was harboring, that he'd use against me the minute he saw Mom. I looked at the soggy bread floating on the empty water.

"I'll get the TV fixed," I said. "But not if you act like that, Sheldon."

So I spent what was left in the tobacco tin. It's how I kept Ducker in the house and the boys quiet.

Ducker got to be a regular thing. And it's more. His friends. The only break I had was Mom's days off. Every night the party was on like clockwork. Soon as Mom was gone to Auntie's ten minutes. Then a worse deal. If Mom went fishing on a day off, the party was all day. I was never one for school, but I wanted this summer over.

Ducker brought his radio. I seen every latest dance. Imagine Justine. She was in her element. She knowed the dances best of anybody and showed it. The boys clapped. It was just boys coming to the house. "Why should girls come here?" Justine said when I asked. "We're the girls."

We had talks, Justine and me. I told her how we couldn't go on like this. She told me not to be so shy. "Don't be afraid to smile," she said. "Don't be worried about your weight."

Then she said how she had a plan for when school started. "I'll show them snobby white girls," she said. "I'll show them Indians from Jack's res, too." She pictured herself walking down the hall with Ducker. She was going to lose fifteen pounds. She was going to wear all kinds of makeup on her face. People would be shocked. They'd be scared of her.

"You already done that plan at Healdsburg," I said, reminding her of how it got her a white boy and a hassle with his family so she hit the mother, knocking her tooth out, and had the cops come and take her to juvee and tell the welfare to take us from Mom.

"Well, everything turned out OK," she said. "You have to see who you are, Alice. Look around and see what you see. See what you can do. How you can be queen. The queen is the baddest. She knows it all. That's how she's queen. Like how I walk at school. Don't be worried about your weight. Some boys like it."

Only thing I was worried about was her plan. I couldn't see the outcome to this one yet. I wasn't a queen. She tried to get certain of Ducker's friends with me. "The kids won't tell, if that's what you're worried about," she said.

This was true. It wasn't just the TV keeping the boys quiet now, it was Ducker. He took them to the schoolyard. He showed them all his basketball stuff. After that, I might as well disappear into thin air far as Sheldon cared. I had to get Ducker to get Sheldon to mind.

If it was Mom's day off and she went fishing, I took Jeffrey to the park and left Sheldon with Justine. Not that I felt right about it. Another thing I must say, I had a friend. Anthony. Not a boyfriend, not in my mind. Anthony just made himself useful tagging along. "Now don't forget bread for the fish," he said, if we was going to the park. Sometimes we did that, on Mom's day off, all of us. What else Anthony and me talked about I don't know. I got used to him. I didn't even think of him being black. Until we run into Auntie's mom and Old Uncle in the park.

I couldn't get out of it. The two old ones sitting on the park bench seen me five minutes before I seen them. The old lady was looking away, the Indian style of looking away. Like you know she seen you and looked away so you don't have to see *her*. In them situations it's a sign to help yourself and keep walking.

I was hardly fifty feet from them, Anthony with me. He was carrying Jeffrey on his shoulders. I knowed the picture they seen. I took the old lady's cue. I turned straight around, in the direction we came, and went behind the tall cypress trees, out of sight. It wasn't just that Anthony was black. I don't even think it was black people that bothered Mom so much. It was anything disturbing. It was what nobody talked about.

I found the sheets that day. I remember. I had my senses. After what happened in the park, I was thinking. I knowed if I tried to wash the sheets in the sink anybody might see the blood. Anybody could walk in. So I burned them out back in the garbage can. Justine never mentioned a thing, even when I was cleaning up. "Me and Ducker had the most fun," she said, after Mom went to Auntie's that night.

Indians say blood is a sign of the devil. Where it spills will be poison everlasting. That's how a place gets taboo. Auntie told me a story once. It was at Great-Auntie Effie's funeral. It was to explain why Mom didn't cry, why Mom didn't like Great-Auntie, who raised Mom and didn't like having to raise her. Great-Auntie got stuck with Mom and her sisters after some man poisoned Mom's mom. But here's what I think of. How Mom and her sisters found their mom in a puddle of salamander eggs and blood. Mom's sister Daisy, she's in jail. Rose, her husband killed her with a hatchet.

With Justine the expected worried me as much as the unexpected. The expected, I worried *when*; the unexpected, *what*. *When* came like a straight shot, now that I look back. Mom came home early from Auntie's that night. After the park, Justine's episode, and all my cleaning the floors and bed. Why that night? Why at all? I can't believe Mom didn't know what was going on before. Maybe she didn't want us to think she was dumb. Maybe she had to keep face for Auntie Anna, if the old lady said something to her. I don't know.

By this time our house was party central. It was Justine's party. She was queen. That's what the boys called her. Dance, Justine, dance. The neighborhood knowed Justine. She was dressing again. She was dressed up every day. Mom saw the party. She stood in the doorway half a minute, then turned around and left.

I unplugged Ducker's radio. I told everyone to get out. Must've been ten guys there. Something came over me so I was fierce. Justine said to shut up: the older sister again. Usually I ignored her, kept on about my business. Like Mom with most things. But this time I was Justine and more. I was going to floor her with the weight of my body. She must've seen because she stopped cold. She tore out the front door with the guys.

Sheldon and Jeffrey, I put in the tub. Sheldon, I slapped in the mouth for no reason. He never made a peep. Neither one of them did. I put them to bed. No TV.

I finished the dishes and put them away. I wiped down the stove and refrigerator with Windex. I did the kitchen table too. Then I put together flour and water for torts. Torts by scratch, Mom's favorite. I was plopping them when Justine snuck past to the bedroom.

I finished. I set the torts on the clean table. I placed a fresh kitchen towel over the pile to keep in the warmth. Then next to a place mat made of paper towels I put a half cube of butter and the sugar bowl with a spoon next to it. Finally, I filled a glass with ice cubes and put it to the left of the place mat, opposite the butter and sugar.

Mom didn't come home until late. Around midnight. I was in the front room. I must've been dozing in the chair because when I opened my eyes, half startled, Mom was past me, turning into the bedroom. I thought of Justine and Mom in that bed together. I didn't hear a sound. Then I dozed again.

It was early morning I heard it: like two roosters woke up and found themselves in the same pen. It started low in the bedroom, then came at full blast to the kitchen. Really loud. I thought of the boys. I pictured them hiding their heads for cover in their sleeping bags. I didn't move from the chair where I'd been all night.

Mom was hollering. "You're the lowest dirty, black-neck squaw. Chink!"

And Justine: "Which one is my father? Tell me, you drunk-slob low-life Indian. Prove you're not the whore everyone says you are."

Then I heard the cupboard and something slam on the kitchen table. I couldn't believe my ears. I knowed without seeing what it was. Still, I didn't move. I don't know, it was strange. Then

Mom comes out, her hair all wild from sleeping, and takes off, out the front door.

"Look how stupid," Justine said, nodding to the shotgun on the table. It was Jack's, what he forgot.

I was still rubbing my eyes, just standing there. I picked it up and put it away.

'Fat bitch thought she was going to scare me with that," Justine said.

"Shut up," I said. "Just shut up."

I turned on the oven and warmed the untouched torts for breakfast.

Mom might as well moved to Auntie's. We hardly seen her, except when she came back to sleep. She put just so much money in the tobacco tin for me to spend. Like when she was drinking, only now we never seen her, and I didn't have to keep the money in my pocket for fear she'd take it out of the tin. Once, when she was drinking, she accused me of stealing the money. I'd spent it, of course, and gave her what I had left: five dollars. She went berserk, hollering in the backyard. Just screaming, no words. Someone called the police. She stopped when they got there, then locked herself in the bathroom, and cried herself to sleep. Later, to bug Mom, Justine said she'd called the police.

Mom strayed, like I said. It was just me and Justine and the boys, and Ducker and Anthony and whoever else. Seemed nothing I could do.

We walked together, all of us. Justine didn't hang back at the house with Ducker so much anymore. She didn't say it, but I knowed she was anxious to try out with other boys what she had tried out with Ducker. Certain things she said. The ways she talked to Ducker's friends and looked at them. Especially Kolvey, who was bigger, more grown, like a man. Signs Justine was up to something.

Anyway, I fixed the lunches. Most days we went to the park. Sometimes we walked other places, like the fairgrounds, where they was putting up the rides. Once we took a bus to the mall.

Anthony would help me with things. He carried the Coolmate so we'd have cold pop. Another thing he did was the shopping. "What do you need?" he asked me. Like we was a pair. But there was nothing between us. In fact, lots of times at the park I went off by myself. I left him where Justine was pulling her stunts and where the two old ones sat and seen whatever they wanted. I took Jeffrey and went behind the cypress trees. He was the only one obeyed me. "Time to take a nap," I told him. It was cool there, away from everyone, and I pulled him close and slept.

It was Anthony who got me up. He told me something was going on with Justine. I was dead asleep on the grass there, and I felt Jeffrey slip from my arms.

"What?" I asked.

But by this time both Jeffrey and Anthony was looking through the trees. Then I seen it too. Some skinny black girl and a couple of her friends, small and skinny like her, stood about twenty yards from Justine. Far enough so they was shouting and I could hear. The black girl was sticking out her hand, curling her finger like a caterpillar walking. "Miss Doris say for Mister Ducker Peoples to come right this minute," she was saying.

The boys was still on the ground, setting there. Justine was standing in all her clothes and makeup. Red lips. Nails. "What's this Miss Doris shit?" she said.

The girl shifted her weight to one side and put her hand on her hip. "Miss Doris say for Ducker to come right this minute if he knows what's good for him."

"Miss Doris eat shit," Justine said.

Then I grabbed Jeffrey. It happened fast. Justine crossed the line. She was face to face with that girl and, with no words, just popped her one upside the head. The girl went over, hitting the ground on her side. Her two friends jumped back, like Justine would go after them next.

"Justine say to eat shit, Miss Doris," Justine said, looking down at that girl, who was setting up now, holding her face.

"I'm telling you, your sister shouldn't done that," Anthony said.

Something in the way he said that scared me. Like I knowed he told the truth.

"There's your grandparents," he said.

I looked to where Anthony was looking. With the commotion I hadn't seen the old ones on the bench, if they was ever sitting there. They was walking away in the opposite direction.

"They ain't my grandparents," I said.

It was in the air. Justine's doings filled the rooms of our house, in every cupboard I opened, every potato I sliced. Like you seen the white of the potato and seen Justine when you was doing everything not to. And it was outside. Like fog settling in the streets. It was between the houses, across at the store. You seen it in the way a bird sat still on the telephone wire.

I made macaroni and cheese and potato salad. Macaroni and cheese is easy: just boil macaroni and melt the cheese. Potato salad, that takes time: boiling the potatoes, chopping celery and onions. Mayonnaise. All that. I did it. And more. Two pies from scratch. And a cake, even if it was from a box. You'd think we was on a reservation and I was putting up food for a funeral.

Mom knowed too. After dinner, she didn't go to Auntie's. How could she explain herself being there when Auntie and them knowed about the trouble here?

I never sat, not once while the others ate. The pies and all that. And I started right in with the dishes. I frosted the cake and set it on the table with a knife and new paper plates. I folded paper towels to make napkins at each place. I put a plastic fork on top of each napkin. I thought of candles and ice cream, but it was too late for that.

I was scrubbing the pots when I heard the first noises and looked over my shoulder and seen the crowd collecting outside on the street. From the sink, if you turned around, you could look through the kitchen door and the front door to the street. I wanted to close the front door, but I didn't move. I mean I kept on in the kitchen. Mom was at the table, kind of peeking out. She had her hands on her knees. Straight arms, like she does when she's going to get up. The boys looked at the cake like they was waiting for me to cut it. I was just about to do that. I thought, What am I doing, forgetting about the cake?

Then Justine came out from the bedroom.

She was in Mom's red dress. That's no getup for the occasion, I thought. Not that I lingered on that thought just then. Mom got up and went into the bedroom, and the boys followed her. The bedroom door closed.

"Don't do it," I said to Justine.

I guess someone outside seen her too, because the yelling and name calling rose up. "Dirty whore. Come out and pick on someone your own size. Slut." All that. I looked once then, and the street was filled with people. Some was near the steps. Young people, old people, kids, filling the air. Shouting.

"You don't have to do it, Justine," I told her again. "Just tell them you didn't mean for them guys to go and say yes."

She looked at me straight. Not like she was mad, or even scared. Kind of like she had a plan. Like she does when she tilts her head and half smiles at you. "I told them yes, I would fight that Miss Doris's sisters, because I ain't scared of nobody. Not three big-ass mean nigger bitches, nobody. They'll see. I'm the queen, remember?"

That's when I took inventory of her getup. The red dress, too big for Justine, was cinched with a black belt, which matched her pump shoes. And she had nylons on and the delicate gold necklace she found in the girls' gym. Her hair was done up just so. Her face, it was a movie star. This I was focusing on, all the while the people outside came closer and louder. The house was surrounded. I thought, Girls fight in old clothes. Like the times in Healdsburg when Justine met in the park to fight someone.

"Anyway," I said, "you can't fight in them clothes."

She was still looking at me the same way. Half smiling, like I didn't know a thing. And she kept smiling and looking straight at me when she reached to the table and picked up the knife. She tucked it in the front dress pocket, her hand on the handle, and walked out.

When that many people is surrounding the house and screaming, everything is clattering. The walls, the windows. It's like things is going to cave in or blow wide apart. It's where the first rip is, you look. And I seen it. A rock through the front window. Glass shattering. A hole wide as a fist.

I was in the doorway between the kitchen and the front room. That was far as I got, and when I looked out for Justine, after seeing that rock come through the window, she was gone. Just the crowd screaming and the empty house. Like the boys and Mom wasn't even there. Like they was rolling away, around the corner, out of reach. Everybody. It all just went so fast. The whole place blowing apart. Then I seen the hole again. I was in shock by this time, I guess. I turned around and started putting dishes away. I don't know what. I opened cupboards and seen the gun. Jack's shotgun. I ran to the front porch and shot it.

I didn't know nothing after that. Just colors. Everybody moving. Voices. People talking to me.

"Dumb-ass bitch. What'd you do that for?"

"Alice, you're the queen now. Nobody's going to mess with you, girl."

"Dumb-ass bitch."

"Hey, Alice. You're bad, girl. Justine never got a lick in."

"Stupid, crazy bitch. Now the cops'll come. Dumb-ass bitch."

They said I just stood there with that gun. Like a statue or something. Like I been there a hundred years.

I thought of that and the other things I heard after, when I started to gain my senses. I was standing in the kitchen, against the sink. Auntie Anna was there by that time, and a good thing. She was talking to two cops in our kitchen. She said the blast wasn't a gun. Some kids threw a cherry bomb at our window and made a hole. They believed her, because they never searched the house. She was in official's clothes, the kind that match her voice when she talks to social workers.

"It's a single-parent family," she was saying. "It's an Indian family just moved to town."

I looked at Justine. She was lifting a neat piece of chocolate cake to her mouth with a plastic fork. Her I'd have to reckon with, on account I upset her show. I looked at Mom and the boys. They was eating cake too. Auntie was still talking, painting that picture of us not capable of nothing. I seen the cops looking at the table while she talked. I seen what they seen, what Auntie was saying. But I seen more. I seen everything.

Sam Toms's Last Song

The day Sam Toms turned one hundred, he woke with a woman on his mind and a plan for a new life. He rubbed his eyes and looked up from the sagging bed to the light coming through the torn cardboard over the window. Six o'clock, he thought. He straightened his arms and stretched his legs. These weren't the times he could spring out of bed and walk tall through the day, even after a night of carousing or who-knows-what. That boundless strength was gone. But he had his songs, and as he watched the morning light in long rays across the room, he had all the feeling of the old days, because at least today he would sing.

The woman was Nellie Copaz. She was a distant cousin of some sort who lived just up the street in the neatest house in the neighborhood: red roses climbing the picket fence, dahlias of all colors, pink and white hollyhocks tall as a man, golden poppies lining the pebble walkway to the front porch. The path to heaven. And inside the smell of home cooking, chili and fry bread, and the soft couch where he lay when she rested her hand on his heart.

He would lie on that couch again. He would eat her cooking. He would pack his suitcase today and move in. That was the plan.

He listened for Linda, his great-granddaughter, in the front room. Nothing. Not a sign of anyone. Not her long, gasping breathing. None of her friends. Out again all night. But it didn't matter now. Toms saw the rays of light across the room like bars he could grab onto and hoist himself to his feet. Today he would do things by himself. Tomorrow it wouldn't matter.

On the count of three he rolled himself up so he was sitting, his feet touching the floor. He reached for his oakwood cane by the nightstand, but his hand landed on the naked lamp bulb there. He reminded himself that he could see perfectly fine. "There, there," he said, taking the cane and bracing himself. He pushed himself to his feet and waited, holding fast to the cane, while the room steadied itself and blood entered his legs. He looked beyond his ample stomach that showed through the open pajama top to his boxer shorts, white with tiny red hearts. He hadn't wet the bed, and as he moved toward the bathroom, he could tell he was swollen like a young man. "There, there," he said again.

He decided he should have his usual bowl of Cheerios with a banana and an extra cup of coffee. A little pep-up. Heck with the blood pressure. What do white doctors know? Sam Toms was an Indian and a hundred years old. Then he thought of his songs. He wanted to warm up, wake that cricket in his throat, as the old-timers said. But Toms was already in the kitchen, and he figured he would eat first.

He didn't need to fast or sweat. No special foods. His songs were the kind you could buy or sell like wine during Prohibition. Use them when and how you wanted. Just don't tell where you got them and, if you're selling, don't expect to get them back. Gambling songs. Love songs. Songs for luck. Toms bought them from dying old men and women who were selling at a bargain. He'd sung them day in and day out years ago, whenever he found himself in a pinch, when he needed more than the eye could see and the hand could hold. The exact status of a down-turned card. The heart of a woman. Now, after all this time, he was singing again.

He got busy with breakfast, peeling and cutting, opening the rattling refrigerator, and, yes, remembering to turn off the stove after he boiled water for coffee. When he sat down at the scuffed Formica table with his coffee and Cheerios all on a place mat with silverware and a napkin, he thought again of Linda. He wished she would walk in. Surprise, he didn't need her, and wouldn't she rant and rave when he walked out in his black suit with a suitcase in his hand. No more two hundred and thirty-nine social security dollars a month to take care of him. Never mind where he was going.

No way to treat a man who'd won out a century. Father of half a dozen families. Grandfather to four times that many. Old Man Toms, who logged the redwoods, built roads where there was nothing but horse trails. Who had enough song power to pass those drunks in the tank a bottle right under the sheriff's nose and collect for it later. No, this place was not for Sam Toms. The Hole, folks called it. Two rows of army barracks separated by a potholed dirt road littered with junk and dirty children. And here in the last unit, with nothing to look out and see but other barracks. No respect, he thought, looking at the tossed blankets over the empty couch where Linda slept. A dog made a neater bed.

He was a pure man, right from Salvador, a grandson of Rosa, baptized by the Spanish padres in the tiny adobe on the creek, the namesake of the town. Santa Rosa. But his offspring? Mexicans, Filipinos, whites. They didn't know the old ways: hard work, respect for the old. Nellie knew. She was an Indian from Rosa too, even if half of her was Coast Indian. She knew songs. He felt power when she leaned over him with a song that led her hand to his heart and pulled him to his feet.

The white doctor said he was going to die. He was scared. And no Greta to take care of him. Greta, the German lady who had cooked and cleaned his house and never lifted a quarter out of his pockets or off his dresser. Good as a wife, he told people. The lady he hired out of the newspaper after his last wife, who was forty years younger than him, went back to Guatemala. Good Greta got him up each morning. She clipped the few whiskers on his chin when they got too long. She ironed his clothes so they were stiff and fresh smelling. She took his arm in the supermarket even though he could walk perfectly fine. Let folks think she was his wife.

"How they do in Germany," she'd say after he complimented her, which was why after Greta got sick and retired, he kept talking about Germany, even though he had no intention of going there.

But his children and grandchildren who came around didn't listen. That is, when they came around at all. They'd bring a pie or a pot of chili stew and vie for him. "Come live with me, Gramps. I cook good." "Pops, you'd have your own room in my house." He'd listen and watch for their eyes to roam the house, searching desktops, always coming back to the dresser where he kept his change. More and more, he found himself alone, staring at the four walls, opening cans of soup and seeing the clean glow from the sink and the kitchen counter fade week by week, month after month.

Orneriness was how he dealt with his family's absence. It drove away whoever still came to see him. "Just rot in your pigsty, old geezer." "Smelly old fool, then don't get out of your chair." Until Linda's mother, Billyrene, found him doubled over on his couch one day and hauled him off to the clinic. No, not a stroke. Well, maybe a small one. Just age. The man is nearly a hundred, after all.

She got special foods and took him into her home. Lost among her countless brood and the round-the-clock Mexican music, he continued to fade. Try Ensure, the clinic doctor said. Baby food, he said. I'm not dead yet. He wanted someone with songs. He called the cab himself, and paid the small fare. With the cabdriver waiting, he carried himself past her flowers, up the steps. And when she sang he knew he'd done the right thing. Something old and true. "Heart sickness," she said in Indian. She opened that place where life was left in him. He could sit up and breathe. She touched and untangled the cramped muscles of his heart. He could feel his pulse. She pulled him to his feet and led him around the room four times before she took him to the front door.

Outside he sucked in the warm morning air as he waited for his cab. Bees hummed around Nellie's flowers, landed, then lifted away, their tiny legs weighted down with pollen. He looked to Grand Avenue beyond Nellie's yard: a black woman hollered from her front porch for her children; a man worked under his car, just his legs and heavy work boots showing on the street.

That was when Toms thought of his songs for the first time in ages.

People said he looked better. He was livelier.

He had a plan.

Before long he couldn't remember whether his plan came from his singing or from his plain thinking. He wasn't going to live in a three-room place with two dozen Mexicans. He'd lost his home where he had lived with Greta, and Billyrene held his pension and social security. He had to find someone else to take care of him. Some conservator who would let him have his money and some peace.

He sang in the mornings. He slipped out while the others slept and made his way to a field behind the barracks, where they lived on Grand Avenue, and with the early light hitting the curly leaves and green acorns, he remembered his songs one by one. He felt the sun warm his blood, clear his senses. Two things he could still do: sing songs and see right into people.

He set his sights on Ernesto, Linda's older brother. He'd seen the cars come and go, day and night, the visitors Ernesto met in the driveway for no longer than you could blink. "You and me, Ernesto, we need our own place."

"You're hip, Gramps."

So he got a new conservator and a new place. First step.

When the social security check came to the new house, Ernesto asked who Sam Toms was. Ernesto matched the name with the papers he signed for the social worker the week before: Gramps. Ernesto cashed the check and turned the money over to Toms. Toms paid the rent and still had money left. Ernesto shopped for Toms, but that was about all. Too busy coming and going for anything else.

Step two: cooking, cleaning, fresh clothes. He sang his songs in the morning still, on the front porch facing the fairgrounds, before the punks rolled up in their low-slung cars with foam dice hanging from the rearview mirrors. The house was on Temple, across from the racetrack. When Toms sang, only the trainers and their horses were out, going around and around the track. Against the sound of birds, with the sun coming over the grandstand in the distance, he sang loudly, then softly, his body lifting and falling with each breath.

He got his answer. It was white, in hard little lumps.

Ernesto could hide nothing. Old Man Toms could still see. Like a hawk. And he wasn't going to beg for someone to tidy up the place or spend an entire afternoon on the phone trying to get someone to wash his clothes. So he kept his eye on two of the greasers, Big Car and No Car, the one who hung around the park up the street. And each day he went into the plastic bag stuffed inside Ernesto's high-top tennis shoe and pinched a few of the little white lumps. They added up.

It happened like clockwork. No Car came over one afternoon when Ernesto was away. Toms was sitting on the front porch. "How much?" he asked No Car and lifted a see-through plastic purse from inside his Pendleton shirt. No Car, who hadn't changed his clothes for a week, fell into the trap. He gave both answers: how much and for what price. Toms unzipped the purse and sprinkled a portion of the cache on his smooth upturned palm. "For washing my clothes," he said. Then he emptied out more of the white magic, in a separate pile. "For keeping your mouth shut."

No Car had the eyes of a child. He was too frightened to lie or cheat, which was why he stayed in the park. He took the brown paper bags stuffed with dirty laundry, and a handful of bills, and quarters for the washing machines and came back with clean clothes for a week. He got the white stuff Toms wrapped in tinfoil just the way Ernesto did for his customers. "Here," Toms said, slipping No Car another wrapper. "I need a hot meal. Go to the deli. Then come back. I have more for you."

He couldn't pinch from Ernesto forever. He needed Big Car. But Big Car was risky, because he wasn't desperate. His eyes were shifty. Toms would have to gamble on the big greaser's greed that he would deliver the goods. "Here you go, old dude," Big Car said, handing Toms the package.

"And keep your mouth shut," Toms snapped.

No Car told Toms he'd been cheated out of thirty dollars in the deal. Maybe fifty. But it didn't matter to Toms. He figured he would more than get it back. And he did. More than warm meals and clean clothes. Old Toms had girls sitting on his lap, girls with tattoos like the ones in the old sideshows who took him behind the horses for a dime. White magic got him a peek, now and then even a feel.

If the girls knew Toms's doings, so did others. Ernesto found out and had a fit. "Old sneak, you got my business," Ernesto complained. "We got to go in together." But that wasn't what Toms wanted.

Step three: Get Ernesto out of the house. He had to figure a way around the social worker, a way to get the checks in his name so he could pay one of the tattooed girls to do things. They'd cook and clean house better than No Car. He planned to just come out and ask the social worker the next time she came around for her monthly visit. Why not? He was healthy now, not like he was when Ernesto's mother found him. Then, without warning, Ernesto disappeared, as if Toms's wish had been enough to do the trick. Ernesto didn't come back one night, or the next morning either. The cars that finally pulled up around noon were black-and-white, and the men wore uniforms. They lifted him off the porch, out of his chair, searched him from head to toe, and tore up his neat house.

They didn't handcuff him like they did sixty years before, when they busted his moonshine operation under the hotel on lower Fourth. He was too old. And they gave him a nice room in the jail, where he stayed until the trial. No Car testified that he got the stuff from Toms and Ernesto. He said he'd seen Toms just before the officer found him passed out under a swing set in the park. Toms sat on the hard wooden bench listening. Occasionally he glanced at the walls and high ceiling of the courtroom.

He looked once or twice at No Car, but not at the boy's too-frightened-to-lie eyes. Ernesto got prison. Toms was too old. He got sent back to Ernesto's mother with someone from the law to check on him once a month.

But Toms still had steam. He wasn't ready to die, to disappear in that crowded house where nobody ever turned off the music. He had clear vision, and Linda walked right into it. Because she was always there, hanging around her mother. She was frightened, afraid to be away from people, not just because Pablo, the hood she had been living with, got shot in the head on their front porch a while back but because she was basically the kind of person who couldn't be alone. Probably this was why she went for the hood in the first place. One of the Rose-land gang. Toms heard people talk about them. Since she moved back into the house, she had yapped incessantly. Why go on living like this? she asked over and over. Her mother was too busy with life to think about things. Toms listened. He told her she needed a fresh start, a new place. They could go in together, and he told her how.

Which is how Toms and Linda ended up with their own place just a few doors down from Billyrene, still in the army barracks on Grand Avenue, still in the Hole.

Temporary, he told Linda, because they had to take what was available at the moment. The social worker and the law people thought it was a good idea. The old man and his great-granddaughter could take care of each other and keep out of trouble. Linda was on probation too: petty larceny.

Linda stuck by Toms, just as Toms had figured. Stuck so close that within two weeks he felt like the spotted mutt with a litter of pups in front of the unit across the way. Sucked dry, day and night. She washed clothes, shopped, cooked, and kept house, even if she wasn't the neatest person in the world. But it was Pablo this and Pablo that. Toms would have shot Pablo if someone hadn't already. And as if Pablo wasn't dead enough, his rivals found where Linda lived and blew out the windows on the back side of the barracks.

"I'm not in the gangs anymore, Gramps," Linda said after she put cardboard over the windows. Which Toms knew was true. She found new friends and stuck to them like a fly on dung. People from some church, and Indians from the Indian Bible study at the YMCA. At first Toms enjoyed the quiet. He could come out of his room, where he used to retreat from her chatter chatter chatter. But in time she came around only to do her duties, and she was never alone. Toms woke with strangers, ate with them, and closed his bedroom door at night to them. Linda wanted an extra five dollars for this, ten for that: for the new church, for the missionaries. Toms swore he found money missing. Of course it would be for a good cause. No way to live, Toms thought.

He hadn't sung his songs since before jail. Oh, maybe those few times at Linda's mother's. But those were feeble attempts. Halfway to the field behind the barracks he hummed in fits and starts. Now he had to sing again. He had to give it all he had. He was failing and he knew it. He couldn't see his way out.

He sang little by little, more and more each day, while Linda was out with her friends. But he'd get tired, close his eyes, and stop. Some days were better than others, but the better days didn't add up to make a difference. On the eve of his hundredth birthday, he thought of Nellie. She could help him again. It wasn't until next morning that he thought of moving in with her.

The idea came to him straight as the light through the torn cardboard over the window. It stirred and rattled his brain, woke his blood, so he felt as if Nellie had sung already. He had a plan. Why not? She lived alone. He had money. They were both Indians. Old Indians. Toms was surprised he hadn't thought this all out sooner. She was so close, just up the street. He hadn't felt better in months, years. Today he would be the one to sing. Right in front of Nellie. For her heart. Peace, he thought. Red roses. Hollyhocks tall as a man. Golden poppies lining the way.

Toms turned from his bowl of Cheerios and squinted at the wall clock above the stove. Seven-thirty. Linda would be back by nine. He still wanted to warm up his voice, wake that cricket, but there wasn't enough time, not if he was going to dress himself and pack. Things took time these days. He had to admit that. He dabbed himself with a washcloth and splashed Old Spice under his arms and on his neck. Sitting on the bed, he lifted one arm into his shirt, then the other. The pants went slowly, one leg, then the other. He labored over every button. When Linda came through the front door, he was tying his shoes.

"OK, Grandpa, what are you doing?" She had seen his dishes on the table and come immediately to his room. "I'm not late. I'm here at the regular time to get you up and fix breakfast."

He straightened, a tad dizzy after leaning over his shoes so long. She couldn't even say Happy Birthday. Did she even know it was his birthday? Did anyone? He was a hundred years old. Toms didn't answer Linda, and she went back to the kitchen. He could hear her doing the dishes.

How could he have thought for a moment about warming up and singing? He still had to pack. At least he could dress himself, and Linda saw that he could. Not to worry about the songs. He had sung on a dime before. And with the way he felt this morning and all that he had done, wasn't luck already on his side? To take care of things now, he only needed Nellie to listen.

He dragged his cardboard suitcase out of the closet and pulled it onto the bed. He packed things for a week, things he would need until he could come back and get the rest. A few pairs of underwear, socks, a couple of shirts, his everyday brown shoes.

Linda went nuts then. She called her mother. Toms listened.

"Is Mama there? Listen, get Mama Where is she? As soon as she gets back tell her Grandpa's going someplace No, he won't tell me."

Luck was on Toms's side. But he didn't have all day. He had to work fast. Linda's mother would stop him, maybe take him back to her house. Why not? She'd done it two times before. He had to get to Nellie and work things out, discuss money and the social worker, before Linda's mother found him. Nellie would have to say she was taking care of him. Lucky he was dressed and finished packing. He buckled the leather strap on his suitcase and made for the phone.

Linda had the phone on her lap. He plopped down on the couch next to her, nearly missing the cushion and hitting the floor. He caught his breath, then took the phone. Linda gasped and threw her arms up, as if a spider had fallen from the ceiling. The number was easy to remember: 555-TAXI. Toms gave the address and said "Now."

"Grandpa, what's the matter? Talk to me."

Toms started to get up, then settled back on the couch. Conserve energy, he thought. He looked across the room to the bare kitchen table. The room seemed so big, empty. Only then did Toms realize that no one else was there, that he and Linda were alone, seated next to each other. Suddenly he felt uncomfortable, as if he should answer her. He wished he were sitting at the table or waiting in his room.

"Pops, haven't you ever had anyone die? Do you know what it's like? I'm doing the best I can."

Toms took hold of his cane, ready to get up. Hah! Had anyone die? He had outlived most of his nineteen children. Didn't she know? Couldn't she see? He was about to tell her, but, thank heavens, the cabdriver was at the door.

With slow, careful strokes of her cupped hand, Nellie Copaz brushed the crumbs left from her granddaughter's breakfast off the kitchen table and into the empty wastebasket on the floor. The girl, who sat watching TV in the front room, was, in fact, Nellie's step-granddaughter. She was Nellie's daughter's husband's child from a previous marriage, and anyone might guess as much, or at least wonder, seeing the ten-year-old's golden hair and complexion.

Nellie set the wastebasket under the sink and wiped her hands on the towel folded over the counter. Then she sat down to work on her baskets. She was behind schedule; she had orders to meet, and these days when she baby-sat, while her daughter and son-in-law were away, she had precious little time to catch up. She couldn't weave uninterrupted for hours at a time. The girl was well behaved, but like so many only children, she depended a great deal on adults for talk and attention. She was all they had to see.

Nellie lifted her large sewing box off the floor and onto the table. Inside she found her baskets and the tight rolls of sedge root and redbud bark she kept in neat little rows. She was meticulous: the polished silver tea set on her counter, the way she turned her sleeves up over her wrists, the exact stitching of her coiled baskets. She even surprised herself when she discovered something she had overlooked: mold on the windowsill next to the African violets or a loose stitch.

Her first task was to finish the basket the mayor had ordered. It was a small canoe-shaped basket with an exquisite design, if she did say so herself. It was inspired, something she felt had power with the first stitch. Now, as she held the basket in her hands and looped the last stitches of sedge, she hated the thought of giving it up. It occurred to her that she could keep the basket and start another one. Just be late. The mayor wouldn't care. She'd still get paid. She never dealt with the mayor anyway, it was always his secretary. But then she wouldn't have a basket in the City Hall's display at this year's county fair. And what could possibly silence the acid tongue of her critics faster than this basket in a showcase with her name under it? No traditional Pomo weaver, they said. No art. No inspiration. Just doing it for white-man money. She could hear their hisses.

The trouble had started years ago when she married Charles Benedict, for which they would never forgive her. Son of the man who mistreated Indians, none worse than Nellie's own mother, who hanged herself in the man's barn after years of abuse. Only Nellie knew the details. They turned their heads when they met Nellie on the road into town. The drunks on lower Fourth shouted things that would shock a sailor. Of course, the son was not the father. But would any of them see that? And now, when the clinic doctor couldn't cure their illnesses, who did they come to with have-mercy-on-me faces? I was wondering, Mrs. Copaz, if maybe you'd sing just a few of your songs for me? And Nellie sang and got them out her front door before she could think and remember their turned heads and hateful words. So when Nellie looked up from her work and saw Old Man Toms through the screen door, she figured he wanted the same thing, another dose of what he paid her twenty dollars for a while back.

"A man's here," her granddaughter had announced.

Nellie saw Toms and tied up the last stitch of her basket. Then she pulled out the half-finished beaded basket the lady on MacDonald ordered. She would get right back to work after Toms left.

She walked through the front room, past the girl watching TV, then stopped at the door. "You're sick," she said.

Toms said nothing. Then Nellie saw the tall cabdriver coming over the pebble walkway carrying a cardboard suitcase.

"Is this the place, old man?" the cabdriver asked impatiently, setting the suitcase on the porch next to Toms.

Toms nodded yes and reached into his pocket for change. Realizing the opportunity to please his client and earn a decent tip, the driver offered to carry the suitcase inside. The lady on the other side of the screen door wasn't exactly a spring chicken either. Not nearly as old as this man, but nobody to be lugging a big suitcase.

Nellie didn't quite know what had happened. Toms gave the man four quarters, exact fare, then looked to Nellie, who stared at the cardboard suitcase on the clean hardwood floor of her living room as if it were a moon rock.

She still hadn't figured things out when Toms was in the kitchen sitting across from her at the table. She was thinking she would have to sing for him in there because the girl was on the couch in the front room. Nellie rarely had the people she sang for into her kitchen.

"How do you do, Miss Copaz?" Toms said. "Pretty little girl you got out there."

He spoke as if he had just run into her on the street. Formal, she thought, taking in his pressed black suit for the first time. She felt uneasy, caught off guard.

"Do you want me to sing?" she asked finally.

"How many rooms you got here?" he asked.

Then it clicked. The suitcase. The black suit. The fancy talk. She forgot the old man across from her with half his face sagged to his neck and remembered the person Sam Toms: joker, moonshine man, big mouth, womanizer. And didn't he have songs?

Her blood boiled. She felt as if she would burst. She'd known his children. She was their age, probably thirty years younger than him. And here he had come thinking he could move in with her and who knows what else. What was she, an open hotel? A doormat? She wanted to holler, blast him right out of the house. She thought of asking him one more time if he wanted her to sing, just to give him the benefit of the doubt. But she didn't holler or ask the question. She surprised herself.

"Two bedrooms," she said.

Toms nodded approval.

"But my granddaughter sleeps in one," Nellie added quickly, gesturing with her chin to the girl in the front room.

Toms raised his eyebrows, then followed her chin. "Gee," he said. "I got them in all colors too."

"Oh, yes?" Nellie said. She pushed the loose gray hairs on her forehead under her red bandanna. Just then Toms thought she was beautiful. Something in her gesture. He hadn't really looked at her before. She could be his wife.

"I'm rich," he said.

Nellie folded her hands on the table.

"Real rich," Toms said.

"Oh, yes? How rich?"

"Pension and social security. You think that's all? Wrong. Two hundred and thirty-nine bucks for keeping me."

"Hah," Nellie said. "I bet you don't have ten bucks in your pocket."

Toms grinned, showing his white dentures. He was on a roll. He reached into his coat pocket and plopped three twenties, a ten, and some change on the table. Nellie studied the money a moment. Then she gathered it up and dropped it into her canoe basket.

"Well," she said, peering into the basket, "what's this? How do I know I'd get any of it? You got too many grandkids."

"I'll sign it over. Everything. It'll be yours."

"Yes, but what's going to stop those seventeen thousand grandkids of yours from coming around for it?"

"I'll sign them out. Just talk to the social worker. Get papers."

"They'll still come around."

"No, sign papers for that too. Keep them away."

Nellie considered. "All of them?" she asked.

"Every last one," Toms answered with resolve. "What good are they to me anyway? Just take my money, leave me hanging around."

"Well, that is a shame."

"Yes," said Toms.

"Yeah." Nellie sighed. "You got a point. The young don't think of the old no more."

"That's what I say." She had been testing him, playing around the bait, and now he felt she had taken it hook, line, and sinker. She wasn't just impressed with his money; she understood his situation and felt sorry for him. He watched her turning the basket in her hands.

The blond girl appeared in the doorway. "Grandma, can I go to the store now?"

"Finish your program on TV. Go sit down."

The girl was startled by Nellie's adamant tone. Nellie never talked to her that way. She glanced quickly at Toms, then disappeared.

See, Toms thought. His point exactly. No end to these kids.

Nellie looked at him a long while, then back at the basket of money between her hands. "What else you got?" she asked finally. "What else you got, old Indian man?"

He knew what she meant: *Indian.* This was it, the last draw. She asked for it. He'd sing his songs loud and clear, so she could hear, and reel her in. He didn't bother to answer her. He cleared his throat, closed his eyes, and, to his amazement, the songs came loud and clear, just falling from his lips.

He lost track of time. He sang every song he knew. He was proud of his performance, not a cough or even a dry throat when he finished. His tongue and the roof of his mouth felt slippery, smooth. When he opened his eyes, he found Nellie with her head bent, as if in silent prayer. But then he saw that she was holding her basket toward him, which he didn't understand. She held it up, off the table, and tilted just enough for him to see the money inside.

"Pretty good, heh?" he asked, to break the silence. She didn't move. Toms felt something foreboding, frightening. He was looking for words. Then, all at once, she set the basket down and with both hands slowly pulled it close to her. She lifted her face, and Toms saw immediately what had happened. Her face was tight, flushed purple. But she didn't burst. She uncoiled and struck like a snake.

"Thank you, sir," she hissed. "Now I can lift the spells dirty old men put on good-hearted women. You know, in the right hands your songs can be used as medicine. Antidotes." She was looking down at the basket, turning it in her hands again.

She had caught his songs with her basket! She'd tricked him, pulled each song out, so that now he was empty. He felt like a drowning man with no sight of land. He grabbed across the table for the basket, but she snatched it up and held it against her breast.

Toms took hold of his cane with trembling hands and bellowed, "Give me back my money!"

"You dirty fool, why should I? You gave it to me, didn't you? Now you're going to take it away from me, just like you did from your family?" She looked him straight in the face. "Come on, try it," she dared.

Toms pounded the floor with his cane. "Give me back my money."

She leaned forward, the basket against her breast, her hard eyes fixed on him with utter contempt. "You fool. Why would I want a man who'd give his money to a strange woman, turn his back on his own family, and then give away songs that might've done good for somebody, but of course never did because the man is low-down rotten to the core?"

"Give me back my money!" Toms ranted. He felt himself sinking now beneath the force of her wrath. In desperation he lifted his cane and took a swipe across the table at Nellie. She jumped back in her seat and the cane swept over the table, knocking her sedge roots and half-finished beaded basket to the floor. "Son of a bitch," Toms cursed. "God-damned white-man whore. . . . White lover. . . ." He went to swing his cane again but couldn't. His heart tightened, his innards turned this way and that. He was out of breath. The fight was over.

His words echoed in Nellie's ears. She wasn't moving now either. She was still leaning back in her seat, the basket clutched tight to her body, as if waiting for Toms's next strike. But her face was pale, expressionless. In a split second she saw her life in countless scenes and situations, from those days and times on lower Fourth to this very morning. Toms had hit her square in the heart with that which never left her, that which she packed on her back the way a stinky old possum packs its young. Spiteful pride. She was stunned. She was mean and she knew better.

"Grandma, what happened?" The girl was in the doorway.

"Watch TV," Nellie said, letting out a long breath. She set her canoe basket down.

Toms took hold of his cane and managed to get to his feet. Instinctively, he turned and made for the door. He moved like a windup doll, slow, deliberate, in one direction.

Nellie sat looking at Toms's money in her basket. She heard the screen door open and close. She thought of her granddaughter and found her watching TV. She poked at the loose strands of her hair, straightened her bandanna, and got up. She called a cab, then went outside with the basket.

She found Toms standing at the bottom of her steps in a daze, glassy-eyed. She took his arm and helped him to sit down. She set his cane against his legs, where he could reach it. Then she put the basket in his hands and situated it so it rested in his lap. She stood a minute, before going, to make sure the basket didn't tip or fall, spilling out the money.

She had forgotten about the suitcase. Inside, she found it still like a moon rock in the middle of her living room. She dragged it across the floor and out onto the porch. Then she went back in and watched through the screen door until the cab left with Toms.

She thought she'd get back to weaving, pick up where she left off. Then, in the kitchen, she saw her beaded basket and roots on the floor. She had forgotten about the mess. Among the loose strips of sedge and redbud bark she saw crumbs from breakfast that had missed the wastebasket.

"Grandma," the girl said, coming up behind Nellie, "I'm glad that old man left."

No great accomplishment, Nellie thought to herself.

"Grandma, now can I please go to the store?"

Nellie didn't answer her.

"Grandma, I need a dollar for the store."

Nellie turned, half facing her granddaughter. "Look in my purse," she said.

Toms didn't remember the cabdriver steering him onto the couch. The driver, who had taken a dollar bill out of the canoe basket for the fare, offered to call an ambulance or a doctor, whatever Toms wanted. But Toms didn't hear him. At six in the evening, just before Linda came home, Toms was still on the couch, not sure how long he had been sitting there or even if he had gone anywhere at all. He saw the crumpled blankets next to him lit by the dull light from the front window and thought Linda was still there. She was asking him about having people die, and he was trying to answer her.

The Indian Maid

At Sherman Indian School my mother was the only girl who actually dreamed of being a maid. While the other girls went through the motions, learning to polish silver and fold napkins this way and that, my mother memorized every detail of the matron's lessons. 'Impeccable," she said. "I had to be impeccable." She wasn't going to be just any maid, the kind you see pushing carts in and out of motel rooms. She was going to work in a big house with wallpapered rooms and crystal chandeliers, in a movie star's mansion in Los Angeles, far away from Sonoma County. The family would love her so much they would adopt her. Why not? It had happened to other Indian girls. That was what all the reservation girls heard on their first day at Sherman. But the morning after graduation, when work assignments were passed out, my mother found herself with only a ticket home.

She kept her head up. She fought. She swore she wasn't going back to the reservation. She wasn't going to see that row of dilapidated shacks in the middle of an apple orchard ever again. She didn't sleep a wink on the bus. The entire twelve hours she plotted and planned. On binder paper she wrote a hundred announcements advertising her skills and qualifications. She listed her age and weight and the duties she was especially prepared to handle: five-course meals, large cocktail parties, shopping. The response she got was beyond her wildest imagination. The announcements that she tacked to every pillar and post caught the town's attention. An article appeared on the front page of the local newspaper with a full-length picture of my mother in her starched white uniform and cap, the only things she got from Sherman besides her ticket home. The article, entitled "The Indian Maid," described my mother as an eighteen-year-old like any other, full of big dreams and determination. A day later, she was hired by the wealthiest family in town.

Her job was to take care of an old lady, the grandmother, old Mrs. Benedict, who was confined to the top floor of the Benedicts' three-story house. Everything was set up on the third floor: bedrooms, bathrooms, a large dining room, and a kitchen, so my mother never had to leave the floor either. Her room was just off the kitchen, and from her window she could see all of Santa Rosa, downtown and the orchards and farms beyond.

Old Mrs. B, as my mother refers to her now, couldn't walk. Something to do with her back, a kind of paralysis. Sometimes my mother helped her up and sat her in a padded wheelchair, but most of the time Mrs. B stayed in bed. Even so, she was quite dignified. She was dressed every day in fine clothes and jewelry, her white hair set and combed. She sat up in bed with a food tray in front of her as if she were seated at a formal dinner party. She held her silverware, always the correct fork or spoon, just so, not too close to the base of the utensil, and delicately lifted each snapped bean or little square of meat to her mouth. She was a lady.

That's why my mother never mentioned the food she found on the floor. Globs of mashed potatoes. Bloody prime rib. Peas. They stained the expensive rug from India next to the bed. It got so bad that while Mrs. B was soaking in her mineral bath one afternoon, my mother rolled up the rug and put it in a closet. Mrs. B didn't seem to notice that the carpet was gone, or if she did, she never said anything. Mother figured she was ashamed. She worked so hard not to spill her food in front of my mother. In fact, Mother never saw her spill a crumb. It happened when my mother wasn't looking, when she wasn't in the room.

My mother was her constant companion. As it turned out, that was my mother's job, to keep old Mrs. B company. Mother didn't have to cook. She didn't even clean. A cook brought up three meals a day. A maid dusted and scrubbed and took down the dirty laundry every morning, including my mother's. The days were long. Mother did her best to keep the old woman company, playing cards and listening to her tell stories about glorious parties in San Francisco that she had attended when she was young: who was there, what they wore, this socialite, that politician. In the evenings, after Mrs. B fell asleep, Mother went to her room. Sometimes the younger Benedicts gave parties that lasted late into the night. Voices, loud laughter/and the popping of champagne corks echoed up the stairs and traveled through the hallways. Mother sat on her bed, listening and looking out her window at the soundless lights of the town.

The Benedict house was elegant, stylishly furnished, though nothing like what my mother had seen at Sherman in the pictures of movie stars' homes. No thirty-foot ceilings and marble columns. No lily ponds filled with brightly speckled goldfish. Mother didn't see much of the bottom two floors or of the grounds outside. There was one chandelier on Mrs. B's floor, and it was in her room. One day while Mrs. B was telling a story, she looked over and found my mother staring up at the chandelier.

"Zelda," Mrs. B said, "do you like that?"

Mother felt embarrassed, as if she had been caught behaving disrespectfully, ignoring Mrs. B as she talked. She nodded yes.

"Do you like crystal, Zelda?"

Mother nodded again.

"Spell it, spell crystal: C-R-Y-S-T-A-L."

"C-R-Y-S-T-A-L," Mother repeated.

"Again," Mrs. B said.

"C-R-Y-S-T-A-L."

"Perfect. Now do you like pretty jewels?"

"Yes, ma'am."

"Then get me up. I'm going to show you something."

Mother got Mrs. B out of bed and lifted her into the wheelchair.

"Now push me to the locked drawer below my dresser. The key is under the dresser. Now get it. If anything is ever missing, well know what happened, won't we?"

Following Mrs. B's instructions, Mother unlocked the mahogany drawer and took out a black box, which she placed in Mrs. B's lap. Mrs. B clasped the box in her hands and looked at Mother. Mother looked away, still mindful that she had done something wrong, been neglectful. She thought perhaps in some odd way Mrs. B was punishing her, teaching her a lesson.

"Look, Zelda, look over here." Mrs. B's voice was commanding.

When Mother looked, she couldn't believe her eyes. In the box, neatly placed on a bed of maroon cloth, sat beautiful jewels, dozens of them, rings and earrings, pendants and bracelets, all sizes and shapes, jewelry my mother had no idea existed in that house. Each morning she had dressed Mrs. B with the same string of pearls and earrings, the same pendant on her dress. When my mother focused on the open box, she saw that most of the stones in the fancy ornaments were blue or purplish in color. The stones reflected all the light in the room.

Mrs. B ever so carefully picked up a ring and held it between her thumb and index finger. "Amethyst," she said to my mother. "Spell amethyst: A-M-E-T-H-Y-S-T."

"A-M-E-T . . ." My mother stumbled. She was nervous and confused. Eventually she spelled amethyst correctly. Then she learned to spell two more stones, sapphire and blue topaz.

The next day at the same time, around three o'clock in the afternoon, Mother learned two more: lapis lazuli and aquamarine. It became a regular event each afternoon, an hour-long lesson. Mother learned to distinguish the fine hues of blue and purple. Mrs. B would begin each lesson by picking up the ornaments one at a time and asking Mother to identify their stones and spell them correctly. Eventually Mother learned words that described the properties of these gems. Transparent—capable of transmitting light so that images and objects beyond can be clearly perceived: T-R-A-N-S-P-A-R-E-N-T. Opaque—not reflecting light, lusterless, obtuse. Coruscate—to flash, sparkle. Then one day Mrs. B said the word "propitious," and my mother was confounded, unable to associate it with jewels in any way. It wasn't a color or a property. Propitious—indicating a favorable condition or an auspicious outcome: P-R-O-P-I-T-I-O-U-S.

Of course Mother didn't ask any questions. She was still under the impression that these daily lessons were a form of punishment or, as they would say at Sherman, behavior modification, for her disrespectful behavior. Yet she didn't feel the hurt in this punishment, no unkind words, no reproach from the teacher. She learned countless words and took pride in her ability to know so much. There seemed no end to what she could learn.

Around this time Mrs. B had a visitor, a grande dame like herself, a Mrs. Strathmore from San Francisco. Mother gave Mrs. Strathmore her bedroom off the kitchen and slept on a cot in the hallway. During this visit my mother had a lot of time to herself, since Mrs. B was occupied with her company. The afternoon lessons were suspended. Still, Mother went over in her mind what she had learned. She sat at the kitchen table picturing each gem and spelling out loud its name and properties.

One afternoon on her way to retrieve the lunch trays that the cook from downstairs had brought up earlier, Mother detected a quarrelsome tone in the two ladies' voices. She ducked back, outside the bedroom door.

"Really, Helen, you must face it," Mrs. Strathmore said to Mrs. B. "You have failed. You're locked up here."

"I'm not locked up anywhere, Ruth," Mrs. B retorted. "I still have command of my ship. I know that every day of my life, and don't forget it!"

Mother didn't hear any more. She backed away. She didn't want to be nosey. She noticed that the women often bickered. Going in and out of Mrs. B's bedroom, Mother couldn't help but overhear what was going on between them: petty arguments about who said what or what did or did not happen fifty years before. Mrs. Strathmore was old and gray, certainly no younger than Mrs. B, but she still held herself erect, very proud, and she could walk, which she lorded over her bedridden friend. "That's fine, Ruth," Mrs. B said, "waltz in and out of this room. Go ahead, show off. But when the time comes, who's going to look after you? You have no children. Good luck."

On and on it went. Once, in the kitchen, Mrs. Strathmore took Mother aside and said, "I don't know how you can take her meanness. I've know Helen all my life. Believe me, she'll never change," After that Mrs. Strathmore was gone, back to San Francisco.

The afternoon lessons resumed. Mother settled back into her bedroom. Life returned to normal. Then Mother saw something. It happened just as before, when Mother first stumbled upon the two women quarreling. She was rounding the corner into Mrs. B's bedroom when she caught sight of the old woman leaning to one side of the bed, holding her plate over the floor. Mother had just enough time to step back, out of sight. Mrs. B didn't see her. When Mother peeked around the corner, she saw Mrs. B throwing her food on the floor. With agile flicks of her wrist she tossed chicken bones. She scraped off a helping of creamed rice, letting the grains fall everywhere, like heavy pieces of phlegm on the ground.

My mother turned away, sickened. She went to her room and sat on her bed where she had a view of the town. It was evening, the lights just coming up. She was angry, but mostly at herself. She felt worse than an animal. An animal can't know it has been made fun of. She thought of herself on all fours below the bed, grabbing up the spilled food and sticking it into her uniform pocket so as not to embarrass Mrs. B. Worse, she saw herself spelling words, silly as a parrot in the old woman's hands.

She didn't do anything that evening. She didn't say anything. The next day, during the lesson, when Mrs. B sneezed, Mother lifted a ring out of the box and dropped it into her pocket. Sometime after the lesson and before dinner, Mother slipped away. She left the house. Carrying everything she owned in a pillow slip, she started on foot back to the reservation. She had nowhere else to go. With the ring now tucked into her pants pocket, she felt like a fugitive. She wasn't going to give the ring up.

As it turned out, the ring was nothing exceptional, which is probably why old Mrs. B never pursued it. It was an opal, non-transparent. But standing under the streetlight in Sebastopol, ten miles from Santa Rosa and the Benedicts' house, my mother saw how the opal glowed. She turned it in her fingers and saw the starched white color of the maid's uniform that she had left behind.

That night she got to the reservation very late. She slept and dreamed like never before.

Us kids tried to guess what Mother dreamed.

"A man," Billyrene said. "The man she'd marry."

"That she was flying," Faye said. "That she turned into a bird and soared over the apple trees."

"That the ring was really a diamond worth millions," Frances said.

"That another family found her and adopted her," Rita said.

"Yeah," Pauline said. "That she never came back."

Often Mother told us about Mrs. B and the jewel box and how she escaped with the opal ring. "Can you tell me what I dreamed?" she'd ask when she finished. She told lots of stories that we had to figure the ending of. We didn't have much else to do. We didn't have a television. Half the time the electricity was kaput, and then we didn't even have a radio. We played cards by the kerosene lamp, gossiped, told stories.

The first time I remember hearing about Mother and the opal ring was after my sisters had had a horrid fight. Billyrene, Rita, and Pauline, the three oldest, were screaming bloody murder and Jesus this and Jesus that over a dress, a crummy piece of thread even a mockingbird would have the sense not to wear: daffodil-yellow taffeta, low-cut, with epaulets like sawed-off wings. They were tugging the dress back and forth, grabbing it out of one another's hands.

"Girls, girls," Mother called from the sink, where she was kneading dough on a cutting board. "Sit here, sit here." She pointed to the kitchen table and wiped her hands on her soiled apron.

"You too, Stella," she said to me as she sat down.

I was the youngest, and since I had nothing to do with my sisters' battle royal, I felt my mother shouldn't include me in any lecture she gave them. All of us gathered at the table. Mother took the dress from Billyrene and spread it on the table before us. She smoothed its wrinkles and hem with her fingers. "Girls," she said, "there was a time I had nothing to wear but my maid's uniform. I was just out of Sherman with nothing to my name but that uniform. . . ."

That night no one answered my mother's dream question. My sisters were quiet but still fuming under their expressionless faces. "OK, then," Mother said, taking the dress and draping it over her forearm, "no one wears it. Not until I get an answer."

Later, crammed into our one bedroom, my sisters began to talk. Mother couldn't hear. She slept on the couch in the front room, which was also the kitchen. Our house was like all the others on the reservation, small. I was half asleep, stuck in a bed between sweaty Billyrene and snoring Frances, when I heard them whispering. Each gave her answer, what she thought Mother had dreamed. Then Billyrene said, "Who cares? She was just bawling us out, making us feel sorry for her."

Frances coughed and turned on her back, nearly smothering me with her shoulder. "I'm not going to be no maid, if that's her point," she said.

I had an answer, one I knew was right. My sisters never listened to me, I guess because I was the youngest, only eight, and they were older, Billyrene and Pauline teenagers. But just then I didn't want to talk. I didn't want to tell them anything. I wanted to tell Mother. I sat up, squeezed myself along between Billyrene and Frances, and slid off the end of the bed.

"There, now you woke up Stella," Faye said.

"Oh, she's going to tell."

"Wet-the-bed Stella."

"Stinky Stella."

I heard them and just kept going, past the door, until I found Mother. And then I said what made no sense. "Opal," I said. "O-P-A-L."

Mother looked at me. She was holding a butter knife in her hand. Behind her, lunch boxes sat in a row on the sink.

"What did you say, Stella?" She was perplexed.

"Opal," I repeated. "O-P-A-L."

Her face relaxed, as if she finally heard me. "Very good. I didn't even spell that in the story."

I nodded, waiting, but I'm not sure for what. She didn't know what to say or do either. We stood looking at each other for the longest time. Then I said, "Can I see it?"

Her face hardened. "No," she said sternly. "Now go back to bed."

She probably figured it was an excuse to stay up. I don't know. After that I couldn't stop thinking about the opal ring and old Mrs. B's box. Each day after school, before my sisters got home, I asked my mother to tell the story again. I wanted to hear about the part where she found the black box and what she saw when Mrs. B opened it. I pictured the precious jewels and saw Mrs. B, a wizened old woman with a shock of white hair, holding a sparkling pendant in her cupped hand.

"Amethyst," I said once, interrupting my mother. "That was the first one you learned to spell."

"Yes, Stella," Mother said. "It was a ring, and she held it like this." She put her thumb and index finger close together, and in the small space she left between them, I saw the violet gem.

"A-M-E-T-H-I-S-T," I spelled. I was a good speller, smart in school—unusual for an Indian, as my second-grade teacher put it. I could sound out words.

"No," Mother said. When she spelled it correctly, I was amazed. It made perfect sense to me that the violet stone would not be spelled the way it sounded. How could I have thought otherwise? I was learning about precious stones, jewels kept behind lock and key. I was learning their secret language.

Now, after school, I wanted to learn the spelling of each of the stones. I learned them all. Then I went on to their properties: transparent, opaque, translucent. I didn't want to hear the story anymore, just the spellings of fine stones and the big words associated with them. And in my zeal to learn, I either forgot or discounted what I knew earlier when Mother first told the story: that she had the opal ring. After learning about these extraordinary gems, how could a person imagine such a thing? How could a woman as poor and simple as my mother own one of them?

My sisters didn't know about my afternoon lessons with Mother. They didn't know about my store of knowledge. They took the late bus home, then visited friends. There was nothing for them to do in the house, so I had plenty of time alone with Mother before dinner. Then one afternoon I got caught. I was going over the stones' properties with Mother, spelling each and giving its definition, when I heard someone behind me, someone coming from the bedroom. I turned and saw Billyrene standing in her pajamas and a robe. Apparently she had come home early from school, sick, and was in bed.

"Getting them all right, little miss A-student?" she scoffed.

"Opaque," I yelled back.

The lessons at home spilled over to school. Where once I was a good speller, now I was an excellent speller, the best in the class. Advanced, is what my teacher said. I competed in the county spelling bees and brought home ribbons I tacked above the kitchen table. Everybody who came to the house, my sisters' friends, cousins, everyone saw my ribbons. And since I was a special student, I had to look the part. No more hand-me-downs. No blouses with patches on the sleeves. No skirts with hems let in and out, sewn with a different color thread. I still had to shop with Mother at the mission store, but now I picked out what I wanted, what was right for me. Dresses that were sophisticated, with pleats. More than once I nabbed St. Rose uniforms, castoffs from girls who attended the local Catholic school. I developed an eye for such things.

In fact it was my quick eye that spied the little cigar box outside the mission store, a dark box heaped with other giveaways in the metal tub by the front door. My mother was up ahead, browsing the pawnshop window. Folded in her arm was the pair of black slacks she had just purchased in the mission store, a pair of plain slacks just like the ones she was wearing, like she always wore. I looked back at the little cigar box. Without blinking I grabbed it and shoved it into my coat pocket. There was no reason to act so secretive. The box was a giveaway, free. I just didn't want anyone to know that I had it, not even my mother.

My first concern was where I was going to hide the box. With five older sisters packed into one room, my options were limited. I had to go away from the house. I thought of old-time Indian women who hid their acorn caches in hollowed-out tree trunks. That's what I did. I found a tree about a mile beyond the apple orchard, a redwood with a crack in the trunk where I could reach in and out.

The first thing I put in that box was a piece of paper, actually two pieces of paper, each folded neatly to fit, with the names and properties of all the precious jewels. I wrote them down. I went to the tree religiously, every day after school, and sat in the cool shade reading over my lists. I didn't take lessons from Mother anymore. I didn't need them.

For the longest time I had nothing in that cigar box but my pieces of paper. Then, slowly but surely, it began to fill. A few pennies, maybe a dime left over from lunch money. Then fifty cents Mother gave me for the fair. Soon the dollars I made selling lemonade on the highway. Then the real money, the fives and tens each day for picking fruit: apples around the reservation, prunes and pears in Santa Rosa. By the time I was sixteen, I had another list inside the cigar box, a bankbook, and each day I could sit under that redwood tree and read what was mine.

My sisters and I still talk about Mother and old Mrs. B and the jewel box, mostly on holidays or after funerals, when we sit around telling stories. Remember about Mother and the rich white lady? someone will say. We take turns, each one of us telling a part of the story: when Mother posted the announcements advertising her skills, the way old Mrs. B sat in her bed, when Mother first laid eyes on the jewels. Each guesses what Mother dreamed when she first got back to the reservation. For Faye, it's still that Mother turned into a bird and soared over the apple trees. Faye uses that word, "soar." Rita still thinks it was that another family found Mother and adopted her. And Billyrene is still convinced it was a man, some dashing young fellow Mother would meet and be happy ever after with. The grandchildren sit and listen for as long as their patience allows. Mother nods approvingly, but she never tells us what it was she dreamed.

At times in the past, family talk with my sisters was upsetting, particularly for me. Maybe for everyone, but I used to feel picked on. Even in my late teens I'd be reminded of my ribbons and straight A's. "Miss Goody Two-shoes" and "white girl," my sisters would say, deriding me. "Still keeps her money shoved up her big ass." No matter where we were or what we were talking about, my sisters would start in on me.

One day when I was twenty, their scorn reached new heights. We were picking prunes on a ranch north of Santa Rosa, near Fulton. Fruit picking was not a regular job for me. I was a trained secretary, two years of junior college preparation, and I had a job at the front desk of the county Indian education office. I picked fruit for extra money during my two weeks off in the fall. I didn't have much else to do. Like my sisters, I wasn't married. Unlike them, I didn't have kids. I still lived with Mother, and while most of my sisters and their kids lived with her too, making the crowding in Mother's house something for the *Guinness Book of World Records*, I felt nostalgic for the old days, when we were kids working together in the orchards. Of course nostalgia is nothing but a pair of rose-colored glasses that doesn't let you see the past as it was, and there's no one like my sisters to slap those glasses right off your face. It seemed to happen just about every time I worked with them. They'd start in on me, and this day in the prune orchard was no exception.

It started with the story of Mother and Mrs. B, innocent enough. We were kneeling in our jeans and work blouses, grabbing the purplish fruit off the dusty earth and filling our crates. We were at the end of the story, the part where Mother is standing under the streetlight in Sebastopol looking at the opal ring. I pictured her alone, a solitary figure on the street corner, not a soul in sight, no passing vehicles, midnight in an empty town. Then Pauline said, "She didn't want to come back."

Yes, I thought to myself, seeing in my mind the dirty-faced children and the drunk old men and women of the reservation.

"Drunks," Billyrene said, echoing my thoughts.

I looked up from my work to nod agreement. But she was looking for nothing of the kind, no agreeable rejoinder to what she had said. She was glaring at me, the sweat above her brow glistening heat.

"Go ahead, white girl, say it. Say drunks." She turned to the others. "Maybe she can spell it. Remember how she spelled?"

They looked at her, then at me. They weren't moving.

"Say it," she said. "Say all the drunks, all the welfare slobs, and all the unwed mothers with all their bastard kids."

I went back to my work.

"Stella."

I ignored her. I felt her eyes zero in on me as if they were a pair of binoculars catching every detail of my face. Then her words hit me like clods of dirt chucked against my body.

"Stella," she said. "Mother was a whore."

I wasn't thinking. I looked at her.

"Yes, Stella, you're a bastard like every one of us. You, me, Pauline, Rita, Faye, Frances." She took a breath then went on. "Yeah, our last name is Toms. It was Mother's name all her life. Who do you think *your* father is?"

I was stunned, caught off guard. I was twenty years old and had never given a thought as to who my father was. I'd like to say I figured he had died, been killed in a car crash or something, but the truth is I hadn't figured anything. I looked at each of my sisters.

"You came late," Rita said. "You didn't see what us older ones did. All the men in and out." Her voice was kinder, less harsh.

"She dried up after you came along," Pauline said.

Faye dropped her handful of prunes into a crate. "Haven't you seen the tattoos on her legs? It's the names of all the men she's had. Why do you think she wears pants all the time?"

"There's at least ten of them," Frances chimed in, "and the years, too, the years she was with them."

I looked back to Billyrene.

"Spell that," she snapped.

I sat a long moment, then got up and made for my car. I left everything, my full crate of prunes, everything.

I drove home. I needed to know the truth, that my sisters were lying. I found Mother in her long bathrobe, just out of the shower. She usually showered in the afternoons, while the grandkids napped, and before me and my sisters got home. I told her I needed to talk with her, that it was serious. She sat at the table, the same one we had when I was a kid, only now we lived in town, off the reservation.

She ran a comb through her wet gray hair. Then she crossed her legs, and when the robe, unbuttoned below the knees, fell back, I saw the tattoos. Dark blue lines, scribbling in the flesh of her calf that was flexed now over her other knee. Almost as if she were flashing the marks in my face. I looked away, though she did nothing to cover herself. She just sat, running the comb through her hair, waiting for me to start talking. Maybe she didn't see me looking. Maybe she assumed I knew, like everyone else in the family.

"What is it, Stella?" she asked.

I was dumbfounded. I blanked. I didn't know what to say to her. "Mother," I said finally, "what happened to the opal ring?"

She looked puzzled, hard pressed to believe that the whereabouts of the ring was what I needed to talk about.

"I mean, Mother, we never get to that part of the story. We argued about it today in the orchard. Billyrene, some of us, said you sold it—"

"No," Mother said, interrupting me. "I still have it."

She got up, dropped the comb in her robe pocket, and went into the bedroom. I heard a dresser drawer open and close. She came back and stood before me with the opal ring in her open palm. The opal, mounted on a simple silver ring, was impressive, about the size of a large-scale pearl. But it seemed unreal to me somehow, as if something from that story we told over and over again had come to life. That couldn't be. I might as well have been looking at an eighteen-year-old girl in a white uniform.

"Take it," Mother said, extending her hand to me. "You'll appreciate it more than the others."

That night, cramped on a cot wedged between two beds, I couldn't sleep. No wonder, with all I had heard that day. You'd figure maybe I was thinking about my father; I wasn't. With the opal ring tight in my hand, I thought of my mother, of the tattoos, the names she hung on to, the way she had hung on to a ring, after she had lost everything else.

Not long after that day the county Indian education office lost its funding. I found myself without a job. Nothing turned up in its place. I did everything: put ads in the newspaper, walked into banks and real estate offices, telephoned people. I got a few nibbles, interviews here and there. But sitting in those stuffy beige front rooms with a half a dozen other job applicants, I knew my chances were slim. How could I compete with those slender-bodied white girls? They looked like what the bosses wanted, what a secretary was supposed to look like. Sitting there, with the perfume-sweet girls chitchatting all around me, I stared down at the opal ring, which I had had fitted to my finger, and remembered a word from Mother's story of Mrs. B. Propitious. Not so, I thought, not here.

I didn't have to go back to work right away. I got unemployment. But I couldn't stand just waiting around, doing nothing, so I got on at the cannery with my sisters. It was the worst work ever. It made work in the orchards seem like a holiday. All of us women were packed in there, me and my sisters, Mexicans, and other Indians, cramped together along a conveyor belt spilling apples faster than we could grab them and peel them. The place was a hellhole, a furnace kept hot and humid by the leaky pipes overhead carrying hot water from the boiler. Eight hours, sometimes ten. I counted the minutes. I dreamed of cool air-conditioned offices. I prayed for deliverance.

Then one day it came, a letter with a plane ticket to Tucson. Months before I had applied for a position with a national Indian health program that had offices all over the country. I had totally forgotten about the job. I had given up on it, just as I had with all the others. I couldn't believe it. I had never been out of Sonoma County before, much less on an airplane. I was going to soar, like Faye said. I was going to get out of the rut called home once and for all.

At night in bed I got frightened thinking of my trip. You know, being so far off the ground, things a small-town girl who hadn't been on a plane would worry about. And I didn't know anything about Indians in Arizona. I went to the library on my day off from the cannery and read about the Navahos. Not at all like us Pomos. They lived in adobe huts and wove blankets.

I should have known better. The Indians in Tucson, the ones who interviewed me, were like any others. And they were sophisticated, in suits and ties and sharp-looking dresses, all different tribes. They took me to lunch and drove me around the desert. My enthusiasm paid off. They asked how soon I could start.

I had two weeks to get ready. I didn't tell Mother and my sisters that I had the job. After a few days they stopped asking about my trip. I kept working at the cannery. The work didn't seem so intolerable when I pictured the handsome air-conditioned offices in Tucson. I saw myself in skirts and blouses, answering phones, directing people here and there, sorting important mail from Washington, D.C. My fingernails would be polished. I'd wear lipstick and of course have a new hairstyle. Eventually I'd be able to buy a condominium, but in the mean-time I'd rent a smart-looking apartment, Western-style, with clean white walls, high ceilings, large open rooms that were quiet except for the sounds of birds from the patio outside.

The time drew near, less than a week away. I had my tickets, sent directly from the manager's office in Tucson. The night I decided to break the news I slipped the opal ring into my pants pocket. I had it all planned out. I would tell my sisters first. On the way to work, or during the lunch break when we were all seated together, I'd tell them and then quickly pull out the opal ring. Here, one of you take it, I would say. That way they wouldn't have time to get jealous and start heckling me about my success. They would be distracted, thrown off track, arguing over who got to keep the ring. I'd set the opal on the table, then leave them to fight it out. Ever since the blowup in the orchard that day, my sisters had pretty much stopped picking on me. "Oversensitive," Billyrene would say when one of them started. "O-V-E-R-S-E-N-S-I-T-I-V-E." But I couldn't trust them to hold back after they heard the news.

That night, lunch came and went and I said nothing. I say that night, because we were working the graveyard. It was almost morning when something happened. It was nothing magical or extrasensory. I simply looked up. The pipe above us was bursting. I screamed at the top of my lungs.

People flew in every direction: under tables, out the doors. Eventually everyone was in the parking lot. I was farthest away, out on the road, looking back on the parking lot toward the cannery. Someone was telling people that everything was all right, no one got scalded or hurt. It was a woman, and she was saying the same thing over and over, assuring people in both English and Spanish. People clustered together, women clutching their blouses, rubbing their hands together in the cold air. I saw my sisters at the far end of the lot, by the big trucks. Dwarfed by the enormous vehicles, they looked so small. They seemed far away. If I screamed, they wouldn't hear me. They wouldn't see me. My knees were shaking. I stood for the longest time, looking. Then I felt something turn and fall over in me, like an open plastic water jug flopped on its side.

I made my way to them. But when I got there I couldn't say anything. I was crying, sobbing out loud.

"Stella, nothing happened. It's OK."

"Stella . . ."

"Stella, a water pipe broke. It just splashed the apples. Big deal."

"Stella . . ."

"Why is she crying like that?"

"Stella, c'mon now. No one got hurt."

"Jesus!"

"What's the matter?"

"Why is she crying?"

"Stella . . ."

I reached out and took hold of someone's shoulder. I don't know who, my eyes were so full of water. Then I felt all my sisters around me, squeezing me between them.

"She's moving to Tucson," someone said.

That morning on the way home from work with Billyrene and Frances in my car, I remembered the answer I had for my mother after the first time I heard her tell the story about Mrs. B and the jewel box. I had forgotten about the night when I had jumped out of bed knowing what Mother's dream was, when I spelled opal instead of giving her my answer. She dreamed that she woke up in her family's small reservation house, where she had been sleeping for the first time in two years. The room was empty. She had overslept, on account of the fact that she had gotten back home so late the night before. She got up and walked past the empty unmade beds to the kitchen. Everyone was seated at the table, her brothers and sisters, the whole family. When they turned and saw her, they didn't see an Indian maid in a starched uniform but their sister, hungry and anxious to sit down. They nodded to her place.

They were all happy, I might have told my mother that night. They didn't fight. It was simple, a lesson an eight-year-old could discern. Appreciate one another. Get along. Share.

I looked across from me at Billyrene dozing. Her head was dropped forward, bobbing with the bumps in the road. Frances was snoring in the back. I thought of Tucson, where I'd be in just a few days. Letting go of the wheel with one hand, I reached into my pocket and pulled out the opal ring. I thought of tossing it. Then I thought otherwise. I'd keep it as a reminder.

Secret Letters

My wife tells me about the letters one night during dinner. "If it's not one thing, it's another," she says. "Your relatives! I swear, Steven."

My wife, Reyna, is an Apache. As good as she is, and as happy as our marriage has been, she never misses a chance to put down the Pomo, my people, especially relatives. I figure it's because she is living in Pomo territory, far away from her homeland, and doesn't want to forget who she is. She doesn't want our two children, Shawn and Raymond, to forget either. "They have another side," she always says to me.

I hold a piece of hot buttered corn bread in my hand, halfway to my mouth.

"Yes," Reyna says, seeing she has my attention. "Pauline told me she called the police." My wife pauses. "You know, Pauline across the street, the one who says she's your cousin."

"Yes, yes," I say, and take a bite of the corn bread.

"Well, anyway, now Pauline says her boy found a letter in his jacket. Can you imagine!"

"Eeee, a pervert's after Tony," Shawn says. She is as excitable as her mother.

I swallow hard. The corn bread sits at the bottom of my throat. "You don't know that," I say. "Does anybody know what the letters say?"

My wife and daughter look at each other, then at Raymond. All three look back at me.

My wife smirks. "Well," she says, "at least it's Pauline calling the police this time instead of someone calling the police on her and her kids."

"Does anybody know what the letters say?" I ask again.

"Yes, I do," Reyna says. "All this stuff flattering the boy. Yuck." She turns to Shawn. "It's creepy. A pervert's in this neighborhood."

I feel sick with what I know: the truth of the matter, which is that I wrote those letters, and that boy is my son.

Tonight I don't let my children rush off from the table. "Story time," I say.

They know what I mean, time to hear about their history, their culture. It was my wife's idea, years ago when the children were small, and usually she does most of the talking, telling them at the dinner table different stories and bits and pieces of history from her tribe. I follow her with something I know from my people, from here. But tonight I start up.

Shawn and Raymond eye each other and then look down at the table. Shawn is twelve, Raymond ten. Both would rather watch TV. I ignore their show of reluctant obedience and start talking. But it's not what I had planned to say, not a story about my uncle, who caused problems by talking about people and things he knew nothing about.

"Your great-great-grandmother was a bear person," I say.

"She would put on a bearskin after sundown. In that skin, she could run like a bear, great distances. She found trees full of acorns, good clover-picking places. She helped the people that way, told them where they could find food. She kept watch for enemies. Once, after the white people marched us all to prison camp in Lake County, she saved our lives. Not just us but all the Indians in these parts, everybody who was marched there by the soldiers.

"Some Indians started dancing and singing. I guess the soldiers suspected an uprising. Word got out that they were going to shoot all of us in the morning. That night your great-great-grandmother sang her bear songs. She didn't know what else to do. Then a miracle happened. She crawled over a twelve-foot fence the soldiers put up and walked past the guards as if she were nothing more than a cool evening breeze. They didn't see her. But the Indians did. That's how people learned she was a bear person. Bear people didn't let others know what they were. But your great-great-grandmother was desperate. The people were in trouble.

"She walked on a ways, out of the soldiers' camp, until she came to a creek just below the lake, and there hanging in an oak tree she found her bearskin, its brown fur glistening in the moonlight. It was waiting for her. She put it on.

"Then she traveled to the coast, fifty miles over rough hills and woods, and back again, another fifty miles. In the morning, the soldiers lined us up. Everybody: men, women, and children. They drew their guns. Your great-great-grandmother stepped out of the line. She had a piece of paper in her hand, which she handed to the soldier who approached her.

"See, in those days none of the Indians here spoke English. Our tribe, the Kashaya Pomo, lived on the coast, where we worked for a landowner who was known throughout these parts. He gave us a piece of paper saying we were his property and we were peaceful. Your great-great-grandmother thought of that piece of paper. The soldier read the note, and later the Indians were freed, not just our tribe, everybody."

"After that, people understood how this woman knew about good places to gather food, acorns and clover. It wasn't just something she remembered or something that one of her ancestors had told her. She was a bear person. But no one feared her after that. No one worried she might poison people or kill lone travelers who crossed her path in the night, things bear people sometimes did. They knew she cared about her tribe."

Shawn and Raymond look at each other, knowing I have finished the story. They know the routine. My wife and I don't want our children just to hear the stories, we want them to become a part of their lives, lessons. Engage the stories, says my wife, who is a preschool teacher. Perfunctorily, Shawn and Raymond volunteer answers, lessons the story was meant to teach.

"Don't judge a book by its cover," Raymond says.

"No, dummy, it's not that," says Shawn. "Remember, he was getting on our case about the pervert writing letters to Tony? Well, it might not be a pervert. It might be someone nice or something."

"Yeah," Raymond says, jutting out his chin. "I was right. Don't judge a book by its cover. That's the lesson of the story."

They look at me.

"Both of you are right," I say. But I'm not paying close attention to either of them or to their answers. Too much swirls in my brain, too much that called up this story and let it pour out unawares.

"Can we be excused now?" Raymond asks.

I nod, then get up and clear the table.

There's a part of the story I didn't tell them. I think of this days later. About how the old woman died, my great-grandmother. She was old, nearly a hundred, so her actual dying wasn't unexpected or unusual in any way. It was what happened afterward, after she passed on. The family never got her body home, back to our place on the coast.

As it turned out, she died here in Santa Rosa, while the family was on a trip. Within moments of her passing it began to rain, not just light showers but a downpour that lasted for days. There was lightning and thunder. Creeks swelled and overflowed their banks. The Russian River buried half of Healdsburg and all the towns below to the coast. People had never seen anything like it, not in the middle of September when even a sprinkle of rain is unusual. What's happening? the farmers wondered, seeing their fall crops, their grapes and prunes, ruined in the torrential rains.

The Indians knew, our family and the Indians from Santa Rosa. They knew what was happening. It was the last battle between my great-grandmother and old Juana Maria, the matriarch of the people from Santa Rosa Creek. Like my great-grandmother, Juana Maria was a bear person.

People knew their tribe's boundaries. They knew how far they could go in a grove of willows, which side of a creek to stay on. Everyone was careful not to cross these markers, not to trespass. Everyone except the bear people and a few others like them, the *walépu* and other spooks. At night in their hides and cloaks of feathers, these people went anywhere. But when they crossed paths, one in another's territory, the fight was on. Great displays of strength, magic powers. Fifty-foot leaps into the air. Roars that caused rocks to roll down hillsides. Sharp whistles that pierced eardrums. Anything to intimidate their rivals or to kill them.

So it was between my great-grandmother and old Juana Maria. A year before she died, my great-grandmother told her daughter, my grandmother, that she had battled with Juana Maria for decades. When the family found themselves stopped by a washed-out bridge, when the wagon wheels sank in two feet of mud, they put two and two together. Old Juana Maria had another power, weather power, and she brought on the rains as a last offense. She wouldn't let my great-grandmother ever go home, back to her own territory. Only after the family buried the old woman in Santa Rosa did the rains stop.

"But that really wasn't the last offense," my father said when he told me this story. "There's more. The most important part for you and me." He looked out our reservation-home window to a large tan oak tree, then back at me. "You see, we knew something was up. A month later, after we finished in the crops and before we headed back up the coast, we went back for the old woman, our grandmother. She was in a pauper's plot in the town cemetery, and we went one night with picks and shovels to dig her up and take her home. But someone had already been there.

"The dirt had been turned up, spread around again, maybe just earlier that night, very recently. We dug down and found the coffin hacked apart, splintered wood everywhere. And our grandmother's body had been cut up too. Old Juana Maria had cut out her rib.

"There was no use but to cover her back up. Juana Maria and her people would always have Grandma. And this is what I'm getting at, Steven." He ran his hand over his face, looked out the window, then back at me. "A bear person can use that rib on her rival's family. She can teach her children to use it too. Even if there's no rib anymore, no signs. It's in the blood, the history. And that's what happened to you."

"So there's nothing I can do," I said to my father. I was seventeen years old and had gotten a girl pregnant. I wanted to do the right thing, for the girl and me, and had sought advice from my father. I hadn't expected this story. Now I was frightened.

"No," my father said. "There *is* something you can do. You can say no. Don't marry the girl. Drop it. Forget it."

"Pauline's a nice girl," I protested. "You always said a man must take responsibility for what he does. Isn't marrying her the right thing to do?"

"You can't marry her, Steven." He looked at the floor and then continued talking without looking up. "Steven, they got me too. Zelda Toms, Juana Maria's granddaughter, got me. Zelda is Pauline's mother, right? Pauline's your sister, Steven."

I unbuttoned the top button of my shirt. I took a deep breath, several of them. I understood what my father was saying, the predicament I was in. Still, I didn't agree with what he was telling me to do. "I've got to do something, Dad. I just can't leave her—"

"Look," he said, glaring at me. "She's your sister. Can't you see? This is the final embarrassment. They'll laugh at us forever. All our family will know. They got us in the end. There's nothing nice about any of those people. I know. And now you should know."

He rambled on about our family name, Pen, our dignity, how we weren't a bunch of drunks like lots of other families. "You'll have a career. You're going places. You're a smart boy," he said, pleading now for me to understand. "Of course they're going to go after the best of us."

"Isn't it too late? I mean—"

My father's face hardened. He was glaring again, his eyes fixed on mine.

"I mean, Dad, there must be something to do."

Then my father spoke in Indian. *"Mensi,"* he said. *"Mensi too.* No more."

I had told Pauline I would meet her at Lita's, a coffee shop in Santa Rosa, and tell her my father's response. She said she would wait and see what my father said before she told her mother anything, whether or not we would get married. Like me, she was seventeen. I never went to Lita's.

In the days and weeks ahead, I couldn't think straight. I couldn't focus on my schoolwork. I was lost on the football field. I couldn't remember a play to save my life. I wondered about me, my future, what would happen to me after this. It seemed I had turned a corner, found myself in a new place with no way back. I wondered about Pauline. What would she do? Would she tell her mother? Who would take care of her and the baby? Would it be a freak, some kind of vegetable thrown in both our faces for all the world to see? Or would it appear normal and then grow up deranged, a thoughtless thief, a murderer? I was seventeen, and the word "incest" colored so many pictures in my brain.

Other times I thought of my father's story. I thought of the wars between my great-grandmother, whom I never knew, and Juana Maria, and the ways in which those wars continued, the ways my father understood them to continue. Zelda nabbing him. Pauline nabbing me. The lure of sex. Was this the hook of old Juana Maria's bad medicine? Was this the trap set for us with my great-grandmother's rib? If Pauline told her mother who the father of her unborn child was, would her mother then tell her the connection between us? Would Pauline believe the strange story of our ancestors' rivalry? Would her mother even tell her that part of our story? On and on the battle had gone without either of us knowing it. I was certain she didn't know our shared history, even if she had been caught up in it like me. She didn't know about the wars between our great-grandmothers any more than she knew we were brother and sister, the same father. No one had told us.

It started out an innocent thing, the relationship between me and Pauline. A guy and a girl, like any other. I met her at a dance in Sebastopol, after a game there, an Indian girl in tennis shoes and Levi's, healthy-looking. I liked her right away. She was on the girls' track team and liked sports. We dated, drove around in my cousin's car, talked about sports. We went too far, one too many times.

We talked calmly about the whole thing, what we would do, who we would tell first. We laughed, telling ourselves, given all that had gone wrong, at least we weren't related, not like a lot of Indians around here who found themselves in the same predicament. I was from the Kashaya Pomo Reservation in the north, at Stewart Point. She was a Santa Rosa Indian, southern Pomo or something. Her mom, Zelda, was no relation to anyone at Kashaya, and I guess I never thought of her father because she never mentioned him. People said Zelda was loose, that Pauline and her sisters had different fathers. That kind of household was worlds apart from mine, where my upright father never as much as looked at another woman, even after my mother died.

The day I was supposed to meet Pauline at Lita's I couldn't get her off my mind. I saw her there, in the corner of that small, brightly lighted coffee shop, waiting, a cold full cup of coffee on her table. The big questions came later, the stuff about our histories and what to do. But at night in bed, after all those big questions and all the talking they caused fell away, I saw Pauline again, sitting in Lita's alone.

Then something happened, and I was cut loose, out the other side. No, not what would have been the obvious way out, not abortion. A Mexican. Pauline took up with a Mexican guy, and the next thing I knew they were married. My cousin, whose car

Pauline and I used to ride around in and who was dating one of Pauline's sisters, told me. "What happened with you and Pauline, anyway?" my cousin asked.

"Nothing," I told him. "We just sort of fell apart."

I was jealous at first, hurt. Whether or not Pauline had told her Mexican husband, or anyone else for that matter, that the baby was mine, her plan was to raise it as his. I was cut out, quickly, quietly, too easily for my frayed nerves to handle. What about me? I kept asking myself.

But what about me? I had abandoned her in a coffee shop, left to her own devices. I got what I deserved, a boot out the door. She settled things. There wasn't anything I could do now, even if I wanted to. So walk, I told myself. Go on. Drop it, as my father said. Forget it.

Soon life went on. My father had said I would have a career, that I was going places, and this turned out true, even if I didn't become President of the United States. I went to the local junior college. I played football, started every game. I got good grades in classes that were transferable to any university. Some of my own relatives, those stuck on the reservation, said I turned white. But that wasn't true. I was an officer of the campus American Indian club, which is where I met Reyna, my wife. Reyna and I worked on fund raisers together, organized a powwow, and volunteered our time in the Indian Health Clinic. She was professional, determined, and always proud to be Indian. I fell in love with her. We got married halfway through our second year of college, right after football season.

Those days I didn't think much about Pauline and what had happened. I never saw her. Once I saw her sisters, Billyrene and them, drinking in the parking lot after a football game. They were sprawled against the car, leaning here and there in wrinkled skirts and blouses, talking with a group of older men, men who didn't look like college students. I thought of what people said about their mother.

Reyna got pregnant, and I didn't get the offers I thought I would, not from the Pac Ten schools. Stanford, UCLA, University of Washington—none of them was interested in me. Only a few nibbles from small colleges, no significant money, no scholarships that would pay my way clear.

"That's all right," Reyna said. "We're the team." We put our heads together. She got licensed to teach preschool; I took a government test and got a job with the Postal Service. I became a mailman. That way we raised our children, Shawn and, two years later, Raymond.

Reyna and I often talked about going on with our schooling. Reyna wanted to get a B.A. and teach history in high school. Now that the kids are older and our finances are squared away, she is finally working on her degree. I wanted to coach, teach P.E., and the plan was I would go back to school first. That's what we had always talked about. But I looked the other way when the opportunity to go back to school first seemed possible. I couldn't leave my job, not because I loved it so much I couldn't leave, or because I was expecting a promotion, which was what I told my wife, but because of Tony, my son. I couldn't lose track of him. My daily route took me to his front door. I made sure of that.

Pauline I didn't care about. I can say that with all honesty. As I said, life went on. She had her life. I had heard somewhere that she had had several children, a brood, and, as rumor had it about her and her sisters, most of them had different fathers. Supposedly, her sisters were like that too. I didn't know. I hadn't seen any of them for years. So it was no surprise that I didn't recognize Pauline when I found her standing right in front of me at Day Under the Oaks, the annual Indian festival at the junior college.

She was a large square woman, significantly overweight, with a shock of hair bleached a faded orange color. Kids were everywhere, in strollers, running every which way, snot-nosed, a brood. I guess a couple of her sisters and their kids were there too. I didn't see them. I didn't see anyone except the dancers performing beyond the heads of those people standing in front of me. Until she turned, staring at me. I looked away. I didn't recognize her. But when someone keeps staring at you, someone who's maybe three feet away, you have no choice but to look. I figured she knew me from somewhere. Ha! Funny thing. When I looked, things began to click: her eyes and then her smile.

"Steven," she said.

I focused and then it registered. Pauline. I nodded and quickly took my wife's hand. I looked at our two small children peeking through the crowd to the dancers. I felt ashamed, found out, as if I had been caught at something I had done wrong. Reyna knew nothing about Pauline.

Pauline kept looking, as if she saw how I was feeling and was savoring every long second of it.

"Hi," she said, extending her hand to my wife. She looked at me, then back at my wife. "I'm Steven's cousin, Pauline."

Reyna introduced herself. I didn't know what to do.

Then I saw the boy.

He came through the crowd from up near the dancers, a tall, lanky kid in an oversized white T-shirt, about eleven years old. "Mom," he said to Pauline, "are any of those dancers our cousins?"

Yes, I wanted to blurt out, all of them. At the time a group of feather dancers from the Kashaya Reservation was performing. There wasn't a doubt in my mind about this boy. In fact, my mind had nothing to do with what I knew, nothing to do with what my eyes took in, the familiar nose and eyes, the same hands as mine. It was in the innards, in the heart, a pounding older than time. I let go my wife's hand and held my own, as if I could hold myself together that way.

Pauline quickly turned around, her back to me and Reyna. I couldn't hear what she said, how she answered the boy. But I knew she didn't tell him the truth. She didn't want me to know who the boy was. She never turned around again. Her stiff back told the whole story.

"I've eaten something," I told my wife, and headed back for the car.

I've said that in the days and weeks after I abandoned Pauline at Lita's I felt as if I had turned a corner, found myself in a new place with no way back. Now, I had even forgotten where I had come from. I had had no life before this boy.

I couldn't get him off my mind. Day and night I saw his face, his hands, the white T-shirt, everything about him, and felt the tug inside of me. Sometimes I thought of Pauline and the whole situation. She introduced herself to Reyna as my cousin. Did that mean she had found out we were brother and sister? Or was she only alluding to our relationship in the past? Or was it both? In any event, the boy didn't know any of this, and it was clear by her actions she didn't want him to know. She had become hard, lifeworn. With me, and probably with others, she resorted to cunning indirection and then just her stiff cold back. It was hard to think of her as the blithe Indian girl in tennis shoes and Levi's. But thoughts of her, or anything else, were no contest for those of my son. It wasn't long before the tug pulled me down, before the undertow swept the sand away beneath my feet and pulled me under.

I went crazy. I took action.

I found out from my cousin, the one who had the car and had dated Pauline's sister, where Pauline and her brood lived. I knew he had kept track of those girls.

I didn't have to probe. I didn't have to ask specifically about Pauline. As it turned out, Pauline and her sisters lived in South Park, on Grand Avenue. All of them, in the same apartment complex. Even their mother, Zelda, my cousin said. Something about how a while back the government terminated the reservation in Sebastopol, the one out in the orchard, where Pauline lived when I was dating her. It was small, only a few families left there, and I guess Pauline and her family moved to Santa Rosa and then wound up in South Park, one of Santa Rosa's worst neighborhoods.

I had no trouble finding the place. Just as my cousin had said, a dump at the end of Grand Avenue. It wasn't an apartment complex but two rows of beat-up army barracks with a dirt road between them. Junked cars, dirty kids playing on the road. It was twilight, almost dark, but I had no trouble seeing the picture there. An in-town reservation: blacks, Mexicans, Indians.

Of course, all I knew then as I sat in my car looking from across the street was the pounding in my chest, like a metal detector over a piece of silver.

That fall I signed up to coach Pop Warner for South Park. Driving by the boy's home every night after work wasn't enough. Catching him walk up the road once after three months of watching for him wouldn't do. As I had suspected, he was an athlete, and when I saw him walk out onto the field that first Saturday, I knew I had made the right move. Surprisingly, I was cool, collected. I talked about sportsmanship, the rules of the game. I talked about my own life, probably for no other reason than to tell the tallest boy in the crowd something about me. Yet, as I talked, all the boys looked up to me the same way, one face, one set of eyes, looking for direction, hopeful.

When I had stopped talking, my assistant, a young black man from the neighborhood, handed me a roster each of the boys had signed with their names and ages. This was it, a name. I went slowly down the list, calling out each name. Then he said "Here." Tony Ramirez. I caught myself from staring in just enough time and then paused with each of the boys after that, so my stopping at the tall boy wouldn't look unusual or suspicious to anyone. "Run them through the first drills,"1 said to my assistant.

He was good. He caught well. He passed particularly well. It was clear he would make the team.

And he did, in a big way. He played quarterback. He had the height and a damn quick eye, a hunter's eye. He could find his target in a field of arms and legs and sink that ball in his receiver's hands on a dime. In time, I knew him from head to toe. I knew his hands, how he bit his nails when he was nervous. He bit his bottom lip when he was thinking. And like my father and me, he had big square feet. There was no doubt he was a Pen: the long nose with slightly flared nostrils, the slanty eyes, arched brows, all telltale signs. Maybe a little lighter from his mother's side, but still a dead ringer.

He goofed around, joked with his friends. But he was basically a serious kid, quiet, contemplative. A lot like his grandfather. I talked with him about plays and drew game plans on butcher paper. He always listened and watched and then looked up, out to the field, picturing himself executing the play. His eyes were full like that every time he walked onto the field.

"You could go places," I told him. "How are your grades?"

"Good," he answered.

These were the things I knew about him: the details of his body, his Pen face, the quiet determination, and, when he talked, his husky adolescent voice that bumped and cracked. He called me Coach.

I watched him play. I watched him win. I watched him lose. I bawled him out. Once, I hugged him. Number 7: RAMIREZ.

When the season ended, I couldn't let him go. I had my route changed from Montecito Heights to South Park.

"What kind of promotion is that?" my wife asked. This was right when we had been discussing my going back to college. A few days before, I had made the excuse that I couldn't take a leave from work because I was up for a promotion.

"I'll get to know the district," I said, then added quickly, "and then get to oversee it."

"That district?" she asked.

"My," I said. "Do I detect some snobbery in the Apache's voice?"

"Steven."

"No, Reyna. Look at us. Look at how we're raising our kids. An all-white neighborhood. All-white schools. Coaching those kids from South Park meant something. It reminded me of who I am, who we are."

She sat down at the kitchen counter and looked at me with a self-satisfied grin. I knew that grin. I knew she had an answer for me. She shrugged her shoulders. "So let's move to South Park," she said.

I thought she was kidding. "It's not a bad idea," I said, expecting her to drop the subject.

She stood up, motioned with her hands as if she were lining things up one at a time. "We lease this house, rent a place in South Park. We save money, buy another house, or start a college fund for our kids. They learn about who they are and you go back to school."

She wasn't kidding.

That's what happened, to a T, except for me going back to college. I stressed the saving money idea. Everything else was easy. Within six weeks, I was pounding the streets of South Park with my mailbag each day and sleeping in a house just half a block down the street from my son each night. It's a nice house, really, a modest three-bedroom place with a picket fence and a huge yard, fruit trees in the back. South Park isn't all bad. In fact, lots of young people are buying places and fixing them up.

I thought Reyna would plant a garden. She had other ideas. For one, fixing up what needed fixing in South Park. She started a tenants' rights group and opened the first South Park preschool. She visited the local elementary school and talked about American Indian history and culture. She got to know everyone in the neighborhood, including Pauline and her family, her sisters and all. She referred to them as my cousins, I guess because that is the way Pauline first introduced herself, and no one had told her otherwise.

"Difficult," she said. "God, it's always something over there."

I knew what she meant. Pauline and her sisters took little interest in their children's education. You didn't see them at PTA meetings. They never showed up for scheduled teacher conferences. They paid little attention to the neighborhood, to what happened outside of their own homes. And what they did inside their homes showed everywhere on the outside, empty beer cans, broken glass.

"Mean Pomos," Reyna said. "Just plain old mean Pomos."

I saw how Pauline lived. How could I not? I delivered mail to the barracks every day. She had five kids total, I found out. A boy and a girl just after Tony, and then two smaller ones, one still a baby in diapers. I saw the dirty Pampers spilling out of the garbage can next to her barracks. She didn't seem to have a husband or a boyfriend of any kind. Neither did her sisters, who would flirt every chance they got. Once Pauline opened the door and winked at me. "Hey, mailman," she said. The booze on her breath would've killed a moose. I handed her the mail and continued to the next apartment. "Hey, I know who you are," she scorned.

I wasn't quite sure what she meant. I wasn't going to let her get to me, though I worried at times she might get drunk and blab our affair all over the neighborhood, maybe to Reyna, when Reyna went door to door over this or that for the schools. Even that concern vanished fast enough, though. What bothered me whenever I saw Pauline or one of her sisters was that they broke my concentration, the thought that I might get to see Tony. I arranged my deliveries so I hit Grand Avenue last, at the end of the day, when school was out.

He was a good boy. He seemed unscathed by the world of his mother and the barracks. His eyes stayed clear, focused. It was as if he went through that world the way he played ball, dodging the linemen and backs who would topple him, watching for the receiver who would carry the ball to the goalposts. No gang colors. No dope. I coached him through Pop Warner and Little League. I watched him grow. I saw the hair thicken over his top lip. I heard his voice settle deep and smooth in his throat. I talked to him, when I could, about school and making something of himself. He was always bright, alert. Until a month ago, when he didn't look me in the face.

I had come up behind him in the checkout line at the supermarket. It was a Friday, after work. "Tony," I said, nudging my shopping cart aside.

He turned, startled. "Oh, hi," he said. Then he quickly turned around, away from me, but not fast enough for me to miss his heavy, glazed eyes. I knew what it was right away. Pot, reefer. It felt awkward, the way he was avoiding me. I didn't say any more to him. I let him pay for his munchies, candy bars, and quart of marble fudge ice cream and leave. " 'Bye," he said, hurrying out of the store.

I wanted to kick myself. Why didn't I say anything? Here I had been following the boy for five years, I had moved my family to South Park for him, and now, when he needed me, I did nothing, came up empty. I guess I was scared too. Tony had seemed sacred, untouchable. He wasn't. He could fall. He could mess up. He could lose himself. Where was his hunter's eye? Where was he without it?

I had to talk to him. I got busy in the front yard the next day, a Saturday, and watched for him to pass on the street. He came along about noon, out from the barracks. I called to him from my yard, then met him in the street, away from my house.

He had just gotten up. Below his slicked-back wet hair, his eyes were still sleep-swollen.

'Tony," I said, "you going out for varsity next fall?"

It was a dumb question. Why wouldn't he be going out for varsity as a junior? He played varsity as a sophomore. Both of us knew that's not what I meant to say.

I looked over my shoulder, back to the house, then back at him. "Tony, I saw you yesterday. Were you smoking pot?"

"No," he said, and both of us knew he was lying.

But I didn't go on. He was looking at me in a way that stopped me. It was as if he had put up a fence between us and was gazing at me from the other side of it. He was neither polite nor disrespectful, yet he seemed to be saying, Stay on your side. How could I say anything else just then? In his eyes, I wasn't his father.

"Be careful, Tony," I managed to say.

"I am, Coach," he said, and continued on his way.

I had taken so much for granted. I had assumed too much, grown comfortable with the relationship. It wasn't enough just for me to be near him, coaching him on the field and nodding to him as he passed on the street. Our small talk about a sports career and good grades hardly touched his needs as a young man.

He was human, after all, with eyes and a heart, and I hadn't considered any of that, not when I saw him on the field or watched him pass the house in his varsity jacket. It was clear. I hadn't done enough.

I felt the old tug, the sand give way beneath my feet. I had to do something. I had to connect with him. Sorting mail one morning at the station, the answer came to me easy as pie. I noticed the handwriting on an envelope. It was simple, homey, the neat letters spaced just so, probably an old person's writing. Letters, I thought. Write letters.

There wasn't much to think of. I could type them at work, address and stamp them, and then, in my neat blue-gray uniform, drop them off like any others.

That afternoon, after I finished my route, I sat in the station and typed a letter. It was about Jim Plunkett, who overcame countless difficulties in his life and went on to Stanford and a brilliant football career. I started another letter about the perils of drugs, but I hardly typed two sentences before I stopped. I started a letter about the great strengths of Indian people but didn't get far on that one, either. None of them was right. Too preachy. It would be obvious that I wrote them.

I had to use another tactic. I had to reach him on his level. I would write as a fan, a simple letter from a peer—an admiring girl.

Dear Tony,
I have been watching you for a long time. All my friends talk about how cool you are on the football field. You're going to be great someday, the coolest quarterback ever. Not to mention how cute you are.

Sincerely,
Your Secret Fan

I thought it was just right. It was short and to the point; it was the kind of letter I could build on, which is what I did in the days and weeks ahead. I talked about what certain of the fan's friends said about him, how he was clean-cut and a good student. The fan had an uncle who coached at a Pac Ten school. *He's watching you*, I wrote. *Everybody's watching you.* I kept the letters short and was careful to make the language sound as if it came from a kid. I sealed and stamped the envelopes, dropped them in one of the boxes outside the station, and the next day pushed them through the slot on Pauline's front door.

I imagined Tony reading the letters, intrigued. The message would get through, touching him deeply. He was somebody, and someone cared. Lots of people cared.

The first time I ever heard anything about the letters was when I came up the street and heard some of his cousins, Pauline's sisters' kids, teasing him. "It's probably some fag," a boy said. I nodded to Tony and the other kids gathered outside Pauline's place and then continued on my way, pushing mail into the slots on the barracks doors. I felt relieved I hadn't pushed one of my letters through Pauline's slot that day. But why? Just because Tony and his cousins were there? What did that matter? How would my dropping off a letter implicate me?

I did think of one thing, though. What if the letters never actually reached the boy's hands? What if Pauline got hold of them? Even if she let him see the letters, might she not color what they said, shape the way he read them? It was a problem. Two days later I found the solution: Tony's varsity jacket. It was draped over the metal railing on the porch steps outside Pauline's place. I checked around, made sure no one was looking, and brushed the jacket so it fell on the porch. I worked quickly. I dropped the mail with my letter on the jacket, so it looked as if the mail had fallen backward out of the mail slot. Then with the toe of my foot, I folded the jacket and gently kicked it to the side of the porch.

What was I thinking? What made me think Pauline wouldn't pick up the jacket before Tony? Anyone could pick up the jacket before Tony. How could mail fall out of the mail slot into a jacket on the side of the porch?

Of course these things I thought of later, halfway back to the station.

Now I hear the police are involved.

As I lie awake at three in the morning, it's not the police I'm thinking about. As Reyna had said at the dinner table, usually it's the police who call on Pauline, not the other way around. I doubt Pauline would call the police about anything, much less a harmless letter. Probably just Pauline talking to make herself look important. Cunning indirection. No, it's not the police.

It's this long mad affair, my obsession with the boy and my need to make things right. It was crazy from the beginning. Every plan, every scheme, was as rash and stupid as the idea to drop the mail in Tony's jacket. Pop Warner. Little League. Changing my route and moving my family to South Park. Every plan only got me in deeper, pulled me farther out to sea. Every scheme was doomed to failure. None ever accomplished what it set out to achieve. I wasn't any closer to my son.

Now I lie awake next to my wife, who has been good, who, without knowing the how or why, has made the best of the life I've put her through, all the side paths off the road we had been traveling as a team. She knows everything about me except this. I was too ashamed to tell her. My kids too. An all-white neighborhood, all-white schools. What difference did it make? With a mother as strong as Reyna, how could they ever forget who they were?

Finally, I start to drowse. As usual, I think of Tony. But then I see my father, sitting in the room, next to the bed. "Drop it," he says. "Forget it."

It's a little after three, the next day, and I come up to Pauline's place with my mailbag over my shoulder and a letter in my hand from the state, in other words a welfare check. The door opens. It's Tony. Not thinking, I hand him the letter. "That's all," I say, and start off, down the concrete steps.

"Coach," he says.

I turn. "Yeah?"

"Can I talk to you a second?" He steps aside, inviting me to come in.

I climb back up the steps, go through the door.

Before I know it, I'm sitting on a sofa in a dank, dark room. TV set. A few chairs. School pictures tacked on the walls. Tony sits in a chair opposite me. I slide the mailbag off my shoulder and set it on the floor.

"Which ones are pictures of you?" I ask, looking up at the walls, focusing on the myriad faces.

Both of us know my question doesn't have anything to do with anything.

"Did you write the letters?" he asks.

I look at him. He holds my eyes a moment, then glances away nervously, unsure. I feel that old tug, the current sweeping around my feet. Someone walks by outside on the road.

Enough, I say to myself. I dig in, plant my feet. "Tony," I say, "your mother and I, we . . . I'm your father." Our eyes meet. "I wrote those letters because . . ."

Hardly do I utter these last words when a bedroom door cracks open. Pauline and her sisters, a mob, coming at me. "He did it!" one of the sisters is screaming. "He did it. Pervert. Pervert'

I bolt for the door, scared, as if I had robbed a bank. I fly off the porch, into the arms of half a dozen police officers. Then I hear the boy. "Leave him alone. Let him go. He's my father."

Things are settled in the police station. No surprise, Pauline and Tony had set up the trap with the police. Why wouldn't they suspect me? How stupid I was to think that Tony couldn't read between the lines of my letters. Between the lines; all he had to do was read the lines, period. It was the same stuff I had been telling him all along. Stay in school. Work hard.

Pauline does most of the talking. Teary-eyed, she tells the officers our story. She says she thought I meant no harm given who

I was, but she couldn't be positive I wrote the letters. Reyna takes Pauline's hand. "I should've told my son the truth a long time ago," Pauline says.

"I don't think it's a good idea for Tony to be home alone now," Reyna says. Pauline stands up. Reyna and I follow her out of the office.

At the dinner table tonight my two children, Shawn and Raymond, seem unusually calm, given what has happened. Reyna told them the story while I was across the street, talking with Tony and Pauline. I feel I need to tell them something, my point of view, how I feel. Maybe something Reyna hasn't told them. Not that Pauline and I are sister and brother. We haven't told anyone that yet. It will have to come out in time, I suppose. But they need to hear something now. I must tie up the story for them. But how do I begin? Where?

"What's the lesson in this story?" I ask, unable to think of anything else.

But my children are way ahead of me.

"When's Tony coming to dinner?" Shawn asks.

"Tomorrow," my wife says.

"Tomorrow," I say.

The Water Place

When I got to the house and saw the old ones seated on the porch steps with their heads hung low, I knew I was too late. She had already died. But then a large woman came rushing out and down the steps. "Help," she pleaded. "Please help. You can bring her back. Please." Water, tears and sweat, poured off the woman's face. I shielded my eyes from the hot morning sun.

"I'll try," I said.

In those days I could do just about anything. No miracle was beyond me. Nothing was impossible. I had my songs and a strong voice to sing them with; I could dance for hours without stopping. I rolled back the shade of death and smashed sickness like a flea between my fingers. All that morning and the night before I had heard the voices, the songs singing in my throat. I knew I was supposed to doctor, but when I entered the dark house and saw her stretched out in the flickering candlelight, I knew what I knew the minute I came up to the house. She was gone.

I didn't leave. People shuffled in, the old ones and others from outside. I closed my eyes. The next thing I knew I was singing. I sang three, maybe four songs. I don't remember. I was confused. One part of me was asking myself how I could be singing healing songs for the dead. My throat kept opening, emptying with song. But when I opened my eyes, when I stopped singing, I saw nothing had changed. She lay on that pallet bed just the same, light moving over her lifeless body.

They were polite, the family. They put up food, as if I had healed her. Good food: abalone and venison, seaweed, duck, acorn soup, old-time food. "What's going to happen now?" the big woman kept asking, talking to nobody in particular. "My sister is dead, and my brother and my other sister took off. What about these three motherless girls, my poor sister's children? Tell me, what's going to happen now?"

The young girl sitting across from me asks to hear this story every day. It's always the same. "Can you start with when you got to the house?" she says.

I never get much beyond the part where the family put up the meal before she starts asking questions.

"Did you know which one of those little girls was my mother? Mollie's my mother's name. Do you know which one was Mollie?"

"No," I tell her. "But your grandmother was Sipie."

Today she is quiet, asks nothing after I tell her the story. She struggles with a sedge root to start her basket with, to tie the knot.

"Hold the hard end," I tell her. "Work from the hard end."

"I know what happened," she says suddenly.

I look back at her, confused. "To my mother," she says. But I don't hear what she says after that. I am amazed by what I see in her hands, a perfect knot.

She wanted to learn how to make baskets. That's what she told me.

I found her one day looking over the fence at my flowers. "Do you like flowers?" I asked, coming from behind a stand of hollyhocks. I startled her. She jumped, seeing me, then nodded. I mentioned the names of plants and flowers she looked at. Canna lily. Marguerite. Rose. Rock rose. Chinese poppies. Sweet peas. Wild rose. Hollyhocks. On and on I went. She said nothing. Then she left, just as she came, from out of nowhere.

The next day she was back, and two days after that. I named more plants, varieties of roses. Finally, I asked her in and she came through the gate into my yard. I led her into my kitchen. She sat at the table.

"Would you like some milk and cookies?" I asked, turning to the refrigerator. She was a big girl, probably fourteen or so, too old for milk and cookies, but I couldn't think what else to offer her just then.

She didn't answer me.

I turned back to her. Her dark eyes were fixed on me. "Who are you?" I asked.

She hesitated a long while, then blurted out, "Alice. My mother is Mollie. Mollie *Goode*. Her mother was Sipie *Toms*."

I swallowed hard. I knew who this girl was. What's more, she knew who I was. I felt certain of it. She had probably heard the family's bad talk about me: poisoner, witch, white-man Indian. There was something old-time about this girl, maybe just the way she identified herself, telling her family line. That and her watchful eyes. Yet she took the milk and cookies I served her, something an old-timer would never do with a suspected poisoner.

I watched her. With two gulps, she finished the glass of milk and inhaled the cookies. Then she became still again, only her eyes moving back and forth over my basket materials on the table, the rolls of redbud bark and sedge, the willow rods.

"Would you like more milk?" I asked.

She looked at me. "I want to learn to make baskets," she said.

After she left, my mind whirled. I couldn't get up from the table. I couldn't pick up the plate and empty glass to put them in the sink. Had this girl come to haunt me? Had the family sent her, my family? Sipie's granddaughter. Sipie's family, the last shoe to drop. When I moved from the country to this place on Grand Avenue, I found myself surrounded by my Aunt Maria's other children and their families: Dewey, the one they call Old Uncle, who lives with his sister Ida and her daughter, Anna; Zelda and her daughters. All of us had lived together out on the Benedict ranch above Santa Rosa Creek. Me and my mother; Aunt Maria and her four kids, Dewey, Ida, Sipie, Zelda. Even the old geezer

Sam Toms, who was married to Aunt Maria at the time and is the father of her four kids. That was our rancheria, our place after the Spanish moved us off the creek.

Maria's kids were young, Dewey about six, Zelda just a baby. I was ten, so I remember. And since the incident that sent us flying in every direction from that place involves my mother, I know what really happened, no matter what anybody says. Yes, my mother, Juana, loved one of the Benedict boys. I can even tell you which one, because I saw it all. I went with my mother. Late, after midnight, we sneaked away, left the rancheria. It was early summer, the sweet smell of buckeye blossoms in the air, crickets so loud no one heard us coming or going. We walked along the road and then through the field until we came to the barn, where Benedict would be waiting, holding flowers for both me and Mama, a large bouquet for her and a smaller but identical one for me. If he gave her a dozen large red roses, he gave me a dozen tiny red roses, little buds on short stems, always something to match. Sometimes he mixed the flowers, put wild poppies and lupine in with the roses. The two of them sat on a bench behind the barn. They never said much, maybe on account of Mama's poor English. They held hands and looked over the open fields, listening to the crickets. Once I saw them looking up, both of them at the same time, gazing intently at the night sky, as if they were focusing on a single star or just marveling at the expanse of God's universe.

Afterward, Mama and I didn't go directly home. We walked to the creek and planted our bouquets in a secret place, a small sandbank overgrown with willows and wild grape. I guess Mama figured people would see the flowers if she took them home and then start asking her questions about them. Where else would you get those kinds of flowers except from a white man or out of a white man's garden? Some of the bouquets were enormous, not just beautiful roses but huge, brightly colored dahlias and chrysanthemums, spikes of gladioluses that were as tall as I was. I thought that after we planted the flowers they would grow. It was so dark under the willows and grapevines, I couldn't see the flowers from the nights before.

Mama's romance with Benedict was innocent, old-fashioned. They never did more than hold hands, maybe a peck on the cheek that I didn't catch. But they knew they were in love. Yes, he loved her as much as she loved him. That's how the trouble started. He wanted to marry her. He told his mother and father and they wouldn't hear anything of it. No son of theirs was going to marry an Indian. He told them he didn't care what they said, he was going to marry Juana no matter what. The next day a ranch hand, a white man, came to the rancheria and ordered all the Indians off the place, off the Benedict property. He had a note signed by Mr. Benedict saying we had twenty-four hours to pack our belongings. He said the reason was because an Indian named Juana was misbehaving and fooling around with Mr. Benedict's sons.

Everyone left. Aunt Maria and her family went to the reservation out past Sebastopol. Others went north, up to Healdsburg and Ukiah, and over to Lake County. By evening, hardly ten hours after the ranch hand had given us word, everyone was gone.

Except for me and Mama.

We were still locked in our house, hiding behind the pulled window shades. The whole rancheria had pelted Mama with mean words and hateful looks. Around midnight, she went out, over to Benedicts' barn, only I didn't go with her. She told me to wait in the house for her. I don't know if she saw him, if he told her he couldn't see her. Afterward, he joined the service. She knew, though, that her love affair was over. And she knew she had nowhere to go. She hanged herself in that barn.

Things didn't go so well for young Benedict, either. He came back from the service and married a wealthy girl. But the marriage didn't last. He moved back to the ranch and did nothing for the rest of his days but stand in that barn talking to Mama, right under the wooden beam where his father found her hanging.

But that's not the end of the story. There's my part.

I married Benedict's nephew. Yes, I married a Benedict, Charles Benedict, the nephew of Mama's lover, which only added salt to a wound that had never healed. I knew the consequences. I knew what Mama's family would say, but I married Charles anyway. I loved him, pure and simple, and we would be together today if that tire on his new car hadn't blown, spilling the car and Charles down a cliff neither would see the top of again.

Of course in those days I rarely saw Mama's people, Maria and all them. After Mama passed on, I went to live with my father's people on the old Indian land by the Sebastopol lagoon, east of where Maria and her family went. My father's sister and her husband took me in. They loved me as if I were their own. They found an old man, my father's uncle, to help me when the songs first entered my throat, when I didn't know what was happening to me. They stood by me when I married Charles Benedict. Charles and I had a daughter, Catherine, and my aunt and her husband took us both in after Charles's accident. Later, after I married Alfred Copaz, a coast Indian from Tomales Bay, and had five more children, they comforted me during those long nights Alfred had his fling with Mary Hatcher.

They were good people, my aunt and her husband, but I never forgot about my mother. I never stopped thinking about the old days on the Benedict ranch.

That's why going to doctor Sipie meant so much to me. I wanted to do good, perform miracles, raise Sipie from the dead for all my mother's family to see. It was the first time since childhood that I found myself standing under the same roof with them. The large woman with tears and sweat was Zelda, of course. Zelda and her kids, Sipie's kids, all of them—except for Dewey and Ida. Dewey thought Sipie's death was his fault, that he had poisoned her. Everyone else thought that too. He hid in Ida's house, where he lived; then at night the two of them took off. Ida probably figured folks thought she had something to do with Sipie's dying also, since Dewey lived with her and the two of them had been so close. But that's not what happened.

Dewey didn't poison Sipie. I saw the truth as I stood there singing over Sipie's lifeless body.

I thought of telling the family what I had seen. During the meal afterward, I wanted to spill out the true story. They blamed Dewey, like I said, though none of them mentioned as much to me. But I said nothing. I was confused. I was still asking myself how it was that I had been singing healing songs for the dead. Why had the songs come to me all that morning and the night before if I wasn't going to heal? And I was afraid, too, afraid to get tangled in family matters, afraid to say something I shouldn't, lest the family get angry with me. I had already lost my opportunity to win them back. I had failed. No miracles. Sipie was gone. They were pleasant, as nice as one might expect given the circumstances. But after I left, I never heard from them again. They didn't call, inquire about me. I was afraid to call them.

I went back to my husband and children. I doctored the sick. My children grew. I got old. Finally the kids decided I should move into town, closer to them, so I left the big house in the country. My son built a small shed in the back of this place on Grand Avenue, where I can sit and wait for that little green frog with sparkling black eyes to come and talk to me, the same frog who first spoke to me out on the lagoon at my aunt's place, the one who filled my throat with song. "Build a shed," it said. "Wherever you go, build a shed behind your house. I will live under that shed and call you when you are needed in this world. I will let the songs come." And it turned out true. Someone always built me a shed—my aunt's husband, my husband, whoever—wherever I lived. And no sooner was the shed finished than the frog appeared. The frog still comes. Only now I'm old, like I said, and can hardly sing my songs.

I didn't much like the idea of moving to town. And this neighborhood isn't the best. In fact, it's downright shoddy. But I made the most of it. Set up a comfortable house. And I planted a garden, which to my surprise took off like nothing I've seen before. And now, for the first time in my life, there's no kids to trample it down, no chickens or pigs to dig it up, and everything grows:

roses, gladioluses, sweet peas, you name it. It's a wonder. People stop their cars. Passersby stand for a half hour, just looking.

Even Zelda, who lives up the street. She'll stop and take in the colors, but she won't acknowledge me. Even if I'm sitting on the front porch weaving, even if I'm sitting right there where she can see me, she won't look up, over the flowers. Ida and Dewey, who live down the street, are the same way. I'm used to it now. But when I first came to Grand Avenue it was hard to find that after all these years you're living around your cousins again and then to have them ignore you. Each time one of them stopped, I waited for them to look up. I hoped maybe they would come through my gate and knock on my door. Aren't you our Cousin Nellie? Oh, I wanted to hear them say that! They knew who I was. I could tell by the way they ignored me. Indians are famous for ignoring somebody they don't want to talk to. They stare, look into the distance, focus on something. It's a sign to leave them alone. Which I did. And after a while I just got used to them passing by, coming and going. I gave up hope.

Then this girl stopped outside my yard. This girl named Alice, who told me she was Sipie's granddaughter when she had come into my kitchen. This girl who drank my milk, ate my cookies, and wanted to learn how to make baskets.

I told her to come back the next day.

I had things ready, coils of redbud bark and sedge, willow strands, extra awls. I even set out a lot of the baskets I had stored away so she could see both the twined baskets and the coiled baskets as well as the different designs: anthill, quail top, butter-fly, water bug. I would begin by explaining the different materials and baskets to her. I would demonstrate coiled weaving and show her how to start a coiled basket, how to make a knot, which is difficult for beginners. But I did none of these things. I guess my troubled mind got the best of me. Had the family sent her to spy on me? Were they going to get back at me finally after these years? No, I wasn't asking those questions anymore, not after I thought about this whole mess. Truth is, they didn't care enough to go out of their way to bother me. What concerned me was what they might have told this girl, or what they would tell her once they found out she was coming to see me. White-man Indian. Witch. No-good medicine. Those words got the best of me. So I did what I told myself I wasn't going to do. When she sat down at the table, I opened my mouth. I blabbed. I said something about me being a good person, maybe a couple words. Then I found myself spilling the story about when I went to doctor Sipie.

"Do you know which one of those little girls was Mollie?" she asked before I could finish. "Mollie's my mother's name."

"No," I told her. "But your grandmother was Sipie."

She looked down at a coil of sedge. "What's that?" she asked. "What's it for?"

"That's sedge root. It grows by water. It's important. It's the light-colored part of your basket." I tapped the side of one of my baskets to show her. "You tie the knot with sedge, start the basket that way."

That's how the lessons started. The next day I told her about where to collect the materials and what time of year. I told her where the best willows grew. After that I showed her how to strip the willow branches and how to split and trim sedge roots. Then I explained the different designs: which were difficult, which were easy. "You always have to pay close attention to what you're doing, no matter what," I told her.

It took about a week for me to explain the basics. I talked. She listened. She never said a word, never asked questions until I was finished talking; then it was always the same thing. She would say, "Tell me about when you saw Sipie. Can you start with the part when you got to the house?" I would tell the story and she would ask if I knew which of Sipie's girls was Mollie. "No," I would say. Then, and only then, would she ask something about the baskets. Sometimes she just thanked me for the lesson and left.

That's why I should've listened when she said, "I know what happened to my mother." I should've picked up on her words right then. Never before had she broken routine. But seeing that perfect knot in her hands, I was dumbfounded, utterly speechless. It takes beginners weeks to tie their first knot. Some never learn. This girl got it on her first try, minutes after I showed her how.

Only now, after a few long moments, after I find my mind and the words to speak, can I respond to her.

"What about your mother?" I ask.

"What happened to her. I know what happened. . . . You know, what that big lady was asking, 'What's going to happen to these three motherless girls?' "

"Oh, yes. Yes," I say. She saw that I was lost, that I shouldn't have connected what she was saying to the story of Sipie. She says nothing and looks at the strands of willow on the table.

"Well," I say, "what happened?"

She looked at me. "Don't I put the willow in now? You know, for the foundation."

I'm not going to let her sink back into her silence. She's not going to close the door on me, not after she opened it, even if it was just for a second. If I have to, I'll yank that door open with my bare hands. I'll shake her. I'll scream.

"Alice," I say. "Talk. It's important to talk. Us Indians here are all family. That's the trouble, no one talks. Stories, the true stories, that's what we need to hear. We got to get it out. The true stories can help us. Old-time people, they told stories, Alice. They talked. Talk, Alice, don't be like the rest."

She looks at the willow strands, then she looks back at me and lets go. "My mother is Mollie. Mollie Goode. Her mother was Sipie Toms. My older sister is Justine. Her father is a Filipino and mine is a Mexican. My brother Sheldon's is white. And my other brother, Jeffrey, his father is a Indian from Stewart Point. Justine gets in lots of trouble. Her and Mom fight. Justine likes black boys. Mom hates black people. She hates Mexicans. She hates whites. She hates Indians. She doesn't like it here. She doesn't like it anywhere. It's no place to live, she always says, but she doesn't know what a place to live is. That's what happened to her. She never had a home."

She stops and keeps looking at me.

"Can I put the willow in now?" she asks.

The next day she is back. Same time, two o'clock. She doesn't ask me to tell her about the time I went to doctor Sipie. She sits quietly minding her work. She holds the small steel awl I gave her and coils the first stitches of sedge around her willow rod foundation. "Good," I say, and she keeps working, weaving one stitch at a time.

But her silent concentration gets to me. Even though I have told her a weaver must pay strict attention to her work, even though I have told her that a good weaver must be clearheaded, I want her to talk to me. I want her to tell me what she has heard about me, what people have told her. Why did she come here? Why is she interested in basketmaking? I look down at my own work, the half-finished canoe basket in my hands, and realize I haven't made a stitch since the girl arrived. Then I feel guilty. My selfish concerns about what people think have not only stopped me but they could stop this girl, interfere with her work. As a teacher, I'm a poor example. It's a wonder she came back today, after I pounded those words out of her yesterday. Then I think to myself that I must tell her something more than just what happened to Sipie, something more than a story about her grandmother's death. Something positive. Just one more story, I tell myself, then I'll shut up. Something totally unrelated to me and Sipie and this whole mess. But that's not what comes out.

"Dewey," I say, "the one they call Old Uncle, he was a good man, a good doctor. I heard nothing but good things about him. But he got tricked, taken in by his own father, Sam Toms. That's what I didn't tell the family that day, what I saw as I sang over Sipie's lifeless body. I saw the story like it was a movie before my eyes.

"Sam Toms knew Sipie had a love song. He wanted it. Sipie wasn't the kind to use a love song. From what I heard, she was a good woman, plain, simple. If she ever used that song it was on Steven Goode, her husband, the man she stayed married to until consumption took him. Anyway, somehow Sam Toms knew she had the song. He told Dewey he had given it to her, which was a lie. He told Dewey he wanted to hear it. 'Please,' he said, 'I'm sick. I want to hear her sing it before I die.' Hah! The old geezer wasn't sick at all. He told Dewey to ask her to sing it and he would sit outside the window.

"See, Sam Toms knew Sipie wouldn't sing the song for him. Sipie and Ida and Zelda didn't like their father. They had no time for him and his ways. He'd left them all, right after him and Aunt Maria left the Benedict ranch. But Dewey felt sorry for him. Somehow he got a hold on Dewey, and Dewey did just what the old sucker wanted. He got Sipie to sing her song. And Sam Toms sat right outside the window, reeling in the words she sang, just like fish on a line. Then he yanked, tugged hard to get the last word, and pulled the life right out of her.

"They say they found her later with her insides out. I don't know. I didn't see that. She looked peaceful when I saw her. She was an innocent woman."

When I finish talking, I feel stupid. I don't know why I told Alice this. I grab for straws to make sense. "You know," I say, "after what all's happened to us, it's a wonder what we do to ourselves."

She keeps weaving.

"I mean our history, Alice. Look at what the Spanish did, then the Mexicans, then the Americans. All of them, they took our land, locked us up. Then look at what we go and do to one another. That's my point," I say, making sense at least for myself.

But she keeps on weaving.

Then I'm as frantic as the day before. "Alice," I say. "Alice, do you hear me? Do you understand?"

She looks up quickly. "Yes," she says.

I sigh in relief. But she's not finished.

"I made a new casserole," she says, looking directly into my eyes. "Pasta, tomato sauce with fresh tomatoes, and hamburger. Then cheese on the top. Justine cut up the tomatoes. I cooked the meat. Then the boys put cheese on the top. It was good. It's cheap, too. Old Uncle grows tomatoes in Auntie Anna's backyard."

I look at her. Her eyes are like windows, and what I see in them shames me. A girl standing over a skillet of meat. Her sister nearby chopping tomatoes. Two little brothers. Nothing more, nothing less. This same girl in front of me doing the best she can to put a meal on the table.

There is nothing else there, nothing in her eyes that gets between me and that picture. No stories about Nellie Copaz. If she's heard the stories, they haven't clouded her vision. She sees only the old woman sitting across from her, just as she saw the flowers in my front yard and the different baskets on my kitchen table. She is as clear as water, as open as the bright blue sky.

After that day, I start wondering about her. Not about what she knows or doesn't know, or what stories she's heard. No, I'm embarrassed to think that way now. I'm curious, just plain curious about how a young kid can be the way Alice is, untainted, clear. My grandchildren her age are angry, full of self-loathing. They don't like who they are. Their hearts are clogged. Their eyes don't see. Most kids are that way, and at such a young age. But not Alice.

My mind goes back and forth about her. Sometimes I think she's a dimwit, not all there. She's a heavyset girl, rather plain, with wavy hair, I guess from the Mexican side. She sits sometimes and just stares. She doesn't seem to notice the latest fashions, like the other kids do. She certainly doesn't wear them. She puts together old blouses and pants, hand-me-downs. Sometimes she's missed a button on her blouse, or buttoned it incorrectly. That's when I wonder how smart she is.

Then I think of the way she mentioned her casserole, the way she reminded me of my selfish fears about the family. She has a knack for saying things that land on target. I don't know if she knows what she's doing, but it makes you wonder about her. She reminds me of my own rules, when I break them, like with my carrying on about the family when I should be focusing on my weaving.

In the last few days, she's talked more. Before we pick up our work, she talks about her sister and brothers. Little things they did, kids' stuff. Like something the boys drew and gave to her. Maybe something her sister said. She talks about cooking a lot, and I take it she does most of the cooking around her place. I guess Mollie, her mother, works at the cannery. But whether or not Mollie works, I get the feeling that Mollie's not at the helm. Alice commands the ship. She told me she hopes Mollie will be happy one day. "Things would be better then," she said.

When Alice isn't talking, I'm going full steam ahead. I tell her everything, about my mother and Benedict, about me and Charles Benedict, the whole history. I tell her about my kids and my grandkids, things I probably shouldn't say, like what I think of certain in-laws. It just pours out of me. I run on until she stops me, until I see her eyes telling me that it's time for us to start working. Then I feel stupid, silly, as if things are turned around and I'm the child.

So much is turned around these days. Things I don't tell Alice. My songs, my whole life. I hear my songs day and night. The little green frog sits in front of the shed winking at me. But he says nothing. How can I be hearing my songs if I'm not going to use them, if I'm not going to doctor? The frog tells me nothing, gives me no answers. Nobody comes for my services. And if they did, could I perform? Could I sing? The strings that have held me up all these years are snapping; the binding gives, and my life spills like sand between one's fingers.

I cling to Alice. She is constant. Two to five each afternoon. The songs quiet down. The sand stops spilling. There are things to do, things to tell her. Put this stitch this way, that one that way. Careful with the redbud bark. Smooth your sedge, trim it some more. Yes, I can tell Alice these things. I'm not totally gone. And she listens. She learns. Whether she's a dimwit or a genius, she can weave. I should've known as much with the way she tied her first knot. Her basket, a medium-sized coiled holding basket, grows each day. The design in redbud bark takes form, a large sunflower radiating up from the bottom of the basket. I've never seen anything like it.

"That's not a Pomo basket design," I told her one afternoon.

She said nothing.

"Why a sunflower?" I asked.

"Because," she said. "Because the sunflower is the tallest flower in the garden. You see it and you know where other flowers grow. Like Old Uncle; he's got them in his garden."

"Oh, where he grows his tomatoes,"1 said.

She nodded.

I didn't want to say any more. I didn't want to question her unusual design, criticize her. I didn't want to upset her.

The days go by, and I find that two to five isn't long enough. I need her to stay longer. Too much of me is lost in the time I spend alone between her visits. Madness, songs flowing everywhere. No rhyme or reason to any of it. My legs shake. I can't sleep at night. Call it age. Call it the end.

I tell Alice she needs to learn how to dig the sedge; we should have done that first. I tell her we have to go in the morning, when it's cool. 'That's my basket-weaving rule," I tell her, thankful I can remember it.

She nods.

I plan a trip to the sedge bed on Santa Rosa Creek, to the water place next to the old village, where we lived before the white man came. Nothing but rocks there now, rocks and sedge. And of course the water. The frog came from there, followed the waterways, creeks, streams, sewers to wherever I was. The place is sacred. I think if I dig there things will settle down, be peaceful.

I plan everything: time, what to bring, the hand picks, trowels. I call my granddaughter Darlene and arrange for her to pick me and Alice up at eight o'clock this morning. At noon, Alice and I are still sitting on the front porch. No Darlene. Not even a call. My aluminum walker stands next to my chair. No need for you today, I think. On the other side of me sits Alice, waiting, gardening gloves in her lap, the half-finished sunflower basket upright on her knee, poised there as if on display.

"You don't need to bring that when we go to dig," I said, motioning with my chin to her basket.

She must know the trip is off. Still, I can't say anything. I don't want her to go.

"My mother goes away," she says all of a sudden. "She doesn't come back until the middle of the night."

"What do you mean?" I ask.

"She goes away," Alice answers, then looks back to the street outside my yard. She doesn't say anything more. I don't ask questions. She was straight, matter-of-fact, as if she were telling me the color of a car passing by. At two o'clock she looks at me, and I know it's time to go in and start weaving.

I plan another trip.

"Sorry about today, Grandma," Darlene says over the phone. "I had to take the baby to the clinic. How about the day after tomorrow? I can pick you up at eight then."

"OK," I say. "Please try." I don't like to beg, but these days I'm desperate. I'm doing things that make no sense.

Like the next day.

Alice comes at two and leaves at five. "See you tomorrow morning at eight," I tell her at the front gate. As I turn to go back into the house, my eyes notice something on the far side of my garden. Something missing. The stand of deep blue and purple delphiniums. Pushing myself along the gravel path with my cane, I come to the corner of the yard and find not only the delphiniums missing but also roses, canna lilies, and gladioluses. Roses ripped off the vines, delphiniums and canna lilies torn from the stalks, whole gladioluses pulled up from the earth. This wasn't Alice, I say to myself. Alice takes flowers all the time, but she always asks. She's careful with the pruning shears, neat. I look over the fence and see rose petals on the cement sidewalk. Then I see a trail of tiny blue and purple delphinium petals, a faint trail leading down the sidewalk to the driveway two houses away. Mr. Peoples, I say to myself—what's wrong with him? He could have asked if he wanted flowers.

I don't think about it just then. I go back into the house. But hours later, ten o'clock at night, I can't get Mr. Peoples off my mind. I see him yanking the flowers out of my yard and hurrying off. He's a black man, silver at the temples, tall, so he would have no difficulty reaching the delphiniums and gladioluses. The roses a child could pluck off the fence. When did he take the flowers? Last night? This afternoon while Alice and I were inside weaving.

I turn off all the lights in the house. I sit next to the front window, peeking around the pulled shade, hoping to catch Peoples in the act. Hours go by. Cars pass on the street, kids on the sidewalk. No Peoples. I go back to the kitchen, turn on a light. I sit down at the table, pick up my awl and half-finished canoe basket. But I can't weave a single stitch. I'm thinking of my flowers and Mr. Peoples.

Then I do what makes no sense.

I get my walker and start for Mr. Peoples's house. Right down my front steps, out the gate, and onto the street. It's two in the morning and I'm going along the sidewalk with my walker. At least I thought of the walker. Cane around the house, walker outside the gate, I always tell myself. But I'm not thinking anything else. Maybe I can catch him, see the flowers in his house. But then what? Knock on the window and say, "Give them back"?

I'm not thinking.

I move up the driveway, go along the house until I see flickering light coming through a window. I edge up to the window, brace myself. I hardly have my eyes over the windowsill when I see the silver temples in the dim light, and then Peoples's face takes shape and a big woman next to him, both of them sitting on a couch, close together. I wonder who the woman is, which black woman in the neighborhood. But the woman isn't black at all. She's Indian, and as her face becomes clearer in the candlelight, I see she is a Toms, not just any Toms but Sipie Toms's daughter, same features, unmistakable straight nose and wide eyes. Mollie, I say to myself. My heart races. I think to get away before they see me, since they are facing the window. But that is silly. Sitting hand in hand, they don't see anything but the huge bouquet of flowers in a metal bucket on the low table in front of them.

Next thing I know it's seven-thirty in the morning and I'm still in bed. I'm always up at six. And for the last few weeks I haven't slept very much at all. The songs that pound in the house all night long, the voices. My madness. And that's what I'm thinking as I stare at the ceiling this morning, and why the events of the night before do not enter my mind. The house is quiet, just as it had been last night, only I was too preoccupied with Peoples and the flowers to notice it. Not just quiet but calm, peaceful. I look to see my chair and dresser against the wall, things I recognize.

I sit up, take my cane, get dressed, and put on water to boil. I think of going to the shed out back, waiting for the frog, but there's not enough time before Alice is supposed to arrive. In the meantime, I take comfort in the things around me, simple things like the pan on the stove, the coffee mugs on the sink, my African violets on the windowsill. I pinch myself.

Alice knocks at eight o'clock. I serve her hot chocolate. I drink my coffee. Only with her sitting at my table do I start thinking about what I saw the night before. But I don't tell her anything; I suppose I am embarrassed. What do I say, I was snooping in people's driveways at two in the morning?

At ten Alice and I are on the front porch. No Darlene. Alice sits just as she did the day before yesterday, gardening gloves in her lap, her half-finished basket poised on her knee. Only now I see that her basket is more than half finished. The full flower radiating up from the bottom is complete, its pointy petals showing all around the basket. She jabbers about this and that, something about her little brothers getting new clothes for school. "School starts soon," she says.

My heart drops. I think of her leaving me. School, I hadn't thought of that. Immediately I turn to her. "Alice," I say, "you will have to come later, after school. Maybe about four o'clock."

She doesn't say anything. I need to get a commitment from her. I open my mouth to say something more, but my throat sticks, my tongue doesn't move. I am looking at the basket on Alice's knee and the flowers beyond in the garden. Something clicks in my brain. I think of Peoples and Mollie and the flowers and the way this girl wove with little on her mind but her family, a simple wish that her mother find happiness. And it happened. It came around in a full circle, a picture I could understand, flowers and two people holding hands. This basket has power.

I look away, out to the street, breathe easy. Fear had clogged my mind so I couldn't see what was happening. I couldn't see this girl who sat across from me day after day, just like I couldn't see that singing over Sipie was enough, enough to show the family I was a good woman, whether or not they wanted to see it. Why else did I go there? Even my jealousy over Mary Hatcher didn't take me down the way this fear did. Fear about the family, my own loneliness and rejection.

Something moves in the marigolds, jumps to the edge of the front walk. The little green frog, what else? Then I hear the song and turn, seeing this girl named Alice singing as sure as tomorrow. The frog winks at me and I smile like never before. I'm not too old for miracles.

Afterword

By Reginald Dyck

Greg Sarris's *Grand Avenue* offers tough, urban stories of a long-fought, still-continuing struggle for self-determination. These stories present the day-to-day experiences of a contemporary, fictional Pomo Indian community living in a multiracial neighborhood not far from their traditional homeland. To my mind, no other author more perceptively engages urban Native life. Sarris's fictional ethnographies—although they are much more than that—have a depth that comes from Sarris's own experiences growing up and his long-term leadership within Pomo communities as well as his academic training. Because his characters have lost their *rancheria* (or reservation) and federal status, they have little choice but to make the city their home. There they have formed a new community.

Although displaced, like the majority of indigenous peoples in North America, they are still intact on "an in-town reservation: blacks, Mexicans, Indians" (198).[1] The stories depict poverty, high unemployment, destructive sexuality, and parenting that provides little protection for children. They also present determination, discipline, and various forms of healing. Conditions on Grand Avenue are the culmination of two centuries of exploitation. Recognizing this, Sarris has created a collection of complexly interrelated stories that are neither victim-blaming indictments nor voyeuristic accounts of dysfunctional families. He states, "My books are chronicles of survival, how a people survive for better and for worse. They light the dark places so we can all—all of us, Indian and non-Indian—see where we have been, where we are, and where we might go."[2]

Forced onto the margins of economic production, Pomo individuals and communities face the profound consequences of their position in U.S. society. Without a historical perspective, readers may see characters in *Grand Avenue* as hopelessly trapped in a world of their own making. We therefore need to consider how historically developed socioeconomic structures shape characters' present choices. Nevertheless, key characters are able to sustain themselves and adapt Pomo traditions to new circumstances. Their stories suggest strategies for strengthening urban Native communities as they provide models for finding wholeness in a troubled world.

Pomo Work History

The contemporary conditions that *Grand Avenue* depicts arose from historical processes that were shaped by the economic desires of dominant groups and by the resistance and desires of Pomo peoples. Forced to abandon their traditional subsistence economy, the Pomo adapted to new ways of sustaining themselves. Throughout the stories characters make historical references to forced removals, tribal division, and reservation termination (212, 48, 197). As a result, Pomo communities were pushed into alienated forms of labor that profoundly affected their cultural well-being.

Work for Pomo peoples traditionally meant hunting, fishing, and gathering, which allowed them to form self-sufficient communities. Remnants of this work situation are hardly even a memory for Sarris's characters. Disruptions began in 1811 with the establishment of a Russian commercial settlement, Colony Ross, on Pomo land. This started a long history of Pomo peoples working as farm laborers for others.

At about the same time, Spanish missions began recruiting Pomo converts and subjugating workers. More significant social changes resulted from Mexican land grants and military control, as California became a Mexican Republic in 1822. Enslaved, displaced from their land, and treated cruelly, Pomo peoples suffered great losses. This only increased with the occupation of Pomo land by U.S. settlers at midcentury, at which time the socioeconomic relationship between Pomo Indians and the dominant capitalist society was developed, "a pattern of semipeonage."[3] Because U.S. farmers gained almost complete control of Pomo lands, Indians were segregated onto rancherias. Anglo farmers who needed readily available workers provided these small settlements, which were often part of the former Pomo homeland. In "The Water Place" Nellie explains that the extended family moved to the rancheria on the Benedict Ranch after the Spanish forced them off their traditional place along Santa Rosa Creek. Their racial and economic vulnerabilities are exposed when the owner orders all Indians off his land because his son wants to marry Nellie's mother (212–14). This loss of ownership in a capitalist society meant a considerable loss of control over their lives, a key factor in their moves that eventually led to Santa Rosa.

By the end of the nineteenth century Pomo Indians had lost 99 percent of their land and faced increasing hostility. For the most part, the only work available was low-paying, seasonal farm labor. Indians saw that even the few who did attend college or work in the cities had no chance of gaining the wealth and power that white people had.[4] Further, as non-Native minorities increasingly entered the region, the larger pool of workers meant a shorter work season and reduced wages. Competition for work created ethnic rivalries. We see, for example, in "Joy Ride" that Albert Silva's Portuguese father assuages the shame of his own low socioeconomic status by disparaging Native peoples (94). As Pomo Indians became increasingly less isolated, this racially inflected competition for work continues into the present as some characters working in the cannery feel threatened by "illegals" (128).

Because loss of land forced them into new work and cultural conditions, Pomo peoples could return to their traditional homelands only in wintertime and to a modified form of traditional work and ceremonies. Steven Pen's father lived through this transition when he was a young man. Thus, while his father tells him of the supernatural events he experienced, Steven struggles to interpret his own life in cosmic rather than social terms (189–92, and see below).

During World War II many Pomo people left their rancherias for opportunities in the armed forces and defense plants. Their movement to urban areas intensified after the war when the federal government started its termination policy and harshly reduced its support. Pomo rancherias lost their federal recognition under the California Rancheria Act of 1958. Also fostering urbanization were technological changes in agriculture that lessened work opportunities and created deeper forms of rural poverty. While many Pomo Indians moved to cities, most found only marginal employment. Economic necessity forced them to establish communities in high-poverty, low-rent neighborhoods. In Sarris's stories, seasonal work in the cannery and government checks account for most characters' income.[5]

Because characters have little opportunity to find well-paying jobs, they adapt to their Grand Avenue situation in positive and negative ways. The community has been displaced by migration but not dismantled. *Grand Avenue*'s first-generation urban characters face conditions similar to those many Indians experienced during the relocations of the '60s and '70s. They support each other in significant ways in spite of many interpersonal tensions provoked by their circumstances. Nevertheless, the fact that none openly rebel and few fight for change indicates their sense of powerlessness.

New Urban Indian Realities

Sarris's fiction stands out for its engagement of Native communal life in the city. James Ruppert explains that Indian fiction before the 1990s depicted cities and reservations as "unalterable opposites." William Bevis observed in the 1980s that Native novels consistently conclude with protagonists returning home to reservations or rural homelands for reintegration with their tribes.[6] They end with reservation or rural conclusions rather than urban commencements. N. Scott Momaday's (Kiowa) *House Made of Dawn* is one example.[7]

In contrast, characters in *Grand Avenue* live in an extended-family/tribal community with a common, if fractured, cultural memory. In spite of their distinctiveness, they confront working and living conditions common to other minorities living in similar urban areas. Sarris shows these conditions as having a range of consequences: the absence of marriage, strained extended-family and community solidarity, weakened parenting, and troubled adolescent sexuality.

Sociologist William Julius Wilson explains the consequences of living in high-poverty neighborhoods like the one described in *Grand Avenue*: "[C]oncentrated poverty increases the likelihood of social isolation (from mainstream institutions), joblessness, dropping out of school, lower educational achievement, involvement in crime, unsuccessful behavioral development and delinquency among adolescents, nonmarital childbirth, and unsuccessful family management." These conditions are often inherited; that is, children will generally experience the same neighborhoods that their parents did.[8] Thus, the challenges in creating change, as Sarris's stories suggest, are complexly multigenerational.

The behaviors associated with poor urban communities are not merely personal preferences or individual moral choices. Scarcity of work is a key constraint for the Grand Avenue community Sarris depicts. Social segregation means that characters have minimal connections to "informal employment networks" and thus have little opportunity to gain "the human capital skills, including adequate educational training, that facilitate mobility in a society."[9]

This situation severely limits the life choices of most of Sarris's characters. For the unskilled workers that make up most of the Grand Avenue community, the only job available, with few exceptions, is at the cannery, "the worst work ever" (179–80). That Sarris's characters take a job with unsafe, nearly intolerable conditions suggests their desperation to find work. Because cannery jobs last only half a year, unemployment checks sustain workers—and thus cannery profits—the other half. Donald Fixico (Sac and Fox/Muscogee Creek/Shawnee/Seminole), discussing postwar employment, notes that "Native Americans were pushed into unskilled occupations with high rates of layoffs and seasonal work." Low-wage work like this does not "foster respect, build status, or offer opportunity for advancement."[10]

Healing and basket making are economically significant work for one or two of the older generation, but elders are generally more valued for their social security checks (154, 153, 31, 43, 143). The importance of government programs to the community's economy indicates characters' difficulties in finding full-time, permanent employment. It also plays into derogatory stereotypes of urban Indians.

A Community without Work

What predominates on Grand Avenue is the absence of steady work. Its insidious consequences have become widespread. For one thing, there are comparatively few men in the community. As a result, very few long-term male-female relationships exist in the stories.

Trying to maintain a steady relationship makes no sense when men cannot fulfill their role in it. The result is women having children by many different men, not out of promiscuous desire but from a common need for acceptance that is thwarted by economic circumstances. This is poignantly illustrated by Zelda who, as a young woman, tattooed her legs with the names of the men she had been with and had hoped would stay (88). Her niece Mollie follows her example of multiple insubstantial relationships, and yet, like her aunt, she clearly desires more. Sarris's characters may be forced to go against middle-class values, but that does not mean they reject them.

The absence of men available to create long-term relationships makes it difficult for women characters to offer each other mutual support. A desperate and painful competition for male attention divides and distracts them. We see this in "The Magic Pony" as the women develop strategies for stealing their sister Faye's man: "Nothing stops them when they get ideas, and nothing gives them ideas like a man does" (6). The ability to attract a man is a weapon against the sense of powerlessness they experience at the bottom of the social hierarchy.

Unstable work opportunities also impinge on the few who do marry. Describing herself as having a "blinding drive against hard luck," Anna summarizes the economics of her marriage to Albert Silva: "Two kids become eight, and a husband's earnings become a welfare check" (47, 42). She dreams of an empowering normalcy, yet her hopes diminish as the family struggles to maintain its marginally middle-class status.[11] Albert's lack of work leads to his insignificance as husband and father, as is seen in his absence from Anna's story, "The Progress of This Disease." His own story, "Joy Ride," depicts his separation from his wife and family as nearly complete. He now lives in a world of lost dreams. Similar to many of the women characters, Albert transposes his economic dilemma into a sexual one as he impotently attempts to reassert his masculinity. Within their strained circumstances, neither Albert nor Anna can offer the other emotional support. However, we should note again that Sarris has not merely created stories of personal or cultural failure but rather is depicting the consequences of structurally determined, urban joblessness.

Growing Up Underclass

The consequences of this joblessness for child-rearing practices are disturbing. We see mothers' lack of control over their children most painfully in the relationship between Mollie and her daughter Justine. In "How I Got to Be Queen," Mollie's other daughter, Alice, narrates a harsh interaction between the two: "'Damned black-neck squaw,' Mom says [to Justine]. 'Dirty fat Indian, you don't even know which Filipino in that apple orchard is my father,' Justine says. . . . And if Justine goes on long enough, Mom goes out or watches TV. Like nothing was ever started" (120). The story ends with a racial confrontation. People are yelling and calling Justine a whore as she walks out the front door, knife in hand, ready to fight a black girl she earlier insulted. The police come, and middle-class Auntie Anna finally eases the situation. Mollie plays no role because she has established a pattern of absenting herself from family situations, which she has little power to impact.

The close-knit, extended family on Grand Avenue can also offer little help because it has few resources for supporting the younger generation. The older generation of Zelda and Old Uncle helps with children's physical needs, but in this urban setting they seem irrelevant as role models or agents of family order. Without adequate extended-family support, and overwhelmed by her own problems, Mollie is ineffective in helping Justine negotiate a difficult adolescence. Thus, Sarris shows the troubled ways that a daughter learns the class-inflected behaviors of her mother, and this is one more way that the absence of work shapes generations of lives in the Grand Avenue community.

"Class comes to children through families," urban anthropologist Sherry Ortner observes.[12] However, Justine does not connect her deprivations—the absence of homeownership, their lack of a car, health disparities, and other material hardships—to her family's marginal status. Yet Justine's inability to understand her class deprivations does not mean that she does not experience them or that she does not attempt to resist class strictures. From her mother and aunts she has learned classed ways to strike back with her most readily accessible weapon, her sexuality. Social rewards for sexual repression hardly exist on Grand Avenue; abstinence and propriety will not be rewarded by social advancement. Because their home place is a constant reminder of society's rejection, these characters' experience of sexuality is more insistently tied to personal affirmation, that is, to being desired. This is the compensation Justine seeks as she becomes the queen of a continuing, summer house party. When school starts again in the fall, she plans to maintain that status with a calculated strategy: "'I'll show them snobby white girls,' she said. . . . She was going to lose fifteen pounds. She was going to wear all kinds of makeup on her face. People would be shocked. They'd be scared of her" (130). Knowing the white, presumably middle-class girls will never accept her, Justine can only imagine a social defiance that may seem empowering but is economically destructive. Her outsider status at school leaves her unprepared for adult life outside of her mother's circumstances.

Unable to recognize her conflict as a class struggle, Justine experiences her adolescent sexuality as burdened with misplaced class anger. She attempts to ameliorate her social injuries with counterproductive displays of aberrant (from a middle-class perspective) sexual displays. Yet, rather than challenging class hierarchies, Justine reinscribes them with her "choices." Although her sexuality seems empowering to her, it actually brands her as belonging to the bottom of her high school's, and society's, status hierarchy.

We can easily imagine Justine growing up to become like her mother or aunts rather than the "snobby white girls" she naively tries to challenge. Yet the racially intersected class injuries she experiences can have even more serious consequences. In his related novel *Watermelon Nights*, Sarris presents an even bleaker future for Justine. One of its narrators mentions that Justine, sixteen years old, "got herself killed" when she was caught in the cross fire of automatic rifles.[13] The narrator's offhand phrase suggests the tragic ordinariness of this event in a multiracial, underclass neighborhood where work has disappeared and characters experience the devastating results.

Alternatives

Grand Avenue gives full weight to the burden of socioeconomic conditions that characters face, yet Sarris has also created characters who sustain or develop positive Native identities while living on Grand Avenue. Alice stands out as a character of hope in bleak circumstances, as do her two mentors, Anna Silva and Nellie Copaz.

Although her sister, Justine, fights to gain higher status within a teen culture that is stratified by class and race, Alice avoids this competition. In part because her body does not match dominant standards of beauty, she avoids the destructive sexual competition that entraps her sister. Instead, taking pride in being responsible has become her way of confronting antagonistic, poverty-driven conditions. The story Alice narrates, "How I Got to Be Queen," opens with the family having moved again and Alice taking charge. Acting on values uncommon in this context, she demonstrates hard work, order, organization, responsible child rearing, and conservative dress. She appreciates the difference between her mother and her mother's middle-class cousin Anna, who models for Alice different ways of maintaining dignity in the face of the economic hardships.

Along with Anna, Nellie Copaz has a positive influence as she offers Alice an example and a relationship that becomes mutually supportive. Nellie lives out traditional practices through her healing songs, basket weaving, and storytelling. Her sense of history grounds her understanding of the present: "Look at what the Spanish did, then the Mexicans, then the Americans. All of them, they took our land, locked us up. Then look at what we go and do to one another" (222). And she sees a larger world beyond material circumstances.

From Nellie, Alice learns stories of the past and the tradition of basket making. As a result, she can sustain positive Pomo traditions as she adapts them to new conditions. Sarris reassures us of this by creating two moving vignettes that reveal Alice's strategy of resistance as well as the possibilities for community healing. One is her creating a basket that is traditional, yet of her own design. The other reassuring picture comes in a later story in typical Sarris form, a story about listening to a story and finding out what the listener understood. Nellie tells Alice family stories about poisonings, suicide, a stolen love song, a lost rancheria, and more. Not really understanding her own stories of loss and separation, Nellie "frantic[ally]" asks, "Alice, do you hear me? Do you understand?" (222). Alice replies yes, and then seemingly incongruously adds, "I made a new casserole." This casserole tastes good and is cheap, Alice explains. More importantly, all the children helped make it. In Alice's cooking-story response to Nellie's stories of poison and healing, Nellie sees that past conflicts and present conditions do not have to trap either her or Alice. Communal well-being here takes the form of a family of kids who, although their mother is out looking for love, can still cook a good meal together. It also takes the form of an elder teaching and learning from a young character who represents a hopeful alternative for her Grand Avenue community.

These contemporary ways of providing for individual, family, and community needs echo the traditional, self-sustaining work activities that flourished before other, alienating structures were imposed. They are possible because two older characters are able to have a transformative influence on a younger member, who in turn creates a nourishing home for her siblings.

Twice-Told Tales

Alice's character is developed in two stories, "How I Got to Be Queen" and "The Water Place." Nellie reveals her life story as she narrates the later as well as "Waiting for the Green Frog." Her character is developed further in other stories, which reveal her complex relationship to the Pomo community. Plots, characters, and character/narrators are woven together into a "novel in stories" in which the conclusion of one story is often complicated by intersecting events and perspectives from others. For example, only by linking "Secret Letters" with "The Indian Maid" can we see the multigenerational, interfamily relationships that allow the Pen father and son to sustain their class superiority through their sexual irresponsibility with Zelda and her daughter Pauline Toms. We also see that while the stories these characters tell of these experiences evoke traditions, they do so in self-interested rather than community-building ways. (One could further complicate these two short stories by intersecting them with "The Progress of this Disease," which provides family histories shaped by other Pomo stories of traditional beliefs.)

Retelling traditional stories "allows for a continuous reinvention of the tradition in those communities," Sarris explains in his theoretical work *Keeping Slug Woman Alive*.[14] And not just the stories, he makes clear, but the storytelling process itself must be contextualized. The transitory moment that engages speaker and audience has its being in a lived social experience. In representing the ways that changing material conditions shape his characters' stories, Sarris shows how daily life on Grand Avenue participates in contemporary U.S. society. His characters, not necessarily knowingly, engage its structures as they use their stories to make sense of, and justify, their lives as they teach their children ways of doing the same.

In "Secret Letters" the father uses a traditional Pomo story to help his son Steven Pen face a life-changing decision. Yet in the short story that contains this storytelling, Sarris includes a cautionary skepticism about such storytelling. Steven Pen's father passionately tells his son a cosmic bear-person story about a rivalry between two extended Pomo families. The father extends this traditional conflict to include the dilemma Steven faces concerning his pregnant girlfriend, Pauline Toms. The father adapts a story of conflicting cosmic forces in a way that solves his son's dilemma and maintains the Pen family's socioeconomic status.

The father explains to Steven that powerful forces have been at work in the longstanding Pen-Toms family rivalry: "Great displays of strength, magic powers. Fifty-foot leaps into the air. Roars that caused rocks to roll down hillsides. Sharp whistles that pierce eardrums. Anything to intimidate their rivals or to kill them" (189).

Although the contemporary events that follow seem a mere shadow of this cosmic struggle, the father makes a connection. First, he explains that as a young man he abandoned his pregnant, underclass girlfriend, Zelda Toms, whom he feared would entrap him in a life of poverty (191). Now, a generation later, he warns his son Steven to follow his example when faced with the same situation, a pregnant girlfriend from the rival Toms family. As the father tells it, his abandoning Zelda Toms was not self-serving social climbing but a strategic maneuver in a cosmic rivalry. His storytelling offers the same interested absolution to his son.

Sarris shows that storytelling can participate in complex struggles over class identity. Although traditional Pomo society included social divisions, they took new forms as the people became increasingly entangled in capitalist socioeconomic relations and as socioeconomic advancement became a possibility for a few. Sarris warns that stories "can work to oppress or to liberate, to confuse or to enlighten," and so readers must carry the burden of moral discernment.[15] Rather than explicitly praising or condemning the Pen family's decisions, Sarris helps readers recognize the powerful, yet at times conflicted or destructive, uses of stories. He also reminds us that, although stories can help us broaden our understanding, no one "has access to the whole."[16] Steven's father offers one side of the story; Zelda and her family tell another. Both sides are encased in their narrators' stories, which offer further complexities to the storytelling process.

As narrator of "Secret Letters," Steven incorporates his father's story into his own. Having continued the process of class differentiation by leaving Grand Avenue, moving into a white, middle-class neighborhood, and becoming a successful family man, Steven now wants to break down cultural (but not socioeconomic) boundaries that separate him from the son born from his liaison with Pauline and whom she has had responsibility for raising. This requires a new storytelling strategy.

Steven and his Apache wife, Reyna, conclude family dinners by telling their children stories from their respective peoples (186–88). Their earnest self-consciousness (although without much self-reflection) about sustaining cultural ties suggests a significant shift in the work that stories are called upon to do: help the children know "who we are" (200). Rather than differentiation, Steven's storytelling is intended to foster Indian unity. Steven's excerpted version describes the children's great-great-grandmother as a bear person, rescuing imprisoned Indians about to be shot by soldiers. Because of the rescue, the bear person's secret powers were revealed. Yet, "No one worried she might poison people. . . . They knew she cared about her tribe" (188). A miracle is needed because soldiers have captured the Indians, but this is only background for the central drama of unity: "the Indians were freed, not just our tribe, everybody" (188). Presented as a decontextualized, morally uplifting folk tale, the children dutifully find an appropriate lesson to the story, the equivalent of eating all their vegetables.

Steven's "palatable" storytelling indicates that he has not resolved the dilemma of his own past action or of his present relationship to the Grand Avenue Pomo community. Defensively (and ironically) he asserts as narrator that the household his old girlfriend Pauline grew up in was "worlds apart from mine, where my upright father never as much as looked at another woman" (193). Moral boundaries, self-proclaimed and socially reinforced, buttress economic ones: Steven notes that he has gained the social success his father wanted, while Pauline, as expected, has fallen. Her physical appearance symbolizes for him her social and moral status: "She was a large square woman, significantly overweight, with a shock of hair bleached a faded orange color" (195). With this understanding, Steven can comfortably exclude Pauline from his family story. Strategic storytelling, Steven has learned from his father, can allow us to live with contradictory desires: for him, unity and exclusion. Yet repressed contradictions return as his and Pauline's son, Tony, draws Steven back across class and cultural lines, and challenges his family's story, which offers no conceptual grasp of underlying conflicts within his present situation.

Steven and Reyna's efforts to integrate themselves into the vibrant but troubled Pomo community offer much to admire, and yet Sarris shows that considerable self-reflection and difficult negotiations across class barriers are still needed. For this to happen, Steven would need to confront not only his past sexual relationship with Pauline but also his present classed relationship with her. In "Secret Letters" Sarris engages readers in the project of understanding how an extended family of storytellers adapts to changing conditions. The storytelling process can teach radically subversive lessons, but it can also tame a family's founding stories by safely cleaning up their contexts.[17]

Like the stories it contains, "Secret Letters" itself comes with a context: the other stories in the book. *Grand Avenue* presents a thickly textured representation of contemporary urban Indian life by weaving together situations from story to story. Readers become actively engaged in the process of storytelling as we identify these connections and construct meanings that emerge from reading the stories as ongoing processes. Thus, our understanding of "Secret Letters" is made more complex as we consider "Indian Maid," with its stories of Zelda and her daughters, as part of its context.

In contrast to "Secret Letters," the stories told in "Indian Maid" are not cosmic in scope. They are stories about work. Yet they function similarly to the more traditional ones in "Secret Letters" by providing a basis for family unity. It is not that these stories have a common meaning for family members. Rather, Sarris emphasizes the competing interpretations characters develop out of their differing experiences. Nevertheless, family stories offer a common symbol, a flag of sorts, around which to rally. Both short stories focus on the interaction of individual and family desires. As narrators of "Secret Letters" and "Indian Maid," Steven Pen and Stella Toms retell the past in ways that help them come to terms with their present social and cultural positions. Sarris calls upon his readers to consider each character's discursive maneuvers.

The character Pauline Toms links the present situation of the two short stories. As noted above, her life after Steven's abandonment seems typical for Grand Avenue, at least from the Pen perspective. In "Secret Lives" Steven comments that while away he "had heard somewhere that she had had several children, a brood, and, as rumor had it about her and her sisters, most of them had different fathers." Pauline, he states, lives in "a dump at the end of Grand Avenue. . . . Junked cars, dirty kids playing on the road" (195, 198). For Steven this is a differentiating and reassuring welfare story.

As in "Secret Letters," Pauline does not tell her own story in "Indian Maid." Instead, it is mediated by Stella, her younger, class-conscious sister. Sharing Steven's socioeconomic desires, Stella presents Pauline in similar ways. In her telling, Pauline is just one of the older sisters who tormented her for refusing to become like them. Stella sees in them the failed life she is determined to avoid.

Yet Pauline's story looks quite different from both Stella's and Steven's version when we contextualize it with Zelda's story. This, however, is not a simple interpretive move, since competing versions of Zelda's story create the central conflict in "Indian Maid." Stella's story of her mother's past is considerably different from the account given by her sisters. Both versions recognize that Zelda, like Steven's father, had dreams of socioeconomic advancement. She hoped to escape from "the dirty-faced children and the drunk old men and women of the reservation" (176) by attending Sherman Indian School, dedicated to training Indian maids.[18] Acculturated there to "kill the Indian," she finds a job with "the wealthiest family in town," which continues her education in class and racial hierarchies.

Zelda's elaborately detailed account of being an Indian maid has become a foundational family story, often repeated. It ends with Zelda returning "like a fugitive" to the reservation. That night she "dreamed like never before" (170). In concluding the storytelling, Zelda would ask her daughters what they thought she dreamed of. The older sisters imagine their mother dreaming of what they themselves want: escape, wealth, a man to marry, or acceptance in another white family. Their answers, so different from the way both Zelda's and their own lives have turned out, imply that such dreaming can only end in defeat. These answers are quite different from the optimistic ending that Stella confidently asserts. The meanings Stella and her sisters create for their mother's story reflect different times in the larger story of Zelda's life. "Mother was a whore," Pauline and the other daughters exclaim to Stella years later. "All the men in and out" is what they learned, along with the lesson about their mother's crushed ambition (177). This version of the story helps reconcile these sisters to their present conditions on Grand Avenue.

One of those in-and-out men who taught Zelda about her place in society was Steven's father. After returning from working as an Indian maid and having few opportunities to provide for herself and her children, Zelda has sexual relationships with various men. We know from "Secret Lives" that Steven's father was one. Abandoning Zelda when she was pregnant with Pauline worked to Steven's father's economic advantage as he bootstrapped his way, more or less, into socioeconomic respectability. Zelda's story makes clear that she, too, was ambitious but lacked his opportunities. Steven's father's cosmically justified yet self-serving abandonment is part of the reason she fails.

After she returned to the reservation, and the reservation was subsequently terminated, Zelda then moved to Grand Avenue (197–98). Her story of humiliation and defeat is repeated, with variations, by most of her daughters, but not by Stella. Because she was too young to know about all the men her mother had, she sees her mother differently. Also, her positive work experiences shape the meaning Stella finds in her mother's Indian Maid story. Zelda's Indian-hating employer had taunted her by displaying her jewels to her poor young maid. When Zelda escaped, she took an opal ring with her, but as it turned out, it had little monetary value. From their mother's work story, Pauline and the other older sisters learn that, in spite of her ambition to improve herself, their mother was used and then discarded like cheap jewelry. Stella, however, recreates a different story, one about jewels and their secret language, a story of classed desire.

Like Steven, Stella tells a story of economic mobility overlaid with a desire for connectedness to the family from which her desire for success has alienated her. Unlike her mother, Stella is able to get a junior-college education and a decent job, just as Steven does. Her escape from Grand Avenue is possible because of new employment opportunities at federal Indian agencies. She can trade "all the drunks, all the welfare slobs, and all the unwed mothers with all their bastard kids"—the view of Grand Avenue she shares with Steven (177)—for a new vision of personal power: "I saw myself in skirts and blouses, answering phones, directing people here and there, sorting important mail from Washington, D.C. My fingernails would be polished" (180). Her storytelling strategically leaves out circumstances that would contradict the lesson of self-advancement that justifies her leaving her family behind.

Stella's story, "Indian Maid," concludes in a way similar to Steven's "Secret Letters." At the end Steven feels assured of an enlarged family eating dinner together; Stella imagines Zelda's dream upon returning to the reservation: a meal where everyone has a place at the table, even the one returning in a maid's uniform whose class aspirations, like Stella's, had set her apart. In this retelling, Stella finds a lesson similar to the one Steven wants to teach: "Appreciate one another. Get along. Share" (183). It is a message of inclusiveness that elides troubling complications. Stella's avoidance echoes Steven's. Pauline still has no real place in Steven's story, just as in Stella's story Pauline and her sisters have been manageably abstracted into loving, distant family members. The message of inclusiveness creates an unconvincing conclusion when we see the acts of exclusion at its center.

As we read for the ways that the stories within *Grand Avenue* are interwoven, we discover more depth in these characters' lives within community. There is nothing simple about becoming or being part of this urban neighborhood. Sarris challenges us to see characters and events from the multiple perspectives presented in this "novel in stories."

Spiritual and Material Stories

As the *Grand Avenue* stories make clear, the material conditions described above shape not only characters' social experiences but also their spiritual imagination. This is true for Anna's adapted apprehension of Christianity, as well as for her cousin Faye's improvised traditional beliefs. Sarris presents a range of spiritual apprehensions and experiences, which affect characters both positively and negatively. In the opening story, "The Magic Pony," Jasmine sees her Auntie Faye as "plumb nuts" because of her "weird stories." Yet she also acknowledges that Faye's considerable knowledge about poisons and cures does give her something to believe in. And this reveals to Jasmine her own emptiness (4, 23).

Faye's beliefs are adapted from the Bole Maru, or Dream Dance cult, a "late-nineteenth-century nationalistic and revivalistic movement among Pomo Indians and their neighbors." Sarris explains that this "blending of different religious and cultural ideas laid the foundation for a fierce resistance that exists today in many places." While Pomo peoples accepted aspects of the dominant culture that, in fact, helped them to survive, their "leaders inculcated an impassioned Indian Nationalism in the homes and roundhouses [spiritual centers]." Sarris notes that groups which adapted to external circumstances were able to survive as a people.[19] Conditions are different in the contemporary Grand Avenue community, but Sarris's fiction expresses a similar position about the necessity of spiritual adaptation.

When Jasmine tells Ruby, "Your mother's crazy. . . . She's a freak and so are you" (8), she is grasping for an explanation of her confusing world. Jasmine rightly sees disaster coming but feels powerless to intervene. She sees her Aunt Faye as similarly powerless. Because the world seems a dangerous place to Faye, she attempts to protect her daughter, Ruby, and niece Jasmine by reimagining tribal tradition in a form she can control: her wall painting of a forest and crosses together with her explanatory stories.

Sarris recognizes the fragmentation of beliefs that result from the historical and continuing colonization experienced by contemporary Pomo Indians.[20] The Dream religion developed as an act of recovery. When in the 1870s Richard Taylor developed this new form of traditional beliefs, "he called people from far and near to hear his Dreams. . . . Dreaming new dances and songs, sacred activities would keep them alive after the white people had taken everything but their souls to Dream."[21] In the present, however, traditional beliefs have become "a free-for-all about the self," Sarris explains.[22] Faye's individualistic adaptation of traditional spiritual understandings does not adequately provide her the sustenance she needs. Community is missing. Faye's painful alienation is emblematic of a larger community displacement. "The balance has been tipped," Sarris states, as people were removed from their land and culture, and thus lost the ability to read the landscape as a text for living.[23]

Another traditional belief, poisoning, or the casting of a spell on someone that makes them sick, is regularly referenced in Sarris's stories. Herman James, Pomo informant for *Kashaya Texts*, told a story of Poison Man set "in the old days [when] there were no white men." Associated with "the One Below," he made everyone afraid with his deadly but mysterious knowledge and power of poisoning. This was passed on to the children, and James stated in 1958 that "we too are still afraid of what we call poisoning."[24] This fear had an important impact on precontact Pomo culture "by inducing isolation, ensuring strict usage of hospitality rules, and inducing strict rules of etiquette." Pomo beliefs "gave the people a feeling of cultural unity and spiritual strength in a way that is vital to the balance, growth and maturity of individuals."[25]

In the present of *Grand Avenue*, no characters are now poisoners, and only a few are concerned about it. Faye alone, of her generation or the younger one, actively believes. For her, however, traditional beliefs about poisoning are no longer about respect, balance, and humility, but about fear. Like Nellie, a generation older, she accepts that the "poison hasn't gone anywhere. It's everywhere so people can't see, and what they can't see they don't believe" (89). Nellie combines this belief with her commitment to basket making and songs as forms of healing. Lacking this balance, Faye engages in a kind of self-created Pomo belief system. Her painted forest and pink crosses do provide her with a structure of meaning that explains the social exclusion she feels as she struggles to change her material conditions. This individually adapted belief structure gives her a semblance of control, the power of explanation, yet it proves sadly inadequate. In a crisis moment, Jasmine recognizes the fear in Faye's eyes that she will lose everything: "She had told stories to save herself—now she was telling them to excuse herself" (23–24).

For the Pomo community on Grand Avenue, Christianity has become the most common belief system, although many characters seem interested in neither traditional nor Christian beliefs. Unlike Faye, Anna Silva accepts Christianity rather than traditional beliefs, yet both experience their beliefs as simultaneously reassuring and alienating. Matching their individualistic drive to improve themselves, they interpret their different belief systems in similar ways. They adapt established beliefs to their personal needs rather than submitting to socially sanctioned forms. *Grand Avenue*'s urban characters often turn to individualistic responses to cultural colonization since they lack the protection of the relative isolation that rural rancherias used to provide.

Jasmine concludes her account of living with Faye's family with new understanding and appreciation. Rather than seeing Faye and Ruby as "stupid fool[s]," she now sees that they have created a place of refuge within their belief systems. Yet Faye's hopes for a new life are not fulfilled. Further, her daughter, in the story "Slaughterhouse," reluctantly accepts a job and place in society as a prostitute because she can find no alternative, a fate similar to her grandmother Zelda's. In these short stories and others, Sarris shows (some) characters striving to find a place to belong, not only on Grand Avenue, but in the cosmos. We readers must look for the ways that some characters find meaning within the material world while others struggle to live out a worldview that includes adapted spiritual traditions.

Reading Responsibly

Sarris concludes his prologue to *Keeping Slug Woman Alive* by stating, "And there is more to the story. . . . The story is now yours too."[26] Like the others', my stories here have been selective. I have emphasized the ways that characters' storytelling knowingly and unknowingly engages socioeconomic structures and desires. These, in turn, shape at least some characters' spiritual experiences. Further, I have emphasized the importance of intersecting stories so that we can better see what is at stake in each telling. Like Sarris's characters, we create, retell, and adapt stories for a range of reasons, some community-enriching and others self-serving. *Grand Avenue*, in its multiply motivated dialectic of storytelling, shows that Sarris is well aware of this. And yet the storytelling needs to continue.

One of the great strengths of *Grand Avenue* is its depiction of the consequences that Pomo peoples have experienced as they have been forced away from traditional means of production on their homeland and into the impoverished neighborhoods of northern California cities. Yet Sarris intends his fiction to affect more than readers' understanding. By helping us grasp past and present realities, his "chronicles of survival" prompt us to look for what actions we should take. As citizens as well as readers, we need to responsibly find ways to help address the structural problems *Grand Avenue* presents while recognizing the effective strategies of resistance that characters, as well as Native communities and nations, continue to enact.[27]

Notes

1. All page citations for the novel *Grand Avenue* appear in parentheses within the text.

2. Greg Sarris, "A Conversation with Greg Sarris," *Watermelon Nights* (New York: Penguin, 1998), 9.

3. Lowell John Bean and Dorothea Theodoratus, "Western Pomo and Northeastern Pomo," *California*, vol. 8 of *Handbook of North American Indians*, ed. Robert F. Heiser (Washington, D.C.: Smithsonian Institution, 1978), 299. This is the basic source for the following historical overview. The Federated Indians of Graton Rancheria website is also a useful source of information: www.gratonrancheria.com. See particularly the "Timeline" and "Our People" sections listed under the "Culture" tab.

4. B. W. and E. G Aginsky, "Conclusion," *Deep Valley* (New York: Stein and Day, 1976), 209–10.

5. For further details, see Reginald Dyck, "Structures of Urban Poverty in Greg Sarris's *Grand Avenue*," *American Indian Culture and Research Journal* 34, no. 4 (2010): 13–30.

6. James Ruppert, "Fiction: 1968 to the Present," in *The Cambridge Companion to Native American Literature*, eds. Joy Porter and Kenneth M. Roemer (New York: Cambridge University Press, 2005) 187; William Bevis, "Native American Novels: Homing In," in *Recovering the Word: Essays on Native American Literature*, eds. Brian Swann and Arnold Krupat (Berkley: University of California Press, 1987), 585, 592.

7. Although James Welch's (Blackfoot/Gros Ventre) *Indian Lawyer* (1990) gives a relatively positive depiction of urban Indian life, its accomplished, middle class, professional protagonist does fulfill the pattern Bevis explains. Leslie Marmon Silko's (Laguna Pueblo) fiction gives a harsher depiction of urban Indian life. The cities of Gallup, New Mexico, in *Ceremony* (1977) and Tucson, Arizona, in *Almanac of the Dead* (1991) are both corrupt and corrupting. Sherman Alexie's (Spokane/Coeur d'Alene) *Indian Killer* (1996) depicts Seattle's urban conditions as being nearly as destructive as Los Angeles' in Momaday's *House Made of Dawn* (1968). While Gerald Visenor's (Anishinaabe) fiction often enough has an urban setting, its focus is on language and ideas rather

than material conditions. Louise Erdrich's (Turtle Mountain Chippewa) novels often include urban settings, but the characters living there are alienated from their tribes and reservations. Clear examples are Beverly "Hat" Lamertine and King Kashpaw from *Love Medicine* (1984, rev. eds. 1993, 2009).

Alexie's story collection *Ten Little Indians* (2003), written almost a decade after *Grand Avenue*, offers a useful comparison. Characters in both books lead urban lives. However, while Sarris's characters live in a Pomo enclave, Alexie's are separated geographically and psychically from their tribes, even if some spend time with other Indians. "So, you tell me kid, what kind of Indian does that make me?" asks one of his characters, a former self-identified Native poet, now working as a forklift operator, who has not had contact with other Indians for years. Many of Alexie and Sarris's characters embody this question but within quite different social situations.

8. William Julius Wilson, *More Than Just Race: Being Black and Poor in the Inner City* (New York: W. W. Norton, 2009), 46, 52.

9. William Julius Wilson, *When Work Disappears: The World of the New Urban Poor* (New York: Vintage, 1996), xiii, 24.

10. Donald L. Fixico, *The Urban Indian Experience in America* (Albuquerque: University of New Mexico Press, 2000), 75; Wilson, *More Than Just Race*, 63.

11. I use *class* as a relational identification within a multifaceted hierarchy of status. Castle McLaughlin's essay, "Nation, Tribe, and Class: The Dynamics of Agrarian Transformation on the Fort Berthold Reservation," *American Indian Culture and Research Journal* 22, no. 3 (1998): 101–106, offers a useful explanation and example of using class as an analytical concept. McLaughlin's justification of her use of the term is appropriate here as well:

> By evoking the term *class*, I am not suggesting that Indian communities can be understood solely in terms of material conflict and social hierarchy or that these define reservation life, nor do I wish to impose a "totalizing" theoretical construct. But I know of no other term that so well acknowledges the relationship between resources, power, and the landscape of competing sociopolitical identities that is episodically visible and subjectively experienced at Fort Berthold.

12. Sherry B. Ortner, *New Jersey Dreaming: Capital, Culture, and the Class of '58* (Durham: Duke University Press, 2003), 40.

13. Sarris, *Watermelon Nights*, 8.

14. Greg Sarris, *Keeping Slug Woman Alive: A Holistic Approach to American Indian Texts* (Berkeley: University of California Press, 1993), 70.

15. Sarris, *Keeping Slug Woman Alive*, 5

16. Ibid., 40, 46.

17. One of the strengths of Sarris's writing is the complexity of his characters. Although Steven Pen fails Pauline, he does offer something important to the tribe by returning to Grand Avenue and integrating his family into the Waterplace Pomo community. Sarris continues Steven's story in *Watermelon Nights*. Now as tribal chair, he and the council aim to regain federal recognition and their land. The goal is to strengthen the tribe's self-determination. "We can control our fates," Steven optimistically states, "be one as a people again, have a home that is ours and truly ours" (Sarris, *Watermelon Nights*, 58). Yet the admirable hope that Steven generates comes again at the cost of strategically eliding conflict from his story. For further analysis, see Reginald Dyck, "Practicing Sovereignty in Greg Sarris's *Watermelon Nights*," *Western American Literature* 45, no. 4 (Winter 2011): 341–61.

18. For historical context, see Alice Littlefield, "Learning to Labor: American Education in the United States, 1880–1930," in *The Political Economy of North American Indians*, ed. John H. Moore (Norman: University of Oklahoma Press, 1993), 43–59; and Clifford Trafzer (Wyandot), Matthew Sakiestewa Gilbert (Hopi) and Lorene Sisquoc (Cuhilla/Apache), eds., *The Indian School on Magnolia Avenue: Voices and Images from the Sherman Institute* (Corvalis: Oregon State University Press, 2012).

19. Greg Sarris, "Living with Miracles: The Politics and Poetics of Writing American Indian Resistance and Identity," in *Displacement, Diaspora, and Geographies of Identity*, eds. Smadar Lavie and Ted Swedenburg (Durham, N.C.: Duke University Press, 1996), 27, 33–34.

20. Greg Sarris, interview with the author, November 29, 2006, via telephone.

21. Greg Sarris, *Mabel McKay: Weaving the Dream* (Berkley: University of California Press, 1994), 8–9.

22. Greg Sarris, interview with the author, November 29, 2006, via telephone.

23. Ibid.

24. Robert L. Oswalt, *Kashaya Texts*, University of California Publications in Linguistics 36 (Berkley: University of California Press, 1964), 213, 215.

25. Bean and Theodoratus, "Western Pomo," 297; Vinson Brown and Douglas Andrews, *The Pomo Indians of California and Their Neighbors* (Happy Camp, Cal.: Naturegraph, 1969), 46.

26. Sarris, *Keeping Slug Woman Alive*, 13.

27. One of the effective strategies for the Federated Indians of Graton Rancheria (FIGR) has been the effort to regain federal recognition. In 1992 Sarris was elected chair of the Federated Coast Miwok, which later became the FIGR, and began leading the effort for tribal recognition. According to the FIGR website, the purpose was to "protect their aboriginal territory and their cultural and political identity." At the end of 2000, President Clinton signed legislation restoring their federal recognition. In 2002 the Bureau of Indian Affairs ratified the FIGR base rolls and constitution. With that, the tribe began reestablishing a land base. See the FIGR website, www.gratonrancheria.com.

Made in the USA
Middletown, DE
02 February 2022

60248006R00144